The Hen Race

A fifties railway childhood

By Alan Durham

With Best Wishes

Alan

Published by HEN RACE PRESS

Copyright © Alan W Durham
E-mail: alan@henracepress.com
Website: https://henracepress.com

Painting for cover illustration by Sara Hayward MA (RCA)
Cover graphics by Martin Driscoll
Layout and printing by Aspect Design

ISBN: 978-0-9930309-0-1

This book is dedicated to my lovely wife Tana Durham.
Without her it would never have been written.
My grateful thanks for her continuous support, encouragement,
advice, incredible proof reading and correcting skills.
Also for allowing me the use of her wonderful photograph of
chickens (Chapter 6).

For Alex Durham with my love

THE HEN RACE

Introduction

This book is inspired by love.

Love given selflessly by parents, grandparents and family.

Love and care given by a railway community; a community in which the author spent a decade of his life.

It is also about quiet courage, often in the face of considerable adversity.

This is an historical novel based in the nineteen forties and fifties. It is fiction, loosely based on the experiences of the author and his close family members. Many characters and stories are products of the author's imagination so any resemblance to any person living or dead is coincidental and unintentional.

Any factual inaccuracies are entirely the author's fault.

Some people commenting on life during the nineteen fifties may say that we had very little. They would be wrong, we had everything. We had love, protection and care for and from others.

In Memoriam

I found an old address book, strung with a scarlet band.
Inside a tatty letters box, 'twas in my Father's hand.
It was part of the diary he wrote in forty four.
Mostly names of army men, his friends throughout the war.
The men in it are very real, ID'ed with nick names all,
Chalky, Jock and Taffy and 'ever whistling' Paul.
It tells of young men injured whilst battling through their day,
Two of them, with black edgings, are labelled K I A.

Chapter 1

HALTHORPE

Tom knew he was a Viking. He was also the Big Chief of the Sioux nation. He lived with his parents, Connie and Phil York, and a black cat called Felix, in a railway cottage in the hamlet of Halthorpe. The name was all that was left of the farmhouse and cluster of workers' hovels, compulsorily purchased for a pittance, to enable the expansion of the rail network and the growth of wealth across the vast flood plains that form great stretches of the East Riding of Yorkshire.

Old Halthorpe was demolished and the new hamlet of Halthorpe was created by and for, the convenience of the railways.

Tom remembered his father explaining where the name came from:

'About a thousand years ago this part of England was invaded and populated by the Vikings. They were a war-like people who crossed the sea from Denmark, sailed up the Humber in their longboats and landed here. The Vikings killed many of the native population, so they could settle, live and farm here themselves. They used Danish names for the villages they created. In their language *Thorp* means little village or hamlet. So Halthorpe is the name for the little village of Hal. He was probably their head man or leader.'

'But where are the Vikings now, Dad?'

'I think we are probably descended from them, mixed up with other nationalities that moved into this area. Over the centuries the different peoples married and had children, so we're all a bit of everything. Some of the folk around here probably look a bit like the Vikings; some a bit like the Normans and some Anglo Saxon. I like to think we've got a bit of Viking in us.'

'Am I a Viking, Dad?'

'You look like a little Viking with your red hair, pale skin and blue eyes. I think you are.'

The hamlet Tom loved and grew up in was built where four lines of railway split, enabling two of the tracks to convey traffic to and from York and the other two to service Leeds and beyond. The wedge of land marooned between the two sets of tracks was where the workers' cottages were built. Many families had to contend with having one railway line abutting their front garden and another running next to their back garden fence.

A road formed the base of this housing triangle. At each of the two points where the railway lines crossed the road was a gatekeeper's cottage and large set of five-bar gates. These were kept closed across the road to allow free movement of trains. Pedestrians could cross the lines through side gates when no trains were visible. Vehicle and cart drivers had to ring a bell for the gatekeeper, whose job it was to contact the signalman and if no trains were due, open the gates to allow the traffic to cross the lines safely.

The railway, and the hamlet that existed to serve it, was surrounded by a patchwork of pasture and fertile, red clay, arable fields. There were no hills in this landscape, apart from the occasional molehill. Tom remembers his mam often referring to the countryside as 'flat as a pancake, but good for bike rides.'

Trimmed thorn hedges surrounded the fields. These were interspersed with willow, alder and oak trees. The only features of any note were the embankment that carried the bridge over the tracks near the station and the Delph, a large pond, which had formed when soil was excavated for the embankment.

A narrow fenced footpath leading to Halthorpe Railway Station lay between the railway side and the pond. The path was called the 'Duck Walk' because walkers and cyclists had to progress in single file.

When Tom crossed the York tracks he had a mile walk along a country road to Normansly village and its shop, school and chapel. He thought the stone surface was great, because it was ideal for striking sparks from the metal heel protectors his Dad always nailed into his new school shoes to give them 'a bit of extra wear.'

The crossing over the Leeds line led into Green Lane, a grassy track used by farmers for access to their fields. There was always plenty along Green Lane to interest a curious boy like Tom. Brightly painted gypsy caravans camped there in fruit picking season. Children and anglers used it to gain access to the Delph. The hedgerows hid birds' nests and hedgehogs.

This part of the East Riding had evolved from remote inaccessible marsh land with few roads, into a vast agricultural plain. This transformation was thanks to the ingenuity of Dutch engineers who had drained the marshes and constructed great earth and stone banks along the sides of the Humber. The only lingering memories of the landscape's marshy past were the dense, low autumn and spring fogs that hugged the ground so snugly that any person over five feet tall could stand within one and see over it. This spooky phenomenon enhanced local legends that the area was inhabited by witches.

Phil used to say, 'It's like sticking your head through the top of a cloud.'

Connie would remark, 'These low fogs play havoc with the throats of opera singers.'

Tom found this surprising as he was sure his mam had never met an opera singer. He wondered if she had read this nugget of wisdom in the *Hull Daily Mail*.

Halthorpe consisted entirely of terraced railway cottages. When Tom lived there from the late nineteen forties to the end of the nineteen fifties, cinder pathways surrounded each terrace. These access ways needed little maintenance, as they were constantly topped up when residents cleaned out their fire grates.

'Tom be a love and empty the ashes on the back path. Put them in that hollow near our gate. When it rains there's a puddle and I splash my legs when I swing in on my bike.'

The cottages were all plain, uniform and uninspiring. They were constructed with red brick walls, grey slate roofs and sash windows.

Each had a backyard separated from its neighbours by a high creosoted fence. The yard contained a coalhouse, a lavatory and a gate leading onto the back lane.

The 'lavvy' had a small frosted glass window and a planked door drilled with ventilation holes, which made each visit a draughty affair.

Inside was a wooden box with a planked seat. This had a hole cut in it, suitable for purpose. On the inside of the lavvy door was a hook from which dangled a loop of string holding many six inch square pieces of torn newspapers. These fragments of assorted literature gave the lavvy its posh name 'the reading room'.

Connie called it 'the music room' when Tom was sitting in there. He enjoyed the resonance when he thumped his feet backwards onto the wooden box. Many of the songs he heard on *Two Way Family Favourites* he blasted out from the lavvy, usually with a totally unique interpretation of the lyrics and little respect for the music. His version of the Toreador song from Bizet's *Carmen*[32] was thumped out very regularly, as he loved the beat.

'Lavvy Door! Now Guard me! Lavvy Dooor! Lavvvy Dooor!'

Quite a few variants on this theme floated out of the lavvy door *'Hel-lo Mam! Wha-a-ts for tea? Wha-a-t-s-s fo-r tea?'*

'Someone's happy anyway,' said Edith Thomas to Connie. Edith was standing on an old Hull Brewery Pale Ale beer crate so she could peep over the fence top and chat.

'Always is when he's in there,' Connie agreed, smiling at her neighbour. 'I'm pleased we're getting *Carmen* this week, I was getting sick of listening to 'Run Rabbit Run'[33] and the blooming farmer's gun going Bang, Bang, Bang, Bang.

'When's he coming out, is what I'd like to know?' she continued, shouting towards the green painted lavvy door. 'Come on, get a move on!'

'Toreador! Now guard me! I'll soon be done! I'm wiping me bum.'

'That's quite enough of that thank you Tom,' said Connie, laughing quietly as Mrs Thomas put her hand over her mouth in faux surprise, 'Get out of there now!'

Under the seat of the 'toilet' was a cube-shaped galvanised metal box. This tank was removed when necessary by opening a small wooden door in the rear wall of the lavvy.

The tank was emptied once a week by the council 'lavvy men', into an odorous, open-topped, riveted receptacle fixed to the rear of their lorry. The escape of noxious gasses was so intense when this event took place, that all doors and windows were tightly closed and washing, even if still wet, was taken inside for fear of tainting.

'Don't get in the way Tom, I've got to take the washing in. You grab the socks, knickers and underpants. Quickly now and don't drop the pegs in the yard.'

There was a considerable amount of liquid fluidity and movement within the lorry's large effluent tank. The contents were poorly retained by its curved sliding lids. Everybody kept well clear when the lavvy men turned their vehicle around, as spillage was usual and frequently abundant.

As a child of four or five years old Tom was fascinated by this lorry, with its loud chugging engine, its ponging, slopping tank and its cheerful chain-smoking operatives. His fascination was so intense, that when asked by the vicar at a Sunday School prize giving what he would like to be when he grew up, Tom replied:

'I want to be a lavvy man.'

His parents were the only two people in the chapel who were not surprised.

Tom and his parents lived in a 'three up, two down' cottage. Downstairs was a sitting room with a cast iron range, a scullery with a terracotta tiled floor and a pantry. The scullery had a small metal copper for heating water. A small fireplace was built under it.

The house had no electricity, gas, plumbed-in water supply or central heating.

Water came from a shared pump situated on the back wall of the lavvies. The pump, which was fed from an underground well, was always reliable, except in the winter when it would occasionally freeze up. A kettle of gently poured hot water usually thawed it out.

Pumping water was part of the daily routine. All the residents carried water from the pump to their homes in enamel buckets. The children helped with this activity and learned very quickly how to give the pump handle the correct stroke and pressure to bring up a good quantity of water. They also learned the hard way that if you pumped too vigorously you were liable to trap your hand and skin your knuckles on the pump housing.

'Tom be a love and fetch some buckets of water and fill the copper up, will you?'

'How many?'

'Five will probably do. Try not to spill on the scullery floor.'

When Tom was about five or six years old, the Halthorpe residents were delighted when the railway board said they were going to install piped water. They fulfilled their promise by installing a tap next to the pump. It was to be a further three years before they fitted cold water taps over every household's scullery sink.

The front doors of the cottages were never used because people had to walk past their back doors and round the side of the terrace to get to the front. The only time Tom could recall his front door being opened was when it was painted. This happened every five or six years when the British Rail painters visited. There was never any choice of colour. All the woodwork was painted the same, a shade forever labelled in Tom's mind as 'railway green'.

The scullery was an intensely used working area. Many activities of daily life took place in this compact space. These included washing, bathing, baking, chicken plucking and sausage making. A lead pipe took waste water from a deep terracotta sink to the drainage gully in the yard outside. This drained into a soak-away, which did not always work efficiently because of the heavy clay soil it was built in. Heavy rain, together with water from the sink, frequently flooded the gully and spilled over into the yard. Tom's pragmatic parents used this opportunity to give their back yard a quick swill down.

Outdoor coats and scarves hung behind the back door. A bucket of coal was kept next to this. Next to the bucket stood a box of kindling and a pile of newspapers that were crunched up for fire lighting, or torn into squares for use in the lavvy. A large galvanised 'tin' bath hung on the wall near the copper. A much-scrubbed whitewood table stood under the window. On baking days, the paraffin lamp that normally stood on the table top was carefully placed underneath.

The pantry was a chamber of delight for Tom, A cornucopia bursting with good things. Neatly stacked equipment and ingredients necessary for near self-sufficiency on a very limited income was arranged on floor-to-ceiling shelving. Tom was fascinated by the stuff his mam used for cooking, the pans, casseroles, roasting tins, cake, bun and Yorkshire pudding tins, mixing bowls, baking trays, whisks and wooden spoons. Then there were the blue paper bags containing flour, sugar, dried fruits and pulses, slabs of butter and cheese wrapped in greaseproof paper, racks of eggs, jars of homemade jam and chutney. Freshly baked loaves and fruit teacakes nestled in a cream enamel bread bin. Icing sugar and cake decorations were kept safe from damp in pre-war toffee tins. A half bottle of funeral whisky was stored on one of the higher shelves, whilst bottles of milk cooled on the terracotta tiled floor. From autumn through winter a bucket of eggs preserved in isinglass kept the family going until the hens started laying again in spring. After the pig was slaughtered, sides of bacon and legs of ham hung from the ceiling, and sausages, black puddings, pork pies and brawns were kept in a small meat press.

The pantry was kept cool by the small window that was only closed in the worst of winter weather. In summer, flies were kept out by a fine mesh screen that was fixed to the frame.

The magic was complete for Tom, when he burst through the back door from school, or from playing. His yell of 'Mam! I'm hungry', would be met with 'Have a look in the pantry. There are some freshly baked cherry buns, or I can do you some bread and dripping.'

This was followed quickly by '...but wash your hands first. There's clean water in the bowl. Wash them properly! No wiping dirt on the towel.'

'Yes Mam, I will and I won't. I'll have a bun Mam, please? Which tin?'

'Quality Street. And keep your fingers away from that coffee cake in the Highland Shortbread tin! It's for Sunday tea. Your dad's favourite. And no sticking your fingers in the butter cream. I'll know!'

'Thanks Mam.'

In addition to his love of Connie's baking, Tom also consumed considerable quantities of bread and dripping. So much, that he frequently exhausted the supply she saved from the Sunday joint. The earthenware jar it was stored in had to be topped up regularly with a donation from their next door neighbour, Mrs Thomas.

'He still enjoys his bread and dripping then?' she'd say.

'Honestly he's like a bottomless pit,' Connie would laugh.

The cosy living room was not much bigger than the scullery. The main feature was the black-leaded cast-iron range, which was crucial to warmth and comfort. The kettle stood on a trivet that could be pushed over the fire when boiling water was needed for tea. The oven next to the fire was used for roasting and baking. It was a temperamental beast, but Connie quickly learned the dishes that worked best and cleverly stuck to family favourites. Vegetables and puddings were steamed and stews simmered on the hotplate on top of the oven.

Meals were eaten at the mahogany dining table, which would be covered with an army blanket to protect the polished surface from hot dishes. On top of that Connie would spread one of the pristine white table cloths that she and Maisie had embroidered for her bottom drawer when she lived with the Wilkinsons at the farm.

When the table was not being used for meals it was Tom's den. The heavy brown army blanket would be unfolded and draped across the table, reaching almost to the wooden floor. Many cowboy and indian fights were thought up and staged in this much-loved private space. Between battles, the cast-lead fighters slept in the toy box, which Tom kept in the cupboard under the stairs, next to the clothes horse, ironing board and his mam's hand driven sewing machine. Hooks behind the cupboard door provided additional hanging space for outdoor clothing and the family's two dark pink, rubber hot water bottles.

An old hand-me-down oak sideboard stored cutlery, spare linen, knitting, clothes to be mended and socks to be darned. Next to the fire were the coal scuttle and an armchair that was used by all the family but vacated for Phil when he came home after his shift. For Tom the sofa was multifunctional; sometimes a boat, sometimes a car and sometimes a trampoline.

On the rare occasions Tom sat still, he was usually listening to the radio. The Bakelite wireless sat on the windowsill. It was powered by a large accumulator battery. This was collected every week by the local grocer and taken away to be recharged. By modern standards it was a very inefficient power source but in those times, with careful rationing, resting and coaxing it could be persuaded to deliver a week's supply of *The Archers*, the occasional *Listen with Mother* and at least an hour of *Two Way Family Favourites* on Sundays.

Tom's tiny bedroom was above the scullery. Although the room boasted a small cast iron fireplace, the fire was never lit for fear of setting the bed alight. The only other furniture was a simple wooden chair which served both as a clothes hanger and a bedside table for Tom's bedtime glass of water. Under the bed was a small enamelled chamber pot. One of Tom's tasks every morning, after he was dressed, but before breakfast, was to carry this receptacle downstairs.

'Now carry that carefully,' Mam would say 'no slopping when you get to the bottom of the stairs, and no running with it!'

Whatever the weather, he would carry the 'jerry' carefully out to the lav and empty it, without splashing, into the lavvy pan, then leave it in the scullery for his mam to wash out, then dry, ready for the next night.

Connie and Phil's bedroom was above the sitting room. Their double bed, large five-drawer chest and wardrobe, were second hand, like most of the furniture in the house. In the austerity years following the Second World War, new furniture was scarce and wages were low. The exception was a new wicker bedroom chair that Connie had saved for and bought from the Blind Institute, which staged twice yearly sales at the village hall.

The third small bedroom was used when family and friends came to visit. As Connie kept in touch with friends made during her land girl days, this was fairly frequently.

All the Halthorpe cottages had gardens. The York family's was alongside their home. It was entered from a side gate in the back-yard fence. In those early post-war years surviving hard times was a priority. Rationing was still in place, shops were poorly stocked and few people had money to spare. The garden was vital for survival. Their tenth of an acre of clay soil gave them the means to produce much of their own food. Phil worked the heavy land, digging in chicken manure and soiled bedding from the rabbit hutches. His hard work and careful planting ensured they had soft fruits in summer and vegetables throughout the year.

When Tom's parents became engaged in 1946, the first purchase Phil made towards their married life was two chicken huts. This was so important to him that he kept the receipt secure in a brown envelope for the rest of his life. It was found by Tom over forty years later, after Phil died.

There were two old pig sties with adjoining pens in the garden. These brick structures had low corrugated tin roofing and had been built between the wars by a previous tenant of their cottage. When Tom's father took them over they were broken down, rotting and decrepit. The young married couple with their new baby could not afford to buy a piglet straight away, so Phil was able to carry out the repairs at a leisurely pace over several years.

Whenever the York's cottage chimney was swept, Phil kept the soot for top dressing the vegetables to keep away the root fly. He stored it in an old galvanised metal barrel next to the pigsty wall. Tom was told never to climb on the pigsty roof, it was too dangerous. Of course he did, but only when his dad was at work and his mam couldn't see him.

One day when young Tom was practising his climbing skills, he heard his mam calling. Hurriedly he slid down from the pig sty roof on to the barrel. Unfortunately he didn't know that his dad kept the worst of the weather off the soot by covering the open top of the barrel with a hessian sack. He disappeared into the barrel of soot, clouds of it billowing all over him, scraping the skin from his shins and worse. When he finally managed to pull himself out he ran to the house sobbing.

'Mam, I've fallen in a barrel of soot and I've filled me pants.'

Faced with a bawling, snotty, black, smelly apparition, with blood running down his legs, Connie didn't know whether to laugh or cry.

Telling Phil about it later that night she said: 'He was absolutely filthy. He even had soot up his nostrils. Fortunately the crying and bawling helped to flush some of that out. Thank goodness Mrs Thomas was round at our house having a cup of tea. She helped me sort him out when we'd stopped laughing. We had to get the tin bath out in the yard and wash him in cold water with soap flakes.'

Phil was not best pleased, but Connie managed to calm him down and he saw the funny side of it, eventually. However his demeanour towards his son remained stern. He forbade him from ever going on the pig sty roof again. Tom never did.

Helping his dad in the garden was a regular pastime for young Tom. It was an activity both father and son enjoyed.

'Tom, come outside and help me with the onion sets. They're on the scullery table in a brown paper bag. Bring them with you. Put your wellies on. The ground's a bit sticky.'

'Here you are, Dad.'

'Let's get you started. Watch how I do it and then you can have a go. Plant them at this depth so the neck of bulb is just showing at soil level. Sprinkle a little bit of soot around each bulb, like this.' Phil looked sideways at his son. 'If you need some more soot you know where I keep it, don't you?'

'Yes Dad,' replied Tom, sheepishly. Some memories never fade.

Tom planted and top dressed the onion sets, while his dad dug out and prepared some potato furrows, bottom dressing each trench with well-rotted chicken manure from last year's muck heap.

'Good lad, that's well done. About five months from now they'll have grown into big onions. We'll lift them and hang them in bunches in one of the old pigsties. We should have enough onions to see us through the winter.'

The gardening year was dictated by the seasons. First to be harvested were spring cabbages, salad crops, carrots and spring onions. These were followed by peas, beans, beetroot, carrots, new potatoes, strawberries, raspberries, loganberries, gooseberries, blackberries, blackcurrants, whitecurrants and redcurrants. Autumn's harvest included cabbages, cauliflowers, onions and potatoes. Purple sprouting broccoli, kale, spinach and turnips were cropped into the winter.

More exotic foodstuffs were almost impossible to get during rationing. This proved to be a challenge for expectant father Phil. One anecdote, regularly retold, demonstrated Phil's devotion to his pregnant wife.

'When I was expecting you,' Connie said to Tom, 'I had these terrible cravings. I used to drive your poor dad mad. Once I had this overwhelming desire for an orange. Your dad cycled twenty five miles in bad weather to buy a single orange for me. Sometimes I'd suck a piece of coal.'

'Coal, Mam?'

'Yes, funny isn't it? I always felt better afterwards. Something to do with needing extra minerals, the doctor said.'

'Did you have black lips?'

'Yes and a black tongue. Do you want to try a bit?' she said, reaching towards the coal scuttle.

'Not on your Nelly!'

Chapter 2

SURVIVAL

1954 Halthorpe

Sitting Bull was in his wigwam. His tribal elders were talking nearby. He listened hard and he heard some of their words. *Will I hear a secret?*

His attention wandered and he thought about his battle plan and decided how he would use his braves. He knew he needed arrows and wondered how to get them. The battle would be lost if he didn't have arrows.

The words started again, louder now. Sitting Bull listened.

'Don't cry, you'll be OK.'

'I'll never be OK. I'll always be like this.'

'No, you won't. You're getting better as time goes by.'

'It doesn't seem so to me.'

'You are. Surely you know that.'

'It's been nine years and people still stare.'

'What people?'

'Bloody passengers.'

'People always stare out of carriage windows. They've nothing else to do.'

'Well I wish they wouldn't stare at me, they think I'm a freak.'

'No they don't. They don't mean any harm.'

'And they point. Heartless bastards.'

'They're probably sympathetic and concerned.'

'Well I wish they would mind their own business. I don't stare at them.'

'No I know you don't, perhaps you are more polite.'

'I can't stand much more of it! I'll have to work somewhere else.'

'Don't talk such rubbish. You're just having one of your bad days.'

'This is not how I want to live. People staring, wanting to hide, not enough money.'

'Well it beats hen racing!'

'I suppose so. Yes that was worse. Anything is better than that.'

'You'll be all right. At least you're alive. You're strong and you've got me and Sitting Bull, and I saw Mrs Russell in the village. She wants you to tidy up her front garden.'

'Sitting Bull? Is he out with Tonto?'

'No, he's in his wigwam.'

'He's quiet…do you think he's asleep?'

'No, not him…earwiggin' more like.'

The Elder raised his voice.

'Hello Sitting Bull…are you there?'

Tom did not reply.

'Hello Sitting Bull. Are you there?' said the Elder again.

'He must be asleep, he's not answering.'

'You've got to use the secret code. Sitting Bull, him cannot speak without it,' piped Tom from under the table.

The Tribal Elder wiped his tears away, laughed and walked across to the living room table.

'What's the code today?' whispered the Elder.

'SOS.'

Three fast taps were promptly rapped out on the table top, followed by three slow taps and another three fast taps.

Two small hands pushed under the blanket edge, followed by a head of ginger hair adorned with a Magpie feather. The face below the hair was heavily freckled and sported a gap-toothed grin.

'Ugh!' said Sitting Bull, standing up and folding his arms. 'Who wishes to speak with the Big Chief of the Sioux?'

'How! Sitting Bull,' said the Tribal Elder, 'do you want to help me feed the hens?'

'How! Dad,' said Sitting Bull, 'Can I feed Esmerelda?'

'Sure,' said the Elder, 'but you'll have to help me make some mash first. Don't give her too much, and watch out, she's broody. She'll probably try to peck you.'

'Mam? What's earwiggin?'

'Listening in to other people's conversations, when you should be minding your own beeswax.'

'Mam? What's minding your own beeswax?'

'Not being nosy, cheeky,' said Connie, as her loved ones headed for the back door.

'Mam? Can I have some pins?'

'What for?'

'Arrows.'

'You can have six, but I want them back.'

'Mam? What's for tea?'

'Egg and Chips.'

'Dad? Can I collect the eggs?'

Connie laughed as her irrepressible son burst into song, grabbed his dad's hand and dragged him towards the hen run.

> 'Chick, chick, chick, chick, chicken, lay a little egg for me.
> Chick, chick, chick, chick, chicken, I want one for my tea.
> I haven't had an egg since Easter and now its half past three
> So chick, chick, chick, chick, chicken, lay a little egg for me.'[34]

Sitting Bull was six years old when he heard the words from under the table. He was forty eight, the Tribal Elders were dead and he'd received a letter from a stranger before he understood.

***

Near Eindhoven 19 September 1944

'Christ Almighty, don't they know we need our beauty sleep?' grumbled Taff, shivering under his blanket.

Aircraft engines roared above the hussars, wrecking any chance of further sleep that night. The men sheltered under a tarpaulin bivouac alongside their tank, in the wet mud to one side of a road. Their role as a reconnaissance tank crew meant their little squadron was always in the forefront of the fighting. They were several miles ahead of the main division. Their push through Eindhoven had been a success, and they had stopped to grab an hour or two of rest before moving forward again. Always aware they were surrounded by the enemy, they couldn't light a fire or show a light, so as darkness fell they kipped down.

Only two nights ago, in the pitch black, Phil had felt around with his boots until he found a flat patch of grass to settle down on. When he had awoken next morning he had been horrified to find he had slept with his head between the feet of a dead German infantryman.

Taff's cheery wake up call of 'morning Phil, don't you know that sleeping with the enemy is a court marshal offence?' had done nothing to ease Phil's shock and horror when he'd opened his eyes and saw the bloodied corpse. Shooting to his feet, he had sworn at Taff for his black humour.

'I can honestly say that's the first time I've had my parentage questioned before breakfast,' Taff had laughed, as he'd rubbed Phil companionably on his shoulder. 'I'm sorry I gave you a shock mate. It set my nerves on edge when I saw him. Mind you I think we're having a better morning than he is.'

Now, persistent droning overhead was alerting the men's attention.

'Look! Jerry,' said Phil pointing, 'flying low under the clouds.'

'Flying Pencils and Stukas,' observed Taff.

'Those fuckers look as though they mean business,' said Jock. 'I hate those bloody Stukas, diving on folks and making that horrible wailing noise. It's enough to give you the shits.'

'I don't think they're after us,' said Paul, laughing at Jock. 'I think somebody else is going to catch it.'

'My money is on Eindhoven,' said Chalky. 'We're so far inside enemy territory, they wouldn't be able to sort out their guys from ours in the dark. Those buggers up there are looking for bigger fish than us.'

'Thank God for that,' said Jock. 'I haven't had a sheet of bog paper in over a fortnight.'

'Yeah it's got to be Eindhoven[1],' agreed Paul. 'A lot of our lads and loads of Yanks are bivouacked there.'

'I reckon you're right.' Taff said. 'Look, they're dropping flares.'

'I bet the bastards are after our supplies,' said Phil. 'If they blow up our ammo, they'll really slow us down.'

The phosphorus flares lit the sky to daylight brightness as they drifted down from the long, slim Luftwaffe Dornier fast bombers. Whilst the hussars watched the sky from the shelter of their tanks, the flares were illuminating the roads and buildings of Eindhoven, making it easy for the Stukas to swoop down, searching for their prey, their eerie 'Jericho Trumpet' sirens howling.

The allied forces, which only a few hours ago, had been celebrating a successful push through, and liberation of the city, found themselves under heavy bombardment. They scattered to find cover where they could. Townspeople hid in their cellars or ran from their homes, desperate to find safety. Army drivers risked their lives, by driving ammo trucks away from the supply convoys that were parked around the square.

Early October 1944

The troopers clustered around their Cromwell Tank. They were exhausted. Another day's push was over; they had stopped advancing for now. Their clothes were damp and smelling. Their bodies itched. It was a week since they'd had a decent wash. It was raining, as always. The light was fading.

'Another couple of hours and it'll be dark,' said Taff, his boots squelching in the mud as he surveyed the nearby ditch. 'I'm sick of these marshes and the bloody, bastard mossies,' he continued irritably, clapping his hands at the flying pests. 'I smell like the inside of a Turkish wrestler's jock strap. The 'Peel country' has very little 'appeal' if you ask me.'

'Very good Taff,' laughed Paul,' I think I'll put that little gem in the letter I'm sending to my mother.'

'Should you really be telling your mum about jock straps?' queried Phil.

Paul grinned and shook his head, 'Perhaps not,' he said, resuming writing, whistling all the while.

'What grub have we got?' asked Chalky, looking hopeful.

'Nothing exciting boyo,' said Taff, 'a few broken biscuits, some tea leaves and bugger all else really!'

'I'm so hungry, me belly thinks me throat's been cut,' said Chalky. 'How do they expect us to fight when we've got no food? Not only have we got Fritz trying to kill us every day, our own side seems determined to starve us to death.'

'HQ radioed earlier and said food supplies will catch up with us next week,' said Paul.

'Next week! Bollocks! I'll believe that when I see it. They said the same last week and what did they send us to eat? Sod all!' exploded Jock. 'I never thought I'd say it, but I'd kiss Monty if I thought he had a tin of bully beef under his beret.'

Jock stepped into the shallow ditch, and began the long process of filling a bucket with water. It was a tedious job because the water kept muddying up. The only way he could get enough, was by baling it out of the ditch half a tin mug at a time.

'We'll have a brew in a few minutes,' said Paul. 'A mug of muddy tea is better than nothing.'

Chapter 3

Lives

Daily life, household activities and behaviour in Halthorpe were driven by the women, who all followed the same routines.

Halthorpe children quickly learned the tricks of daily behaviour. On Mondays, when washing was hanging in every back yard, running around was never appreciated. It was a good way to end up being chased by an irate mother, or a neighbour brandishing a yard broom.

'Will you clear off out of here? I've already told you twice. Go and play somewhere else. Now!'

Washing day was always a physical toil. The fire was lit under the scullery copper, which had to be stoked up throughout the day. The copper was filled with countless buckets of water that had to be brought in from outside. When the water was bubbling hot, it was bucketed into a large, galvanised metal, washing tub. This tub was about the size of a dustbin. Soap flakes were dissolved in the hot water before the clothes were added.

Washing was agitated by hand using a device called a posher. This was an upside down colander-like object, on the end of a sweeping brush handle.

The technique was to hold the handle firmly and plunge the posher repeatedly up and down in the washing tub, circulating the water and soap flake mix. The water in the tub flooded through the holes in the posher and added to the agitation. As Tom grew bigger he often did some 'poshing' to give Connie a break from this muscle straining activity.

'Tom will you have a go with the posher? My back's killing me.'

Great care had to be taken to drain the posher into the tub after using it. Tom soon learned that if he didn't, a large quantity of hot soapy water poured out and soaked him from the waist down.

When Connie decided that the clothes were clean, she fished them out of the wash tub with a whitewood stick, dumped them into the stoneware sink, and gave them repeated hot water and cold water rinses until all signs of soap had gone.

The washing was then loaded into a large white enamelled basin and carried out into the backyard. Surplus water was squeezed out of it by repeatedly feeding each item back and forth through the mangle.

The mangle was a heavy, metal framed device, fitted with two parallel, wooden rollers. It stood about three feet high. There was a gap between the rollers, into which the washing was fed. Care had to be taken to ensure the clean washing did not trail on the backyard. As the roller handle was turned, water sprayed out of the clothing being compressed by the rollers. When helping Connie with the mangling, it was usual for Tom's socks, shoes and legs to become wet through.

Halthorpe children were frequently 'collared' to turn the handle. They rapidly learned it was not a job that could be rushed. Patience was the secret to good mangling.

'Tom don't turn the handle so fast, it's not a race. You'll bung the roller bars up. Use your other hand to hold up the sheet so it doesn't drop in the dirt, and put your foot on the bottom bar of the mangle to stop it 'walking' across the yard.'

'OK, Mam. Then can I go out to play? Please?'

The mangle frequently jammed. Shirt collars, sleeves, shorts, trousers and buttons always presented challenges. These had to be fed through very carefully. Jams could usually be resolved by reversing the rollers, but occasionally the blockage was of such magnitude, that the backs of spoons, other blunt kitchen implements and occasionally pliers, had to be engaged to release the jammed clothing. This was never a pleasant task, but doing it on a cold day with wet, frozen fingers was misery.

When the clothes had been squeezed they were hung on rope lines strung across the yard, then lifted up and into the breeze with wooden poles. The wash tub was topped up with more hot water and soap flakes, more clothing was added and the whole process started again.

A rainy washing day was detested by all.

'Tom! Will you stop running around the wet washing please? I keep telling you. I cannot believe I have to tell you again! You'll be in trouble! Why don't you play in your den? In fact I don't care where you go, as long as you get from under my feet!'

'Sorry Mam.'

On rainy days wet washing had to be hung throughout the scullery and the living room. Suspended in front of the living room range was a Gnu rack clothes airer. This wooden slatted contraption was fastened to the ceiling with pulleys and ropes. It was in almost constant use in wet weather and during the short days of winter.

Tuesdays were also good days to avoid the living room. The Gnu and the clothes horse were festooned with airing washing and a red faced Connie was labouring over the ironing board.

Connie ironed in front of the range fire, because she heated her pair of smoothing irons on the trivet which was hinged and could be swung over the burning coal. The cast iron 'irons', became very hot and had to be handled with a thick cloth to protect her hands from being burned.

'Mam, why do you spit on the iron?'

'If it sizzles and evaporates straight away, I know the iron's hot enough. Then I give it a quick wipe with this cloth to make sure the iron has no soot sticking to it.'

Each smoothing iron had a different mark on its back so you could alternate them and know which one was heating up and which one was hot. The symbols on Connie's pair were similar to those used in a deck of playing cards; one had a raised diamond and the other, a club.

The ironing of each garment was done quickly because the irons were heavy to handle and they cooled down rapidly. Women had to be strong. This was heavy repetitive work, involving lots of lifting and bending. The ironing basket was always full, so the job would last for hours.

Tom and Phil always looked forward to Wednesdays. This was baking day so it made sense to keep on Connie's good side.

Every Wednesday Connie did battle with the range. Keeping the fire burning and maintaining a draft of hot air under and around the oven was always a challenge.

Regulating the temperature was vital to successful baking and only experience of the range's performance could help the baker. Windy days were a problem because the fire might draw too much and cause the oven to overheat, or the chimney may back draft, pushing puffs of black smoke into the living room. Rainy, heavy days were tricky because the fire would be slow to burn and it was difficult to get the oven hot enough. A handy supply of kindling was needed to boost heat quickly if needed.

'Tom, fetch some more kindling for me will you?'

'We've not got much left, shall I chop some more?'

'Bring me what we've got before you start chopping.'

'Yes Mam.'

'And don't chop your finger off.'

Despite these difficulties Connie baked bread every week and usually meat pasties, scones, jam tarts, sponge cakes and buns. Her productivity was such that she kept the family supplied with baking and provided for an old couple in Halthorpe who looked after their grandchildren on their meagre pension. She also contributed to the Village Hall, Chapel and Women's Institute fairs and fetes. Well-behaved children who came to the house were often rewarded with freshly baked scones and buns.

In Tom's house there always seemed to be little bits of dough, pastry or cake mix left over, which could be made into tiny misshapen treats by grubby little hands.

'Mam! Can I make some scones?'

'Yes get the baking board your dad made for you.'

'Shall I sprinkle some flour on it?'

'Yes but on the board, not the scullery floor.'

'Where's my little rolling pin?'

'On the shelf in the pantry, where it always is.'

'Can I use a cutter?'

'Why not use the square shape your Gran bought you this time?'

The tiny scones and pastry balls made by Tom often had a slightly grey tinge, due the number of times he had managed to drop them on the scullery floor. Tom did notice that other family members weren't very keen to share these culinary gems. He didn't care; he was always delighted with them.

'Can I have those scraps of pastry to eat?'

'Yes but not too many, you don't want belly ache do you?'

'OK.'

'Do you want to clean out this mixing bowl?'

'Yes please.'

'Go and get a teaspoon from the sideboard then.'

Halthorpe children became adept at disappearing on Thursdays. Those who hung around could find themselves wielding a yard broom, beating a clip rug, brushing the stair-mats or running the Ewbank around the upstairs floors. If you were asked to hold the steps while Mam washed the windows you would find yourself being sprinkled with vinegary water. It was definitely a day for playing away.

After play, when Tom ran back home for tea, all the rooms would have been cleaned and the beds upstairs changed. The lavvy, scullery and the living room floors would have been scrubbed and the backyard swilled.

Woe betide young Tom if he clomped into the house in muddy wellies or brought in a bucketful of sticklebacks, or a frog, for his mam to admire.

'Yes Tom! That is a lovely frog, now take it and put it back where you found it. You can show your dad when he comes in. No! Don't put it in your pocket.'

Fridays were 'anything goes' sort of days. Jobs that needed catching up were tackled. This was a time for working in the garden, bottling and pickling, repairing socks and making clothes, painting and papering, plus all the usual maintenance jobs.

From Tom's point of view, Friday was a brilliant day because his dad or one of the neighbours would bicycle into Normansly and bring back fish and chips.

Unfortunately Friday was also bath night. After the evening meal, the large, grey, 'tin' bath was taken down from its hook and laid on the scullery floor. Water was heated in the copper and decanted into the bath.

In the winter months the scullery was cold. The little fire, set deep under the copper, didn't give out much heat. The bath water cooled rapidly in the chilly room. The galvanised metal seemed to absorb cold from the terracotta floor. Bathing could be a very shivery affair.

Tom was always the first in.

'Aahh! No Mam! I had a bath last week.'

'And you're having another one this week, you mucky little perisher.'

After Tom's, usually very fast, bath, he was dried – wriggling and giggling, with a rough towel and popped in his jim-jams in front of the living room range, to keep warm. More hot water was added and Connie would have her bath. After that, more topping up and it was Phil's turn.

When Phil had bathed and dressed again, he would bucket the water out of the bath, dry it out and hang it back on the scullery wall.

Saturday was the day for more leisurely activities. Sometimes Connie went shopping to Goole. Money was tight so this was not a frequent excursion. Connie and Tom would attend bring and buy sales, fetes, flower shows or other events held in Normansly village hall. On rare occasions, the Yorks would go to Hull for 'the Sales', or for a treat, enjoy a trip to the rebuilt Cecil cinema. The original cinema had been flattened by German bombing in 1941. Connie and Phil were greatly taken with *The Glenn Miller Story* and Connie particularly enjoyed *The King and I* because she fancied Yul Brynner. The cinema was a great favourite with Tom. He loved to watch the organist who would rise up out of the floor, playing music before the beginning of the film.

Sunday was Chapel day. Mam would go to the morning service and Tom to Sunday School. After his wartime experiences Phil hardly ever went to chapel or church, because he wasn't convinced about the existence of God or the integrity of formal religion. He'd had a Church of England upbringing and was a member of the church choir during his early teens, but his religious belief ended in 1944.

Life in the Halthorpe community had other factors helping to regulate activities. All the men and some of the women worked for the railway and had to work railway hours. Many people worked shifts and on meeting with a neighbour most people began conversations with the words…

'What you on this week?'

'Two 'til ten. You?'

'Nights.'

'Swap over Saturday?'

'Can't wait! Nights are boring, but Sunday will be a bugger!'

Swap over days were always a problem, especially if a rest day hadn't been built into the roster. A railway shift worker could work from 10pm on a Saturday night until 6am on Sunday morning. If his shift swapped to afternoons, work started again at 2pm on the same day and finished at 10pm. This meant the person had worked sixteen hours in a twenty four hour period. It also only left an eight hour gap to travel from and to work, have two meals, get washed, shaved and rest.

Children were well warned not to play under or around the bedroom windows of shift workers who were trying to sleep.

The railways operate seven days a week, every day of the year. The trains always run, so employees had to work extra hours to cover for other people being on holiday, sick, or if there were staff shortages. Twelve hour or double shifts were a mixed blessing, because while they brought in much needed extra money, it was very easy to fall into an all-work-and-no-home-life cycle.

Generally wives did everything they could to help their men through these hard, long hours. Extra lunches were packed. Favourite baking was done. Children were kept out of the way when the men came home.

The York's neighbours were a couple in their early fifties, Reg and Edith Thomas. He was a signalman, a job vital to the efficient and safe running of the railways. Due to weekend leave and staff shortages, Reg regularly worked long shifts on Sundays when he and Edith would have preferred to enjoy a leisurely roast dinner together.

Edith, a lady deeply set into her routines, still cooked Sunday lunch when Reg was working, but could not bear him to miss out. So on each of these days, Tom was paid sixpence, to take him his meal. Thinking about it years later, Tom realised that this was his first paid job.

To give Mr Thomas time to enjoy his food, lunch had to arrive at a slack period between trains. At ten minutes to one precisely, Tom would knock on Edith Thomas's back door. He would be invited to wait in her scullery while she decanted piping hot gravy from a pan into a small gravy boat. The gravy boat was wrapped tightly in a spotless tea towel and wedged into a deep wicker basket. Frequently a jug of custard and a slice of fruit pie, similarly wrapped, were also jammed in. The basket was quite heavy because Mr Thomas's dinner would be contained in a pre-heated glass casserole dish and covered with a lid. Also included in the basket was a large china dinner plate, a pudding dish and cutlery. Mrs Thomas would cover everything with another tea towel, before dispatching Tom off.

'Hurry up. We don't want Mr Thomas to have a cold lunch do we? And don't swing the basket, you'll spill his gravy.'

It took Tom about fifteen minutes to walk to the signal box. He had to cross the first set of lines and then hurry the half mile along the Duck Walk. Reg Thomas would come down the signal box steps and cross the second set of lines to collect his basket.

This handover was the high spot for Tom because the visit always ended in the same way.

'You're definitely the best man I've seen today,' Mr Thomas would say, then, 'look what I've found behind your ear!' He would laugh, ruffle Tom's hair, and miraculously a silver sixpence would appear and be placed ceremoniously into Tom's eager hands.

The effort Edith Thomas went too, to give her husband his Sunday roast lunch was extraordinary and was a true expression of her love for him.

Reg Thomas and all the other workers lived their lives ensuring that trains ran safely and on time. The children soon became used to the train timetables and it wasn't unusual for parents to say things like…

'You can play until the big goods train comes through. When it whistles, you must come straight in, because your tea will be ready.'

Chapter 4

INFLUENCES

As a child Tom was protected from the harsh reality of the Second World War. He was lucky because he was born three years after that terrible conflict ended. Thanks to the commitment, courage and sacrifice of his parents' generation, he never had to live in a country threatened by war.

Connie and Phil didn't have his good fortune. They were both exposed to the horrors of wartime. Yet Tom heard his mother say on many occasions that in lots of ways the war years were happy years. She would reflect on how the people of this country had pulled together in a time of great adversity. Tom remembers her saying...

'The worst of times bring out the best in people.'

Connie was brought up in one railway family and married into another. She was raised in poor circumstances. Her family never had a great deal, but Connie was bright, intelligent and vivacious. She said she only had one regret in her life. She had passed the school certificate and won a place at Grammar School. Unfortunately her parents Dick and Dorothy were so poor they could not afford the cost of the uniform and travel for their daughter, so she was not allowed to go.

Connie left her village school when she was fourteen. She was offered a job as a housemaid for a husband and wife doctors' practice in Hull. Although the doctors, who were both Jewish, were very kind to her, she was not fulfilling her potential. Despite that, she found that working for them was very convenient, because she could bicycle to work each day from her mam and dad's house.

When her job suddenly ended, she was sad and worried for her kindly employers. As Jewish people, they were greatly alarmed and frightened by the letters they were receiving from their family and friends in Germany, where Hitler and his Nazi thugs were persecuting people of their faith. The doctors closed their medical practice and moved hurriedly to a remote part of Cumberland, somewhere near Lake Windermere. Connie thought about them often throughout the war years, hoping that they were well and safe. She received and sent occasional cards and letters. When Germany was defeated, they returned and she was offered her job back, however her life had moved on so she didn't accept.

It was June 1939. In anticipation of the commencement of hostilities, and the need to recruit men who worked on the land into the forces, the Government had restarted the Women's Land Army[2]. Connie, who was just seventeen, travelled to a recruitment office in Hull and signed up to become a land girl. She was one of the first women in Yorkshire to do so.

Training was minimal, as she was expected to learn on the job. She was billeted in a farmhouse and had free board and lodging, so her earnings were sixteen shillings for a minimum of forty eight hours work a week.

Connie was assigned to the Great Hall Estate Farm in East Yorkshire. The land looked towards Goole and its docks, and stretched along the banks of the Humber, near its confluence with the River Ouse.

In 1940 Connie was issued with the Land Girls' manual[26]. She was also expected to learn the Land Girls' song:

> 'Back to the land, we must all lend a hand,
> To the farms and the fields we must go,
> There's a job to be done,
> Though we can't fire a gun,
> We can still do our bit with the hoe.'

October 1939

The train huffed and hissed its way into the station, until with a final screech of brakes, Connie's carriage halted next to the platform. She grasped the leather strap dangling down the back of her compartment door, released it from its button and let the window down. Taking care to ensure that her new hat didn't fall off, she leant out and felt for the handle.

She opened the door, picked up her case and stepped down onto the platform. She was the only passenger to alight. The platform was deserted. *Not much doing here.* The guard opened his van door, jumped out, manhandled half a dozen empty milk churns onto the stony surface, looked up and down the platform, climbed aboard once more and gave two sharp blasts on his whistle. He nodded at Connie as the train chuffed past her.

Widemarshe Station was no more than a platform with a decayed seat in need of a coat of paint and a sign bearing the station name. A gap in the fence, with a stone path leading down to the road, was clearly the only way out. Beyond, Connie could see no houses, just a landscape of fields and woodland.

A signal box was located down the line, next to some crossing gates, where the road crossed the tracks. Connie watched the signalman climb down the wooden steps from his box. He pushed the gates, climbed back up the steps again and closed his door. He did not look in Connie's direction. The road across the lines was now open, but no vehicles or pedestrians were waiting to cross.

The letter she had received stated quite clearly, that if she arrived on the six o'clock train from Hull, she would be met at the station. She sat down on the seat, stowed her battered suitcase next to her and waited. It was very quiet now the train had gone. She decided to eat the apple her mother had given her.

After a while, she realised it wasn't quiet at all. Birds were singing all around her and she could hear cows lowing. Somewhere in the distance she could make out the sound of a horse's hooves clopping on the road. A few minutes later a good looking chestnut horse, with a white blaze down its forehead, trotted briskly across the railway crossing. It was pulling a polished wooden trap. Even from where she was sitting Connie could see that the yellow painted wheels gleamed. The trap was being driven by a severe looking middle-aged man, carrying a horse whip. He was wearing a trilby hat, a tweed jacket with matching waistcoat and trousers, polished brown leather boots and strapped, canvas puttees covering his lower legs. A girl, wearing a sweater, trousers and a headscarf, was sitting next to him.

The horse and trap clattered past the signal box and pulled up on the road behind the platform. The man and the girl dismounted and walked through the gap in the fence towards Connie.

'You must be the land girl,' said the man, frowning at Connie.

She nodded and smiled nervously trying to remember her manners.

'Good evening. I'm Henry Wilkinson, Great Hall Estate Farm manager,' he continued. 'This is my daughter Maisie.'

Connie held out her hand. 'Pleased to meet you, Mr Wilkinson. I'm Connie Aldridge.'

Henry's hands were huge and calloused. He shook hers vigorously. His severe expression softened.

'Sorry we weren't here to meet you lass. One of us,' he said, casting a loving glance at his daughter, 'had to brush Tantivy's tail before we set off. She's very proud of that horse and we couldn't possibly come and meet you with him looking a mess.'

Connie looked at Maisie and smiled. The girl looked about twelve. She grinned back.

'I think your uniform is very smart.'

'Thank you,' said Connie, adopting a jaunty pose, 'do you like the hat?'

She was wearing her new Land Army kit, and was feeling very sophisticated in her green wool jacket, brown jodhpurs, cream smock, green tie, brown brogues and her splendid broad brimmed hat. It was all a far cry from the housemaid's uniform she had been wearing only a few months ago.

***

1955

On the wall in Railway Cottage was a framed photograph of Connie in her Land Army uniform, standing between two enormous Shire horses. Tom liked to hear stories about her time on the farm.

'Tell me about the horses, Mam.'

Connie would smile at the photograph, wander over to it and polish the glass with a duster, while she told Tom about them.

'I loved those horses. They were gentle giants. I did lots of ploughing with them.'

'What were they called?'

'Castor and Pollux.'

'They're funny names.'

'Mr Stansfield, who owned the farm, was an educated man and apparently named them after twins in Greek mythology, because the two horses were the same age and looked similar.'

'How did you know which was which?'

'That was easy, Pollux had white socks.'

'Did you do spud bashing with them?'

'Potato picking yes,' smiled Connie, correcting him. 'They used to pull the carts while we gathered the potatoes up. They used to walk on, using their own initiative, as we worked down the field; they were always in the right place. Who told you we used to call it spud bashing?'

'Dad.'

'I thought so, that's an expression left over from his army days when they had to peel potatoes for the army cooks.'

'What's initiative?'

'Using their brains. They were very clever.'

'When you were ploughing with them, were they difficult to steer?'

'No, not at all. They knew how to plough better than I did. They were very good natured and ever so patient with me when I was learning.'

'Was the plough heavy?'

'Yes it was, but I was strong in those days. It was a bit tricky when you set off, because you had to push down, to get the plough into the earth. Then you had to give a good lift at the end of the furrow to get the plough up out of the ground. Other than that it was OK.'

'Were you falling over the soil all the time?'

'No you walked down the furrow left by the plough.'

'Did you ever trip up?'

'Sometimes,' she laughed, 'but the boys usually stopped and waited until I got myself upright again.'

'Are they still there on the farm, Mam?'

'Yes I think so, but they'll be getting on a bit. They don't work anymore. They probably just get paraded round the ring, with their brasses on, at local agricultural shows. After the war Mr Stansfield bought another tractor to do the ploughing and heavy hauling. During the war years we had a little John Deere tractor but we were always short of fuel so we couldn't use it all the time. Using the boys meant we could keep on top of the work. The last time I saw Uncle Henry, he told me the boys were in the top pasture living a happy retirement. Mr Stansfield loves them and will never part with them.'

'What sort of tractor is it?'

'What, the new one? Fordson Major I think.'

'Is it blue? Same as my tractor?'

'Yes I think it is,' laughed Connie, giving the photograph one last polish before they wandered into other areas of conversation.

Sometimes she would tell Tom about the Italian prisoners of war, who were regularly marched from their camps to work in the fields.

'They were very good looking and always singing.'

'Were you allowed to talk to them?'

'Yes, a couple of them spoke some English. They liked to chat.'

'What were they called?'

'Well there was Guido; he was their leader, very handsome. He was always the first to start singing their songs. He had a lovely voice, he usually sang in Italian. Another was called Giovanni. He was from Naples. He stayed here after the war and married a girl from Howden. I still see him occasionally when I shop there. He sells his own ice cream from a big tub on the front of his tricycle.'

'If we see him can I have an ice cream?'

'Of course you can. If you're good!'

One story she told Tom, upset her. He had asked her about the war because his dad was at work. She started to tell him about the day she was working alongside the POWs and they had heard some planes circling above them. Suddenly she stopped talking and tried to change the subject. Naturally this aroused Tom's curiosity and with a callous disregard for her feelings, he applied the pressure as only a child can do.

'Mam, you can't start a story and not finish it, it's not fair.'

'Never mind, it's not important.'

'But Mam,' he persisted and Connie relented.

'Well one day we were working in the fields and these planes were circling overhead. Five of them I think. They were our lads and they seemed to be practising dogfights. They were diving at each other and then they'd veer away suddenly, brushing up on their flying skills I expect. Every now and then we'd hear a burst of gunfire as they were practising.'

She took a deep breath and continued. 'Well something went very wrong. They were obviously using live ammunition, because one of the planes was hit. It caught fire. The engine stalled and then cut out altogether. Smoke was pouring from it.'

Connie caught her breath; her hand went to her throat as she recalled the incident. 'We were all horrified. It was obviously going to crash. Thankfully the pilot ejected from his cockpit, his parachute opened and he started drifting down. We all cheered. His plane crashed into a nearby field and exploded. Unfortunately the wind caught his parachute and he drifted out over the Humber. We could see him desperately pulling on his parachute ropes, trying to steer it away from the river. We ran across the field to try to help him, but he landed in the centre of the river. The current was strong and he was drifting. He was fighting to release his parachute. We ran alongside him on the riverbank but we couldn't get to him. The river was very wide and we didn't have a boat. There was a rowing boat on the opposite bank and people standing near it gawping. I screamed and screamed across the river for them to use their boat, but they never launched it, they never even tried.'

'What happened to the pilot, Mam?'

She had tears in her eyes as she told Tom. 'We ran along the bank, shouting encouragement in the hope that he might find the strength to swim to the side, but he couldn't. After a while he disappeared beneath the water and we never saw him again.'

'Did he die, Mam?' Tom asked.

'Yes, I'm sad to say he did, poor man. If only that cowardly bunch on the other bank had launched that boat,' she said bitterly, 'they might have given him a chance. We'll never know.'

She pulled herself together, and smiled sadly at her son. 'It was in the papers a few days later. He was an instructor, flying with some trainee pilots. One of his students, poor guy, fired his gun at the wrong time and shot him down. They were all young men. It was another tragedy of the war.'

They were both upset by the end of her story, so they went into the garden for a breath of fresh air and to feed the chickens. Tom was soon distracted and dribbling grains of corn through the hen run wire to his favourite, Esmerelda. She was a speckled grey Sussex and was the prettiest hen he had ever seen. Children bounce back rapidly and this tragic story rested only fleetingly in Tom's memory at the time, but is recalled easily now he's older. He doesn't think Connie ever forgot.

***

One day every autumn, for five or six years in the early fifties, a tramp would knock on the York's back door.

'Hello missus. How are you? Can you spare a stale crust?'

'Hello John,' Connie would say. She always remembered his name. 'How are you keeping?'

'Alright when the sun shines and the rain stops,' he would answer.

'Come in.' Connie would smile and open the door wider.

'No missus, I won't thank you, I stinks a bit. I'll stay out in the yard.'

'Will you have a cup of tea?'

'That would be grand.'

'Tom, carry one of the chairs out so John can sit down.'

John was a tall, extremely thin man, probably in his late twenties. He wore a shabby army great coat. The caps of his boots were split so badly his toes poked out. The boots lacked laces and were held onto his feet with loops of coarse, hairy string. His trousers were tied around his ankles with dirty old rags. He wore an old army beret on his head. His hair was long and straggly. His skin, what you could see of it, was filthy.

Connie would busy about bringing him a mug of hot sweet tea and a plate of sandwiches, usually cheese or beef. While he was eating his food, she would ask him where he'd been since she'd last seen him.

'Oh round and about. I just follows me boots where ever they lead me. Usually end up in the same old places.'

'Around Yorkshire?'

'Mostly. A bit of Lancashire sometimes, if I wander over the tops.'

While he was finishing his drink, Connie would wrap him a chunk of cheddar in some greaseproof paper and stick a few buns in a bag.

'Here you are John; pop these in your pocket for later.'

'Thanks missus. That was grand. I'll be off then.'

'We'll see you next year?'

'Expect so!'

'And John, here's a pair of woollen socks and half a crown.' Connie would ball together two of Phil's best socks and slip the coin inside. 'They will keep you warm in the winter months.'

'Thank you missus.' said John. He would stuff the socks in his pocket, raise his beret to Connie, salute Tom, say 'Cheerio' and he was gone.

'Was he a soldier, Mam?'

'Yes he was. He told me once that he had a very bad time fighting in Holland. He has never recovered from all the bombing and the horrors he saw. I think he must suffer from shell shock. He doesn't seem to have anyone who cares for him.'

'Where does he come from?'

'When I asked him, he said he didn't know. People have told him that he's got a Yorkshire accent. I sometimes wonder if he's looking for somewhere that he'll recognise.'

'Does he live outside?'

'Yes he does. He told me that he can't stand sleeping inside a building, in case the roof falls on him again.'

'Where does he sleep?'

'Ditches and hay stacks I expect'.

John only visited the York's once a year and stayed for about half an hour. When Tom was eight, John stopped coming.

Chapter 5

RAILWAY LINES

When Tom was growing up there were six men and two women in his immediate family who all worked for the London North Eastern Railway (**LNER**)[3]. This allegiance to a particular industry was not unusual, especially in rural areas of Yorkshire where employment opportunities were limited.

When Phil left school at fourteen he had a choice of two careers. He had a fine tenor voice, so an undertaker who had heard him singing in the church choir, offered him a job as a mourning singer. His job would have been to walk ahead of coffin processions, and lead the bereaved in singing at funerals and wakes.

He didn't fancy that job, so he took the alternative. He became an under footman in Widemarsh Park Hall. The local squire was a retired colonel with an inflated idea of his own importance and a 'them and us' attitude. An under footman's tasks were wide, ranging from cleaning and charging fireplaces and washing windows, and included standing to attention in the dining room, whilst the colonel and his wife ate the numerous courses they were served at mealtimes.

The hours were long and, because he lived in, the pay was poor. He slept in a coarse, planked, cot bed, built into the unheated roof space above the stables. Phil's diet consisted largely of rissoles made from table scraps. The head cook and her husband, the butler, ensured the majority of the domestic budget was used for their own comfort.

When Phil was seventeen, he collapsed at work and had to be carried home to his parents. He was suffering from malnutrition. It took John and Enid York three months to nurse Phil back to health. The colonel expressed no concern. John York would not allow his son to go back to the Hall.

When Phil recovered he managed to get a job as a junior porter and railway goods yard assistant. In those pre-Second World War days, most agricultural produce was transported by rail. Phil spent a lot of his working hours loading heavy bags of corn, cart-loads of sugar beet and other root vegetables into railway wagons. Because the goods yard had no mechanical assistance, everything had to be done by hand. This heavy work was quite a trial for a slight young man just recovering from a life threatening illness, but nevertheless he got the job done and satisfied his manager.

Phil's father, John York, was a line ganger in charge of a team of platelayers. He lived in a crossings house, so his wife Enid did the gates whenever they needed to be opened to road traffic.

Connie's father, Dick Aldridge worked most of his life in a busy shunting yard in Darlington, coupling wagons and coaches to railway engines. Dick's father and his grandfather Richard had both worked in the same shunting yards. It was dangerous work. Richard died in a shunting accident when he was in his early forties. The steam engine on one set of wagons suddenly jerked backwards, trapping him. He was crushed to death, caught between two sets of wagon buffers while coupling two lengths of wagons together. Accidents of this sort were common.

In his later years, after injuring his ankle, Dick Aldridge was given a position as signal man and gatekeeper, at a small rural station in North Yorkshire. His wife Dorothy worked as the porter. Their house was on the station, with their door opening onto the platform. They were effectively on duty seven days a week. To ensure the station was always manned, they took alternate days off. Each year Connie took young Tom to her parents' home for a summer holiday.

'Grandma, can I have my breakfast in the signal box with Grandad?'

'As long as you don't get under his feet. Would you like a fried egg sandwich?'

'Yes please. Will the cows be coming through?'

'In about ten minutes. Can you hear them mooing?'

'Why are they mooing?'

'They know it's milking time.'

The little signal box was at the end of the platform where the narrow country road crossed the tracks. Dick's main duties were to ensure the safety of the sparse local population, their vehicles and animals as they crossed the busy Scarborough to Hull line.

Farmer Sam Forrest had grazing pastures on both sides of the line. When the grass was rich on the far side of the track, he brought his herd to and from field to milking parlour twice a day. The black and white cows plodded down the lane early morning and late afternoon and waited patiently, until Dick Aldridge, sometimes with Tom, climbed down from the signal box to open the gates and let them pass. The farmer wobbled behind the cows on his bike giving out regular encouraging cries of 'walk on ladies' to keep his beasts moving. Tom and Dick were both convinced that the cows were so set in their routine they could easily do the journey without assistance from Sam.

The only time Dick didn't work for the railway, was during the First World War. He was a mule driver in charge of a team of six, pulling heavy guns through the mud and death-filled trenches, of the Somme. He survived the horrors of that terrible war without comment, but always suffered quietly with a bad chest, a legacy of a German mustard gas attack.

Before Tom's grandma Dorothy married Dick she had worked as a domestic, scrubbing the floors in a Darlington hospital. As a result of this relentless hard work she had a stoical disposition and a lifelong attachment to blocks of dark pink carbolic soap. Whenever Tom stayed with his grandparents, Dorothy always gave him a vigorous scrub down with carbolic soap in their tin bath. The smell lingers in his memory to this day.

Dick and Dorothy eventually retired to a small railway cottage near Fleet Railway Station. It is five miles up the line from Halthorpe. Their cottage was on the side of the tracks, separated from the lines by a three feet wide stone path. The trains thundered past day and night. The intrusive noise, vibration and shaking was at its worst when a train passed on the track immediately next to their home. Then Tom's grandparents would have to stand up and hold the dinner plates, the clock and the radio. This was such a part of their daily routine that Tom was convinced they acted unconsciously. The only time Tom ever heard his grandma complain about this constant disruption was when the 18.55 train came through. This coincided with *The Archers* on the wireless in the evening. She missed two minutes of every episode.

'Why does that blessed train come through every time Walter Gabriel is saying something? I'll bet he was chasing after Mrs Perkins again, the old devil.'

'Who's Walter Gabriel, Grandma?'

'He lives in Ambridge, he's sweet on Mrs Perkins. He calls her "me old pal, me old beauty."'

Grandad Dick and young Tom were very close. Dick was a witty and gentle man. A couple of times each month he would take Tom with him to shop in Goole. Grandad Dick would board the train at Fleet Station. He would hang out of the carriage window as it pulled into Halthorpe and wave through the billowing clouds of steam, to ensure Tom climbed onto the right bit of the train. Tom would pile aboard and they would rattle along looking out at the people, houses, fields, ponds, ditches, wildfowl and other things of interest that appeared along the track side.

'Look there's a little hut. What's it for?'

'It's where the lamp men and platelayers keep their tools.'

'There's a woman hanging out washing. She has pegs in her mouth.'

'Give her a wave.'

'Grandad what bird is that?'

'That's a mother mallard, look in the reeds just behind her, she's got some ducklings.'

'How many has she got?'

'How many can you see?'

'Six.'

'So can I.'

These magical moments were fleeting, but stuck in Tom's memory forever.

'Are we going over the river bridge?'

'You know we are. We go over it every time we go to Goole. Pay attention when we cross, there may be a ship sailing along the Ouse, or waiting for the bridge to open.'

'Will the man open the bridge when we're going over it?'

'No of course not, the train would fall into the river.'

'Will he open it when we're past?'

'Yes he will and he'll put all the railway signals to red, to stop all the trains.'

'Where will the ship be going?'

'I think a lot of them sail to Russia and back.'

'Is it cold there?'

'Very.'

'When we get to Goole, can I have a Sherbet Dip?'

'Yes, we'll buy one in Maynard's.'

'Dad's given me money for a comic.'

'What do you fancy?'

'Beano.'

Dick would buy his ounce of pipe tobacco, a quarter of black bullets, and exchange his western for a different book at the stall in the local market hall. They would have a cup of tea and a scone in the market cafe and Tom would listen fascinated as his grandad used his considerable charm, to chat up the café ladies. It was a time of happiness, love and laughter.

Keeping his family safe always concerned Dick Aldridge. The implications of living so close to four sets of busy railway tracks were never ignored. Tom was always carefully instructed on how to cross the lines safely. It was impressed on him he must always look both ways and never take risks. His grandparents' house was similar to his parents in its lack of water, electricity and inside sanitation. Dick had to cross the lines several times a day to fetch water from the tap, which was located on the far side of the tracks.

His knowledge about the times of all the trains was excellent. However when Dick was crossing the lines one morning, he was taken by surprise. He waited until the scheduled train had passed, then stepped out to cross the lines. An express 'excursion special' was coming the other way at high speed. He tried to run out of its way, but he didn't have enough time or speed and so it hit him. He was flung along the tracks and died from blood loss and trauma injuries. His leg was severed at thigh level. Dick was seventy nine years old. Like his grandfather, he was killed in a railway accident.

Connie's brother, David, was a platelayer. Fred, one of Phil's brothers worked as a lamp man, the other brother, Bert was a signal man. Uncle Fred, was a cheerful man who got a great deal of pleasure and satisfaction from his job. He spent his days working along a set length of track, ensuring that, whatever the weather, the lamps never went out. He would climb up the signal gantries and posts, remove the old used lamps and replace them with newly serviced ones. The lamps were lit twenty four hours a day, every day of the year.

Wet, windy, stormy, freezing cold or snowy weather made no difference to Fred. He had his lamps to change whatever the conditions. People's safety and their lives depended upon him. Tom recalls standing at the end of a station platform, on a very windy day, watching his uncle working on a swaying signal gantry. Some platelayers were working on the track nearby.

The song Fred was singing down to them, improvised from the sea shanty 'The Stormy Winds do Blow',[35] made Tom laugh then and still does now.

> And the raging gales do roar, and the stormy winds do blow.
> While we jolly lamp men, are up and up aloft,

And the platelayers are skiving down below, below, below.
And you daft buggers are shoveling down below.

It is easy to imagine the ribald responses the men shouted back to him.

Uncle Bert, worked as a signalman on a remote country line. The goods and passenger service was invaluable to the scattered, local community. Bert spent a lot of hours alone in his signal box, with only a few trains to service. To pass the time he painted beautiful murals of steam trains on the fireplace and inside walls of the signal box. They were very well executed and admired by everyone who saw them. A decade later, in the 1960s, this line was closed in the infamous Dr Beeching railway closures. The cabin and its works of art were bulldozed.

Tom's father and his two brothers joined the army within months of the start of the Second World War. Conscription had been reintroduced in October 1939 for all men between twenty and twenty-three years old. Railway workers were in a reserved occupation and were exempt from joining the forces, however patriotism was high and public opinion was all for young men joining up.

Phil went to a recruitment office in York and joined the 15th/19th King's Royal Hussars, a tank regiment. During his time working as an under footman he had collected cigarette cards depicting the heavy military machinery and weapons used in World War 1 and these had fired his imagination.

This period coincided with what Winston Churchill called the 'colossal military disaster' in Europe, when the German armies[4] had routed the British forces and driven them to the beaches and harbour at Dunkirk. Three hundred and thirty eight thousand British and Allied troops were evacuated in Operation Dynamo between 27 May and 4 June 1940. This event is always remembered for the courage shown by the 'Little Ships fleet', which ferried the surviving and wounded troops back home across the channel in terrible warfare conditions.

The Little Ships managed to get most allied troops safely back to England, but virtually all British heavy military equipment was abandoned and left in enemy hands. Phil had joined the Hussars at a point when they were desperately short of equipment. Britain had less than a hundred tanks. Phil stayed with the Hussars until he was discharged in April 1945, while recovering from his war injuries.

After leaving the army, Phil had three anxious months of medical examinations and fitness tests before he was once again accepted as suitable and fit for a job on the railways. His background as a member of an established railway family greatly assisted him in getting this job.

He rejoined the **LNER** as a railway porter in July 1945. Two years later he and Connie married and moved into a railway cottage near Goole.

***

'Mam, why am I not on your wedding photograph?' asked Tom, staring at the black and white photo on the mantelpiece over the range. 'I can see you and Dad, and all the family, but not me.'

'That's because you weren't born, silly. It was another eleven months before you popped into the world.' Connie ruffled Tom's hair thoughtfully. After a while she said, 'I loved that dress. I made it from a pattern that was in Woman's Weekly. Uncle Jack managed to get me some parachute silk. The dress was a devil to make though. It had 'shoulder of mutton' sleeves and the bodice had loads of tiny tucks. I used Aunty Phoebe's treadle machine, which was a nightmare to get the hang of, and the silk kept slipping. It took me months! At one point I thought I'd be going down the aisle in my uniform. Still, it was worth persevering. Aunty Phoebe lent me her pearls. She made my headdress from some net and lace she'd kept from before the war. When my dad walked me down the aisle I felt like the Queen.'

'Can I see it, Mam?'

'No love. I gave it to cousin Beryl in Darlington, to wear when she got married. I think she eventually gave it to a friend. Goodness knows where it is now.'

'You had lots of flowers. What colour were they?'

'Yes. I was lucky. Uncle Bert won prizes for his roses. They were in different shades of pink and some white. Doesn't your dad look smart in his demob suit?'

Tom was enjoying his mam's story and cuddled closer. 'Who's that?'

'That's my friend Marie. She was a land girl too. She was my bridesmaid.'

'Where was I born?'

'In a little cottage, next to the river.'

'Was Dad there?'

'He was outside in the yard repairing my bicycle, although how the daft man thought I was going to ride it, after spending twenty three hours giving birth to you, I can't imagine.'

'Was the doctor there?'

'Yes and the midwife.'

'Why was Dad outside?'

'The midwife made him. She said she had enough on her hands, looking after me, without having a husband under her feet.'

'Was he wearing his demob suit?'

Connie laughed, 'No, he kept that for Sunday best.'

'Did you have a party?'

'What are you on about?'

'For your wedding.'

'Oh I see what you mean. Yes we all went back to Grandma York's house. It was a swell do.'

'Did you have jelly?'

'Yes, and we had boiled ham and egg salad, potted meat sandwiches, scones and jam tarts.'

'Did you have Christmas cake too?' Tom was remembering the tiny box containing a wedge of iced fruit cake that had arrived from his mam's Rochdale friend, who had just got married.

'Wedding cake do you mean? Sort of, but it was made of cardboard.'

'Cardboard! Ugh! That must have tasted horrible.'

'We didn't eat it. It was just for the photos. You couldn't get the ingredients after the war, so Grandma York hired a wedding cake shape from a shop in Goole. Grandma Aldridge made a beautiful Victoria sponge to hide underneath. When it was time to cut the cake, we just lifted off the cake shape – and 'bob's your uncle…'

Tom wished they still had the cardboard cake. It would have been good to use it for a magic trick.

***

The Dutch River railway cottage was the York's first home. The grandly named Dutch River was built to relieve the flooding in the lower reaches of the River Don by diverting some of the meandering flow to the nearby Ouse, and away from its natural meeting with the Trent. It is actually just a large man-made drainage canal, built by Dutch engineer Cornelius Vermuyden. It is five miles long and stretches from Thorne to join the Ouse at Goole.

By the time Tom was one year old, his father had transferred to Halthorpe Station, so the family moved away from Dutch River into the railway cottage where Tom was to spend his childhood.

His father's work at the station involved looking after passengers, selling tickets and giving travel advice when the ticket clerk wasn't on duty. He also kept the platforms clean and tidy between trains, checked parcel deliveries and loaded and unloaded wagons in the adjacent goods sidings.

During this period he also undertook first aid training through the St John Ambulance. This training was to be tested to the limit some years later, when he was working at Fleet Station a few miles up the track and was the first on the scene after Dick Aldridge had been hit by an express train.

A great joy in Tom's life was to visit Phil at Halthorpe Station and watch the trains coming in and out. His visits frequently coincided with baking day. If his dad was working an afternoon shift, Connie would send Tom along the Duck Walk with a freshly baked pasty or a couple of cheese scones for Phil's tea.

February 1957

Sitting Bull was singing at the top of his voice and enjoying seeing his hot breath vaporise, creating little wispy clouds in the cold air.

> 'The runaway train came down the track and she blew
> The runaway train came down the track and she blew
> The runaway train came down the track – her whistle wide and her throttle back
> And she blew, blew, blew, blew, blew.'

His song, accompanied by hearty blowing, floated over the icy surface of the Delph and echoed from the frozen embankment as Red Bess tore along the Duck Walk, leaving a slipstream of cinder dust.

> 'The fireman said he rang the bell and she blew
> The fireman said he rang the bell and she blew
> The fireman said he rang the bell – the engineer said, **you did like hell!**
> And she blew, blew, blew, blew, blew.'[36]

As Red Bess galloped around the halfway bend, where the fence fleetingly diverted to avoid a tree which jutted out over the walk, Sitting Bull spotted Charlie Wilson. He was perched on the top rail of the fence, gazing out across the Delph. Sitting Bull screeched to a halt. Charlie was one of his favourites; always a smile, and usually a spare chocolate biscuit in his bait box.

'Hello Tom,' said Charlie, using Sitting Bull's English name, 'good song.'

'How Charlie,' panted Sitting Bull, 'Runaway Train. Michael Holliday.'

'He's very good.'

Sitting Bull noticed Charlie wasn't smiling.

'Are you alright Charlie?'

'Fine Tom, fine. Just looking at the ice on the pond.'

'Dad reckons it's six inches thick.'

'I remember back in 1947, a really cold winter, the Delph was frozen so hard we played ice hockey on it. Mary taught me to skate. It was a lot thicker then than it is now, so no walking on it.'

'Mam says I mustn't go near, it's starting to crack at the edge.'

'Quite right, it's very dangerous.'

'Charlie,' continued Sitting Bull, 'there were Swans on the Delph at Christmas, did you see them?

'Yes Tom I saw them. They were beautiful. Where are you going?'

'Taking my dad his tea.'

'Give him my regards. Take care crossing the line.'

'Bye Charlie.'

'See you later Alligator.'

'In a while Crocodile,' shouted Sitting Bull, spurring Red Bess into action and galloping off down the Duck Walk towards the station.'

'Bill Haley and his Comets,'[37] shouted Charlie after him.

At the embankment end of the Duck Walk he 'tethered' Red Bess in the grass and climbed over the fence onto the platelayers' path, which led under the station bridge. He looked across the tracks at the signal box. Mr Thomas slid a window open and beamed across at Tom.

'How! Sitting Bull,' said Mr Thomas.

'How! Mr Thomas,' said Sitting Bull.

'Going to visit your dad?'

'Yup! Red Bess needed a run.'

'The speed you were going, you'd have passed those darned Apaches and bushwhacked them on their way back to their tepees. Red Bess seems to be running well today,' he continued, 'must be due to this cold weather.'

'She had a thorn in her foot last week, but Dad pulled it out,'

'Hoof, Sitting Bull,' said Mr Thomas, 'Horses have hooves not feet.'

Sitting Bull hadn't the heart to tell Mr Thomas that Red Bess was only a pretend horse. She was actually a little red bike.

Sitting Bull liked Mr Thomas; he knew so much about cowboys and indians. A few weeks ago he'd told him about a man called Davy Crockett who wore a raccoon hat and now there was a song about him on the radio. Sitting Bull had asked his mam for a raccoon hat for his birthday. His mam said that when she had a minute she'd pop over to America and get one.

'Mam's going to get me a raccoon hat,' shouted Sitting Bull across the tracks.

'Ask her to get me one as well, it's a bit cold on top when there's no sheaves in your hay loft,' laughed Mr Thomas, stroking his bald dome.

'Will do,' shouted Sitting Bull.

'Wait for me to wave, before you go across the sleepers,' shouted Mr Thomas, as Sitting Bull set off along the path under the bridge, 'there's an excursion coming through.'

'OK pardner!' shouted Sitting Bull. He stopped and turned back. 'Did you say an excursion? What's pulling her?'

'It could be the *Mallard*. She went up to Hull earlier.'

'I've never seen her. Dad and I can watch her go through together if I hurry.'

Whenever Tom went under the station bridge, he always felt that he'd magically walked into another world. The railway station, where his dad worked, just appeared. You couldn't see any of it from the Duck Walk as it was all hidden by the embankment. Twelve big strides from the Duck Walk fence and there it was – the sleeper crossing, the signal gantry, the two long concrete-edged, gravel-covered platforms that seemed to stretch forever into the distance and the tubs that his dad planted with flowers every summer.

Tom looked both ways, up and down the track, and then under the bridge to where he could see Mr Thomas watching him from the signal box.

Mr Thomas gave the OK wave, his voice echoing through the bridge way.

'All clear, pardner.'

Tom scampered across the sleepers and onto the platform. He scuffed his wellies in the carefully raked gravel and sang as he made two little railway tracks all the way along the platform to the station building.

> 'Born on a mountain top in Tennessee, greenest state in the land of the free.
> Raised in the woods so he knew every tree, killed him a bear when he was only three.
> Davy, Davy Crockett, king of the wild frontier.'[38]

Tom ran towards the ticket office, stood on his tiptoes and peered through the service hatch. The blank tickets were all neatly stacked in their little wooden racks, the date machine perched on the counter edge and the black ticket punch dangled on its string. The fire was roaring in its hearth and Mrs Potter, the ticket clerk, was sitting at her desk writing on a piece of paper. Mrs Potter and her husband Stan, another signalman, also lived in Halthorpe.

'Hello Mrs Potter,' yelled Tom, through the hatch.

Mrs Potter jumped slightly in her chair; she'd been very engrossed in filling in the weekly summary and hadn't anticipated any customers at this time of day.

'Oh! Hello Sitting Bull, it's you. What a shock you gave me.'

'Mr Thomas thinks the *Mallard* may be pulling the excursion. Where's she going?' continued Tom, unperturbed by Mrs Potter's surprise.

'Hull to Leeds,' smiled Mrs Potter, warming to Tom's enthusiasm.

'When's she due through?'

Mrs Potter looked at the big pendulum clock on the wall. 'In twenty minutes if she's on time. Twenty two minutes past four.'

'I hope it is the *Mallard*. She's a 'Streak'.'

'Have you ever seen one before?'

'Don't think so,' said Tom, 'I bet you've seen lots?'

'One or two. Although we don't get many through here; they're mainly on the London, York and Newcastle run. I saw the *Nigel Gresley* once and the *Union of South Africa*, both beautiful engines.'

'Where's Dad?' said Tom, 'he mustn't miss the *Mallard*.'

'He's sweeping out some wagons, in the siding shed, I think.'

Tom had gone before she finished the sentence. He dashed around the side of the porters' cabin and went through the little gate into the station yard and sidings. He had to push hard to open the gate, as it had a big weight on a chain to keep it closed. The gate had a sign:

Trespassers Will Be Prosecuted
Railway Staff Only

Tom had once asked his dad if he was a trespasser.

'No son. You're the eight year old son of a leading porter, so you get a special dispensation.'

Tom didn't know what a special dispensation was, but he felt very important.

The station yard had three sets of rail tracks. Two of them led into the siding shed and the third into the pole yard. Two of the tracks had little spur lines where wagons could be stored if necessary.

Tom ran across the three tracks and jumped onto the fence that surrounded the pole yard. He hung there for a few minutes, watching as a newly trimmed telegraph pole lumbered out of the sawmill side onto the big rollers. The rollers ran across the yard in the shape of a big flattened out V; the poles came out of the trimming and shaping mill at the top end and pushed each other slowly down the gentle ramp, into a bubbling trough of creosote at the bottom. As each pole entered the trough, a soaking wet one was pushed out at the other side then plopped onto the drying racks.

Mr Fry was working hard as usual, pushing the poles into line with a huge metal bar.

'Hello Mr Fry,' shouted Tom, waving.

Mr Fry waved back. Tom's mam had told him that Mr Fry had accidentally cut the top of his thumb off at work, but as always Tom couldn't manage to see if this was true. He was too far away. Tom was desperate to see what it looked like, but it seemed that his ghoulish curiosity would never be satisfied because he was forbidden to go in to the dangerous confines of the saw mill.

According to Phil, Mr Fry had been a very brave man during the war.

'He was a commando and went on some very dangerous missions. He killed lots of the enemy with his commando knife. He crept up behind them and slit their throats.' Dad always made him shiver with excitement when he ran his finger across Tom's throat to show him how it was done.

After the telegraph poles had dried on the racks for a week, they were lifted onto the bogeys kept on the siding line and towed away by Puffing Billy, the shunting engine. Puffing Billy pulled and pushed the loaded bogeys, one by one, into the station yard sidings and then collected them all together, until there were sufficient to form a train.

Today the little engine was sitting idle on the spur track that ran between the siding shed and the pole yard. Tom jumped down from the fence and walked alongside her, tapping the three big wheels with his hand. *Have I time to climb into the cab?* She wasn't really called Puffing Billy[39] – that was just Tom's name for her. Charlie, who knew a lot about engines, said she was a J-72 and that her class had been built to the same design for over fifty years. She had a tall tapering chimney and a large, dome-shaped lump on top of her boiler. The cab had a circular window looking forward at both sides so the driver and the footman could see where they were going. She also had a little built-in coal bunker that held two tons of coal.

Tom loved to watch her when she was steamed up and working, huffing and puffing moving the bogeys. If the load was really heavy, her wheels would spin and squeal until she found purchase on the rails, then she would puff importantly away, belching clouds of pure white steam.

Suddenly remembering the *Mallard*, Tom hurried along the track side and through the big open door into the siding shed. Two high sided goods wagons were alongside the loading platform. Steady brushing noises were coming from the nearest wagon.

'Dad,' shouted Tom.

A porter's cap appeared, perched atop a smiling red face.

'Hello Sitting Bull, what are you doing here?'

'Mam sent me with your sandwiches and a scone, Charlie Wilson sends his regards, Mr Thomas says the *Mallard* is pulling the excursion and Mrs Potter says she is due through here at 4.22pm which is nearly now,' Tom babbled without taking a breath.

'I see,' said Phil, slightly taken aback by this overload of information. His mouth twitched at the corners. He looked as though he was fighting the urge to laugh at the panic stricken expression on his son's face.

'What time is it now?' he said, unbuttoning his jacket and reaching into his waistcoat pocket for his fob watch. 'Fourteen minutes past four, plenty of time, I'll just finish this wagon and we'll go and watch her go through.' Phil returned to his sweeping.

'Not a man to be rushed, is your father. Slow but reliable,' Mam was always saying.

Shifting from foot to foot, Tom fretted while his dad continued his methodical brushing. Putting the little bag of food down on a sleeper, Tom dashed out of the open doorway to look across at the signal gantry. As he watched, the main line signal juddered and was pulled into the up position by Mr Thomas.

'Dad! She's boarded,' screamed Tom.

'We're alright, that means she's just left Brough. The signalman will have dinged his bell through to Reg Thomas as she passed his box. We've got four minutes.'

Phil climbed leisurely down from the wagon and followed the running figure of his son back across the siding yard, only pausing to pick up the little bag of sandwiches that had been left behind. When he reached the station platform, Tom was peering down the tracks.

'Can you see her?'

'No Dad, not yet.'

Phil took out his watch out again. 'We should be able to spot her anytime now.'

'There she is,' yelled his son. His slight frame was jumping up and down so excitedly that Phil felt obliged to grab one of the flailing arms, just in case the lad fell onto the tracks.

'Can you see her Dad?' yelled Tom, wanting his dad to share his pleasure at spotting the distant dot with its tiny plume of steam.

Phil peered down the line, with his hand dramatically shielding his eyes. 'Yes that's her, she'll be here in a minute, she'll be doing at least seventy miles an hour when she comes through, so don't blink.'

Mrs Potter came out of the ticket office and stood next to them.

'Don't forget to wave at the driver Tom, he might give you a whistle,' she said.

Tom's arm went up ready.

The engine driver reached for the whistle halyard and pulled long and hard. The sound whirled around the station buildings and echoed back from the bridge and the embankment walls as the gleaming blue engine whooshed towards them. *Wow she's beautiful.* Tom felt the thrill and rush of her speed, admired the dazzle of her streamlined casing, and the grace of the long sweeping arch over the wheels. As the cab flashed by, he caught sight of her number, 60022 proudly emblazoned on a red background. The pull of her slipstream tried to sweep him off his feet as one hundred and sixty five tons of steam engine roared past him. It was only five yards away.

The excitement was overwhelming. He jumped up and down, up and down yelling 'I've seen the *Mallard*, I've seen the *Mallard*.'

Phil and Mrs Potter laughed at his antics, delighted to share this moment with him. The train screamed under the station bridge, trailing huge billows of steam and smoke, and then it was gone.

Chapter 6

ANIMALS

After they married, Connie and Phil kept chickens for eggs and for meat. They also sold any surplus as dressed birds at Christmas, or, as was more usual, gave them away as gifts to those whose need was greater than theirs. Eventually they also kept rabbits, pigs and ducks.

Their only pet was Felix their cat, although even she was expected to earn her keep by controlling vermin. Living in the country and rearing animals means there are always rats and mice around.

'Tom will you clean out the rabbits?'

'Have we got any bedding?'

'Your dad says we've run out, but he's spotted lots of dead grass in the hedge bottoms down Green Lane. Why don't you take a sack and gather some? Take Tonto with you. I saw him mooching around on the backs, I think he's waiting for you.'

'OK, we can pretend we're hunting.'

'Don't dawdle. You can each have a ginger biscuit, when you get back. Take care going through the railway gates, listen and look both ways.'

'Will do Mam.'

Sitting Bull and Tonto (Bernard), both experienced railway children, were trusted to go over the lines at the Green Lane crossing.

The lane, a grassy track, stretched from Halthorpe through the fields to the Widemarsh Road, half a mile away. Tom knew the lane well. He rode Red Bess along it when he bicycled to Widemarsh with his parents for Sunday lunch at Grandfather York's house.

'Come on, I'll show you where the gypos' camp is,' said Tom, running towards the burned patch of grass, where they'd had their fire.

'How many caravans were there?'

'Half a dozen and about twelve horses. Look at all the empty tins in the hedge bottom.'

'Cor! They're all Cross and Blackwell baked bean tins,' Bernard said, poking at the pile with his stick. 'Is that all they eat?'

'And rabbits and hedgehogs.'

'Hedgehogs! You're kidding! They're covered in spines.'

'Dad says the gypos roll them up in clay and bake them in their fire.'

'What, alive?'

'Expect so. When they're cooked they crack off the baked clay and all the spines come off with it.'

'What do they taste like?'

'Don't know. Pork maybe?'

***

The Yorks kept rabbits for meat and fur. Connie made delicious rabbit pies and stews. She also scraped and cured the skins to make mitts. Warm hands were essential when bike riding in chilly East Yorkshire winters.

'Come here son and I'll show you how to skin a rabbit.'

The dead rabbit was lying on its back on the scullery table.

'The first thing you do is open its belly up, with a nice straight cut,' said Phil, cutting lengthways down the rabbit's stomach. He nodded to Tom.

'Now stick your thumbs in and gently pull the skin apart.'

'Uurgh! Are those its guts?'

'Yes, now slide your finger in and pull them out.'

Tom hooked his finger into the guts and pulled, jumping back as they spilled out of the stomach cavity.

'That's good,' encouraged Phil, 'now get the scissors and snip them free.'

'Is that OK?'

'Yes fine, let's get the skin off. Watch me. You've got to get the back legs out first and then it's easy. I'll do the first leg and you do the other.'

Phil bent the back leg and eased the fur over the thigh, and then the knee joint, gently pulling the skin away from the flesh. The leg came free of the pelt and Phil chopped the foot off.

'OK, your turn. I'll just cut its tail off first. I've promised a rabbit tail to Jim Phelps. He wants it to pollinate his tomatoes in the spring.'

'How does he do that?'

'He uses the fine hairs to move pollen from flower to flower. Now careful, think what you're doing. Hold the skin with that hand and gently push the leg out with the other.'

'Yuk, it's very slippery.'

'Grip harder and wobble it a bit, to pull the skin away. That's it, you've got the hang of it now.'

'It's coming free Dad.'

'Well done. Now pull the skin off all the leg and I'll chop the foot off.' When they'd skinned the rabbit up to its neck Phil chopped the head off, without cutting the skin. 'I'll trim the skin neatly in a minute. Go and get a plate, put the rabbit carcass on it and put it in the pantry. Then go and tell your mam that you've skinned your first rabbit.'

***

Usually Phil and Connie kept around two dozen chickens and a cockerel. The birds were housed in a wire run and were locked into their huts each night to keep them safe from foxes.

During the day, the ferocious looking cockerel, with his bright red wattle, strode around the run, looking important, but being completely ignored by his hens, unless he was treading them. He could be tetchy so Tom had to wear his wellingtons when he went in the run, to avoid being spurred down the back of his legs.

Each spring, some of the hens became broody, a clear sign that they were ready to sit on eggs. These birds were easy to spot, because they would stay in the hen hut after they had lain, gathering theirs and any other eggs together to sit upon. They were often aggressive and bad tempered and could give a sharp and bloody peck to the unwary.

Phil would close one of the chicken huts and turn it into a broody house by installing a bank of nesting boxes and erecting a temporary run next to it.

'Help me sort out the eggs to put under the broody hens. Leave the pot ones in the hut; I don't want the hens to think they've lost all their eggs. Don't get the very big eggs, they're poor hatchers, take them in to Mam and we'll eat those. The same goes for the small ones because they give small chicks.'

Phil would put about a dozen clean, medium-size eggs under each broody hen. They would sit patiently, all day and night, only standing up occasionally to turn the eggs over. Their urge to sit was so strong that, in many cases, they had to be lifted off their nest each morning and carried out into the run, so they could have a drink and eat some grain. The door to the nesting hut had to be closed, to stop them going straight back onto their precious eggs. They usually clucked around cantankerously for half an hour or so until the broody house door was reopened, and then they would hurry back onto their nests, fluffing up their feathers, before settling down for another day.

Connie frequently had to restrain Tom from going into the broody house, to look under the hens. Being pecked was a risk he was willing to take.

'Leave those poor birds alone. It'll be another week before the eggs start hatching. You'll upset them if you keep lifting them up to look at their eggs. You don't want them to desert their nests do you?'

'No Mam, I don't.'

'If you go back in there today, I'll tell your Dad when he comes home.'

'Oh, alright.'

'Do you understand?'

'Yes Mam.'

After about three weeks, Tom's torment ended and the chicks would start to hatch. Connie and Phil were very busy checking on progress and ensuring that the chicks stayed healthy. When the fluffy yellow chicks hatched they were kept in the chicken hut for about a week and fed on very finely chopped boiled egg and chick crumbs. Any weak ones were gathered up, put into a cardboard box and brought into the warmth in front of the range. They were usually hand fed until they were strong enough to return to their siblings. Tom's job was to guard the box of weakling chicks and make sure Felix didn't get them.

'Don't let that perishing cat get anywhere near them. She'll have one if you don't keep alert.'

'Why? Will she eat them? She's not hungry.'

'She still has her hunting instinct. Why do you think Felix catches so many rats and mice? She doesn't eat them, just dumps them on the back step for us to admire. She just likes to hunt.'

Felix was not a good loser and, after being repeatedly denied access to the chick box, she usually strode, with tail lashing, into a corner of the living room to sit facing the wall, sulking. It always took considerable cajoling and petting to get her out of this bad mood.

When the chicks were big enough, they were let out with the mother hens, into the broody house run, to be 'grown on'. The mothers would scratch up the earth and make little clucking noises to encourage the little chicks, which would dash and dart between their mothers' feet, snatching up little morsels. Scraps of vegetables were chopped up into small pieces and thrown into the pen for the hens and chicks to peck at. Connie often won first prize for her eggs at the village show. When asked how she got the egg yolks so big and golden coloured, she would say: 'It's all down to vegetables. I always give my hens plenty of greens.'

Two or three weeks after the hatchings, the hens usually lost their urge to brood and were put back in the main chicken run to give them a rest. Phil would leave one good well feathered hen in with all the chicks to brood and mother them.

Keeping poultry was a necessity, not a luxury. As a child, Tom sometimes learned the lessons of home economy the hard way.

'Dad, I've just been feeding the hens and Esmerelda isn't there, she must have escaped!'

'Did you enjoy your lunch on Sunday?'

'Yes…awhh!…Dad!'

It was some weeks before the memory of eating Esmerelda faded, and several months before he forgave his father.

***

One year the Yorks were given three full grown Muscovy Ducks. They had been reared as pets at a local poultry farm and were called Tim, Min and Ruby. They were beautiful, large, black-and-white birds native to Mexico and South America, but hardy enough to survive British winters. Tim, the drake had bright red wattles around his beak.

At first Phil put them in with the chickens. This didn't last long, because they were always trying to swim and bathe in the water bowl and made a terrible muddy mess. To solve this problem he built them their own duck run, that included a large concrete bathing trough.

The ducks were happy and started laying eggs. Connie declared the eggs excellent for baking. The next spring Min hollowed out a nest in the corner of the pen and sat stoically upon her eggs. She hatched out three beautiful ducklings, which were reared and sold.

The ducks were not kept for very long, because Phil decided that Tim and Ruby were past their prime. Tim clearly wasn't up to the job and the Yorks couldn't afford to keep non-productive animals.

All three were relocated onto the Delph, as it had a little reedy island, at the embankment end, where they could sleep at night safe from foxes. They lived a happy retirement, with Tom and the other children regularly feeding them scraps of bread.

***

From around 1952 the family always kept one or two pigs. These were slaughtered in early December by a local butcher. Once an animal was killed, the carcass was brought into the scullery and hung, head down, from a large hook fixed firmly into the ceiling. A two-gallon enamel bucket was put underneath the pig to catch the blood. Phil cut the pig's throat and work began in earnest.

The scullery window was kept open to let the winter breezes blow in, so that the room was kept as cold and airy as possible.

Phil opened the pig. The scullery started to fill with the smells of raw meat, blood and offal. Felix the cat appeared, as if by magic, attracted by these irresistible aromas. Phil took out the pig's kidneys, liver, heart, stomach and the long coils of intestines. The kidneys and liver were immediately washed and trimmed by Connie, then put to one side in bowls on the pantry floor. Felix would by this time be enraptured, rubbing her body appealingly against Phil's legs to attract his attention, and giving out her loudest meows and howls.

'Tom, grab hold of that perishing cat and take her outside will you? She's twining round my legs so much, she's going to have me on me back.' Grasping the wriggling cat firmly by the scruff of her neck, Tom would put her out into the backyard. She would lash her tail to show her anger at being forced to leave the scullery. 'Give her this to chew on, or she'll sulk.' Phil would pass Tom a thin strip of fleshy and bloody pig skin. 'We might have a couple of minute's peace now! Careful! Don't trip over the blood bucket!'

By the time he was six or seven years old, Tom wasn't just looking after an excited cat. He was helping by squeezing out the residual contents of the intestines and washing them clean, in buckets of cold water. To ensure both sides of the intestinal tubes were clean, he would turn them inside out by pulling them onto the round handle of a wooden spoon. This was a fiddly job as the intestines were wet and slimy.

'Mam this won't go on the handle.'

'Give it to me and I'll get you started. Do it gently, no pulling and heaving. Take your time. I don't want them ripped.'

'OK, thanks Mam!'

Once the intestine tubes were washed to Connie's exacting standards, they were hung from the ceiling in festoons, to drain. Phil, using an assortment of knifes, cleavers and his hacksaw, chopped up the carcass. The tin bath had been washed out and filled with coarse salt. The joints were laid in it as they were cut.

'Dad, how did you learn to joint a pig?'

'Watching my Dad like you're watching me.'

Connie found receptacles for all the other meat. The floor and the table was constantly scrubbed and mopped down to keep everywhere clean. It was a family production line. The scullery was awash with noise. Felix, despite having been fed a progression of scraps and tasty morsels, persistently meowed outside the back door, desperate to get back in. Phil was enjoying himself, perpetually sharpening knives on his carborundum stone, before returning to his cutting up task. Connie laughed and chatted, doing about twenty jobs at once; Tom held, carried and fetched, all the while asking questions galore. It was a happy and busy time.

On the second day of the pig slaughter, Tom's time was devoted to feeding strips of meat and fat into the 'Spong Mincer', then cranking the handle and producing masses of finely chopped sausage meat. Connie would gather the chopped pork into a large bowl and hand mix in herbs, salt and spices. She would stuff the mixture down the lengths of clean intestine. Every six inches along the length, she gave the tubes of meat a couple of twists and before long they would have strings of sausages.

'Mam can I have a go?'

'Come on then. That's right. Spoon it in with the teaspoon and then push the meat down the tube with the wooden spoon handle. You might find it easier to use that wooden clothes peg. Don't force too much meat in at once. That's right. Well done. Now give it a twist and that's it. There you are, you've made your first sausage.'

'Can I have it for breakfast tomorrow?'

'Put it on a plate in the pantry and I'll cook it for you in the morning' laughed Connie, snipping it out of the string.

Phil knelt over the bath on the scullery floor, sorting out the hams and rubbing salt into them, using the heel of his hand. When he was satisfied that they were cured, he wrapped them in clean white muslin, strung and hung them from hooks screwed into the pantry ceiling.

'Why do you do that?'

'So the meat doesn't go off. Salt is a preservative.'

'How do you know when to stop rubbing?'

'When the meat starts to feel drier; the salt pulls the moisture out of it. I always give it a good do because I don't want the meat to go bad.'

'Does it stink when it's bad?'

'Yes horrible. The only time I ever saw your Grandfather York cry was when the pig went bad.'

'Grandfather, crying?' said Tom, finding it difficult to believe that his kindly but stern Grandfather, with his bristling moustache and ferocious expression, would ever show so much emotion.

'Yes I came home one day, and there he was, sobbing his eyes out while he buried the pig in a deep hole in the back garden. He probably hadn't salted it enough.'

'Why was he crying? Was he sorry for the pig?'

'No I don't think so. As far as he was concerned, he was burying the family's food. The pig would have helped feed us all over the winter. We had very little money and I think he was really worried that we would go hungry. As you know he really loves pork,' continued Phil, moving their conversation onto happier ground.

'He usually carves some fat bacon or ham for his breakfast and has it with a slice of apple pie, to cut the fat.'

'What do you mean? I don't understand.'

'Ham fat is greasy, a bit difficult to chew and can stick in your throat; the apple pie makes the fat more palatable and easier to swallow.'

Phil chopped the racks of ribs into chops. Connie would make parcels of chops, wrapped in greaseproof paper. So that everyone could share in the bounty, these were distributed to both sets of the York's parents and to the family's neighbours.

'Tom, take these round to Mrs Thomas with our love and don't forget to thank her for the little apple pies she left for you yesterday.'

No part of the pig was wasted. Even the blood was turned into black pudding by adding pork fat, onion and oatmeal and gently heating the mixture.

On the third day after the pig was killed, with assistance from Phil and 'hindrance' from her son, Connie produced trays of sausage rolls and pork pies. These were stowed away in airtight tins, with the best 'lookers' kept for Christmas.

The hams were carved for bacon rashers and gammon steaks, or chopped into tiny cubes for baking in egg and bacon pies. The meat usually lasted throughout the winter and well into the spring months.

Chapter 7

PEOPLE

'Mam! Is Gordon the milkman a Chinaman?'

'No love,' replied Connie smiling at Tom and rubbing the back of his head, 'he's as English as you and me.'

'But his skin is yellow isn't it?'

Gordon worked for the Co-operative Society and every day he delivered the York's milk. He was one of Tom's favourites because he was happy to have a quick fag and spend time chatting with the young lad when he knocked for his milk checks. Milk checks were little tokens that were bought from the Co-op to pay for the milk so the milkmen didn't have to carry lots of heavy money around with them.

The milkman was probably in his early thirties, although it was difficult to judge his age. He was a cheerful man, with a deeply lined face, dark shadows under his eyes and a broken smile. Most of his front teeth were missing and the rest were cracked and bent. His jaw was over to one side; this caused his speech to be slurred. He was emaciated. Gordon's cheek bones protruded so much, they looked as though they could break through his fragile skin.

'He's a lovely man, but he's not very well, I'm sad to say.'

'Is his skin yellow, because he's poorly?'

'I think his liver was damaged in the war. People with poorly livers, can be jaundiced. That affects the colour of their skin.'

'What happened to him?'

'Gordon is a very brave man. He's lucky to be alive; he worked on the Burma Railway.'[5]

'Is he a railway man, like Dad and Grandad?'

'No! Not like them. Gordon was a prisoner of war, and was forced along with lots of others to build a railway.'

'Who forced him?'

'The Japanese. He was with our troops in Burma in 1942 when the Japanese invaded and he was captured. The Japanese decided they needed a railway to carry supplies between Burma and Thailand, they're countries in Asia, and so they forced their prisoners of war to build it.'

'Is it a big railway?'

'I think it's about 250 miles long. It runs through the jungle, between Bangkok and Rangoon.'

'What, a jungle with wild animals and snakes?'

'I expect so. I've never been there; it's a long way from here – on the other side of the world.'

'Was Gordon attacked by wild animals?'

'I don't know what he had to do to survive. I just know he had a terrible time. The Japanese soldiers were cruel. They treated their prisoners very badly. Gordon's jawbone was broken when a Japanese soldier repeatedly hit him in the mouth with his rifle butt. There were no doctors to look after the men if they were injured in that terrible place. They made him keep working. His jawbone eventually healed, but it's not in the right position. It must have been terribly painful.'

'Why did the Japanese soldier do that?'

'I don't know. Absolute badness I expect. A very evil man! I will never forgive the Japanese for what they did to our lads. They were a nasty lot.'

She paused and took a slow breath before continuing. 'Gordon worked on building the railway for over a year. Some of the time he worked on a stretch known as Hellfire Pass. The POWs had to cut through a large section of rock to lay the tracks. Gordon told me it was in a very remote area in the Tenisserim Hills, wherever they are! They only had hand tools. They were living on one handful of rice a day, and only had bad water to drink. Most of them had dysentery. They were constantly beaten with bamboo canes by the Japanese, to make them work harder. In the six weeks it took them to cut through the rock, lots of men were killed. Survivors called it the 'Railway of Death'. Even after the railway was built, Gordon was kept in the jungle in case the railway needed any repairs. He didn't get released until the Japanese surrendered in September 1945, so he lived in terrible conditions with very little food for about three years. God alone knows how he survived.'

Gordon eventually had to give up his job, due to his bad health. Tom never knew what happened to him. He deserved to recover. Tom hoped he did.

***

Another regular visitor to Railway Cottage, in the 1950s, was Stan, the fruit and vegetable man. Every week he would drive his horse and cart to Halthorpe. The cart had been cleverly adapted to display his wares. An a-shaped construction ran the full length, allowing deep boxes to be displayed at an angle so Stan's customers could easily see what he had for sale. When he travelled, he rolled down a tarpaulin at both sides and tied it to secure his boxes, making sure the contents didn't escape.

Connie bought fruit and vegetables from him each week. Her purchases always included a bag of apples. When she had paid for them, she would remove one from the bag, split it into quarters with a knife she carried in her apron pocket, and feed it to Stan's horse, Major. She loved Major and he loved her.

This love affair had hilarious consequences one week, when Connie was not at home. Stan arrived with his horse and cart, the neighbours made their purchases, but Major, unwilling to leave without his apple, took matters into his control. He went looking for Connie. Ignoring all Stan's protestations and commands to stop, he trotted along the back lane, halted at the York's back gate and tried to turn in to the backyard. Unfortunately the gate was only thirty inches wide. The head and shoulders of the horse entered the yard, but the shafts of the cart stuck fast. It took a considerable effort by Stan and the neighbours to reverse Major and his cart back out of the gate and onto the back lane again.

On her return, the neighbours told Connie all about Major's behaviour. She was very amused, and could find no fault with the horse at all. As always she came up with a practical solution to the problem. She suggested to her neighbours, that if for any reason she was not there, they could buy an apple for the horse on her behalf and she would reimburse the cost. They were happy to agree and so from then on Major always had his apple.

Drawn together by their mutual love of horses, Connie and Stan remained lifelong friends. They often laughed about the day Major came to call.

***

When the Second World War started in 1939, Britain was importing fifty million tons of food a year. During the first year of the war, in an attempt to weaken Britain, Germany used their fleet of U-boats to attack allied shipping. Within a year they had reduced the nation's annual food imports to twelve million tons.

In 1940, to ensure that scarce food supplies were fairly shared amongst the population, the government introduced rationing. This strategy was also meant to stop the more affluent in society from hoarding food. Some items were still rationed until July 1954, nine years after the war ended.

Many staple foods were rationed. These included meat, cheese, bacon, butter, sugar, cooking fat, tea and biscuits. Potatoes, fruit and fish were not rationed, however imported fruit such as bananas and oranges were impossible to get hold of. Housewives had to cook what was available for their family, often cheaper cuts of meat and offal. This did not always go down well with Tom.

'Mam what's that? It looks yuk!'

'Tripe and onions, it's very tasty. Try it.'

'I don't want to. It looks horrible,' moaned Tom, pulling a face and prodding his dinner with his fork. 'What is it? It's like slimy, white, honeycomb.'

'It comes from the lining of the middle stomach of a cow.'

'Uurgh! I don't want my dinner.'

'Well there's nothing else, at least try a piece. You might like it.'

'It really is tasty,' said Phil, popping a piece in his mouth and chewing hard. 'You should try it, it's quite good. During the war we ate whale.'

'Whale?'

'Yes Vera Lynn even sang about it. "Whale meat again, don't know where don't know when".'[40]

'Huh! Very funny Dad. Can I go out to play now?'

'We can't afford to waste food Tom. If you don't eat it now, you'll get it for your breakfast.'

Everyone in the country was issued with a ration card. This controlled the quantity of rationed foods people were able to buy each week. Young children were allowed more milk and eggs, and after five years of age they were allocated an increased meat ration.

Each family had to register with a local supplier, then had to buy their rations from that shop. When the York family moved to Halthorpe, their neighbours advised them to register with Jim Sawyer, an 'open-all-hours', husband-and-wife grocery business, in a village about five miles away. Jim and Susan worked incredibly hard. Jim always wore a flat cap and a full-length blue overall.

Susan looked after the shop, while Jim cycled around all the nearby villages, taking people's grocery orders. Back in the shop, he and Susan would make up the orders and Jim would deliver them, two days later, in all weathers. The shop opened at 5.30am every day, except Sunday

On the front of his bicycle he had a huge metal box; sitting on the rack behind his bike seat was another. His bicycle was also fitted with two metal side panniers. All of these would be piled high with people's groceries that he would deliver on his rounds.

Every Tuesday evening around 7.00pm, Jim knocked on the York's back door, then breezed into the scullery with a cheery 'hello everyone.'

'Come on through to the living room, Jim.' Connie was always pleased to see him.

He would take out his little red book, find his stub of pencil from behind his ear, lick it, and take down their grocery order. At the same time, he would impart all the local news and gossip, discuss the football with Phil, gave updates on anyone who was ill or dying and tell Connie about any new lines coming into his shop. If the radio battery needed changing, he would dive into one of his bike panniers and swop it for a charged one. Jim also performed another invaluable service in the community in those pre-telephone days. If anyone was ill he would call into the local doctor's surgery and ask the doctor to visit.

It was the 1960s, before Jim could afford a van to do his rounds. Even though Connie and Phil eventually bought a car of their own, Connie continued to buy her groceries from him until he retired, thirty years after food rationing ended.

Jim wasn't the only caller who used a bicycle. During the fifties very few people owned cars so pedal power was the norm. Between surgeries, Dr Frazer did his extensive rounds by bicycle. When Tom was ill with pneumonia, Dr Frazer biked the five miles to Tom's house every day, including weekends, until he was over the worst. Dr Frazer was the perfect kindly country doctor. He was a Scot with a strong accent, a loud voice and a gentle caring manner. He had a big bristling moustache, smoked a pipe and dressed in a hairy tweed suit, with both trouser legs secured in bicycle clips.

'Now laddie, how are you feeling today? Shall I blow on the end of my stethoscope to warm it, before I listen to your chest? When you're feeling a bit better and can ride your bike again, you can come and visit me in the surgery. I've got a big bag of sugared almonds over there. You can help yourself to a couple.'

Dr Frazer was liked and trusted throughout his patch of the East Riding.

Chapter 8

THE DELPH

The Delph is a large man-made pond, excavated to provide soil for the massive earth embankments that support the riveted metal road bridge across the four railway tracks at Halthorpe Station. Looking down at the Delph from the bridge, it resembles a long, thin rectangle lying adjacent to the railway tracks, with only the fenced Duck Walk between it and the Hull to Leeds line. The pond is about five hundred metres long and fifty metres wide.

It is shallowest at the embankment end, where there is a tiny reed-covered island. It is possible that the sloping bottom would have aided the railway navvies to move the soil more easily out of the excavation with their carts and barrows. The signal box for Halthorpe Station overlooks the pond at the bridge end.

Nature has a wonderful way of softening the most unnatural shapes. By the nineteen fifties, the Delph was surrounded by long-established willow and alder trees, interspersed with hazel, thorny blackthorn and hawthorn bushes and brambles. An impenetrable mass of bulrushes, reeds and water iris grew in the shallows. Water lilies, water buttercups and floating weeds clustered the edges all around the pond and bright, sparkling clear water filled its deep centre. Throughout preceding decades, bank collapses and the creation of fishermen's pitches between the shrubs, reeds and long grasses had softened the edges even more.

The Delph was a haven for Tom and the other children when they were growing up. They thought of it as their own nature reserve and play area. Many of their days were spent peering into the waters, exploring the banks, poking sticks down the holes of water rats, having 'adventures' and building dens.

'Look there's a caddis fly larva,' said Jean. She was lying in the grass and hanging out over the bank looking into the water. Her big brother, Roger, was holding her feet so she didn't topple forward into the pond.

'Where? I can't see it.' Tom was lying next to her with one of his feet hooked around the root of a shrub.

'There! Hiding next to that little reed.'

Caddis flies, sometimes called sedge flies are little moth-like insects that have aquatic larvae. The larvae spin a silk-like cocoon tube to live in. To disguise their appearance, they often stick twigs, tiny stones and other bits of debris to their cocoon. The tube is open at both ends so that the insect can stick out its head and legs. It is capable of moving about on the bottom. It can retreat back into its home to hide from predators, but they can't escape fishermen, who use the larvae for bait.

Tom and his pals would roll up their shirt sleeves and delve deeply into the shallows around the margin. They captured these fascinating little creatures so they could admire the diversity of the homes they created.

'Look at this one! It has used an old matchstick as part of its case,' said Tom, holding the little tube in his wet hand.

'Poke this bit of grass down the end. See if you can make it stick its head out,' suggested Roger.

'My brother found one with a shirt button stuck to it,' Bernard said.

The Delph is full of fish. Perch, bream, roach, carp, tench, pike and eels abound. In the nineteen fifties, locals were of the opinion that the Delph had never been stocked by man. Nobody really knew. Perhaps the fish stock had arrived because of natural processes, maybe fish eggs had been stuck to the feet of birds.

Halthorpe children spent hours trying to catch fish with makeshift rods. They were usually content if they managed to catch one small perch, so they were no threat to the adult anglers who came to the pond.

One day an angling club from a town some miles from Halthorpe, put up a sign, stating that any '**children caught fishing in this pond will be prosecuted**'. Phil was infuriated and tackled the secretary of the club about the notice.

'Did you put up that sign, banning our kids from fishing in the Delph?'

'We've every right. We don't want kids spoiling our fishing.'

'Spoiling the fishing!! That is utter rubbish and very small-minded of you, especially bearing in mind the size of the Delph. The kids were here long before you got your license. These kids are all railway children and the railways board will not be impressed by your sign.'

'Well the sign stays. What do you say to that?'

'I'll tell you what I say to that. Until you take the sign down, you will be no longer welcome to walk on our pathways, park your bikes or leave your cars here.'

Further angry words were exchanged, with the final words coming from Tom's very red faced father.

'And what's more if I find one of your bloody bikes on our backs, I shall throw it in the Delph. Now that will spoil your precious fishing.'

The sign was taken down.

The children mostly used bits of bread or little worms for bait. However if a dead fish was floating on the surface, within reach, it would be taken home and thrown onto one of the corrugated shed roofs, that were dotted around the hamlet. The fish would be covered with an old tin box weighted down with half a brick and nature would take its natural course. Blow flies would get at the fish by crawling along the valleys in the corrugated tin, but birds and cats couldn't get near it. The decaying and smelly corpse was inspected every couple of days, until the carcass was crawling with fat maggots. The maggots were collected into little tins, mixed in with a sprinkle of sawdust and shared amongst the children to use as bait for their fishing lines.

Phil and Connie were lifelong friends with a family who lived in Rochdale. They had two sons who regularly visited during their summer holidays. The oldest son Aidan, was mad on all things sporty. Evan, the youngest boy, loved fishing. He was seven years older than Tom. He spent many hours fishing in the Delph and taught Tom a lot about fish and fishing. It was Evan who caught the first pike Tom had ever seen. Tom thought Evan was the best fisherman in the world. Aidan and Evan's father was Tom's Uncle Albert. It was he who first fired Tom's imagination with his tales of the great Sioux warrior chief, Sitting Bull.

Tom loved the Delph and its wildlife. Butterflies, dragonflies and damselflies danced through the air in the spring and summer months and water boatmen skittered across the glossy surface. However it was the birds that constantly caught his attention.

There were several resident families of moorhens; these were always called water hens by his father. Phil used to show Tom their nests of floating twigs and tell stories about how he and his brothers collected the eggs for bank-side fry ups, when they were kids. Tom was fascinated by the way the birds' heads jerked back and forth and their tails flicked when they swam. He thought they looked funny when they were standing on the bank because their feet looked too big for their bodies. He also loved the way they would dive beneath the surface if they were startled then wait with just their beak and an eye protruding until they felt safe. They were like bird submarines. It was always a worry when the moorhens had young, because the big pike lurking in the depths were capable of swallowing their chicks.

Swans and ducks were very frequent visitors. Phil said the swans liked the Delph because its length meant they had a good flight path to land in and take off from. On most days during the winter months huge skeins of geese in V-formation passed overhead on their way to feed in the muddy shallows along the River Humber.

Every year in spring Tom watched for pairs of grebe and dabchicks to arrive. They usually nested at the embankment end of the Delph, in the thick reeds and bulrushes around the little island, where they were safe from the predators lurking beneath the surface and from foxes and badgers, which prowled throughout the night.

The shrub-covered banks were great places for building 'dens'. Many escapades were plotted in the large hollow under the branches of an ancient, white lilac tree.

'I've seen a wasps' nest,' said Bernard.

'Where is it?' Tom's interest was immediately aroused.

'It's in an old rat hole over there. Come on I'll show you.' Bernard led the gang through the long grass and round the big nettle patch to the far side of the pond.

'I hate wasps; there are loads of them this year. They keep coming in the house,' said Jean.

'Wow. Look at them all, there's hundreds. They sound angry,' said Tom, fascinated by the buzzing cloud of black and yellow insects busy around a hole in the bank edge.

'Don't get too near, you'll get stung.' Jean stood well back from the boys, and held her skirt tightly around her bare legs.

'Our Geoff says he's going to dig the nest out and throw it in the pond,' said Bernard, reflecting his older brother's bravado.

'How's he going to do that?' asked Tom.

'He's going to gather up a big pile of dry grass, dump it next to the nest entrance, set fire to it, then stand in the smoke, so the wasps can't get at him.'

'Wow!' said Tom, 'can I help?'

'Sure, he's doing it this afternoon, I'm going.'

'Me too,' said Roger.

***

'Mam,' Tom cried, running into the living room, 'I've been stung by a wasp.'

'Where?' asked Connie, looking up from the sock she was darning.

'On me nose and top lip. It hurts, a lot.'

'Have you been messing with that wasps' nest?' she said, putting down the sock. She stood and pulled her son over to the window so she could get a better look.

'No.'

'Let's have a look at you. Yes they do look sore. You're lucky it didn't get you in your eye. Now where's my Dolly Blue bag?'

Connie always had some Reckitt's Blue bags in the scullery. She called them Dolly Blues. They were made from ultra marine and baking soda. They were used to whiten the washing during the rinses, to overcome the yellowing effect soap flakes had on the whites. Dolly Blues were also excellent for treating stings. 'Now hold still,' she said, dabbing his face with the wet bag.

Tom peered over her shoulder at his reflection in the scullery mirror. 'But Mam me face is blue now.'

'It'll soon fade. It might remind you to stop mucking about with wasps. Anyway it looks like war paint.' She gave the bites another dab and painted a blue circle on each of his cheeks.

'Ooh that looks great. Thanks Mam.' Tom admired his war paint and felt a lot better.

She smiled as her irrepressible son ran back to his mates sporting a blue-tipped nose, swollen top lip and war paint – trophies of his latest adventure.

**

The gang returned to their den under the lilac tree. Their attack on the wasps' nest was discussed and deemed a failure. Roger suggested they needed a hand grenade. Jean thought a stick of dynamite might do the trick. Unfortunately, some would say fortunately, they had neither.

'Let's leave the wasps in peace for now,' said Tom, rubbing his top lip.

Bernard dug in his pocket and produced a tin of baked beans, which he'd snaffled from his gran's pantry.

'Did you get an opener?' asked Jean.

'Couldn't find one.' He rummaged around in the old tin box, they kept in the den. Eventually they managed to open the can by hitting an old screwdriver repeatedly with a rusty hammer, punching holes through the tinplate. When Tom missed the screwdriver with the hammer he hit Bernard's hand, which was holding the tin.

'Owya, bollocks!' Bernard screamed, dropping the can in the dirt. He sucked his bruised hand, while Roger picked up the tin so that Tom could keep bashing at it. They eventually forced a flap open by levering it with the screw driver, then knocking the sharp jagged edges back with the hammer. The friends triumphantly devoured the cold contents with a shared teaspoon.

When Tom returned home later, if Connie noticed that his top lip was stained with a mosaic of dolly blue and tomato sauce, she just smiled and said nothing.

***

Charlie caught the 9.35am to Goole. The train pulled out of Halthorpe Station, puffed under the bridge and passed alongside the Duck Walk. He looked across the frozen surface of the Delph, and enjoyed the noise of the engine chuffing happily along with swirls of steam cascading along its carriage sides. The train swept on through the crisp winter air.

That morning Charlie had decided to wear his de-mob suit. He was pleased it still fitted and looked smart with the shirt and tie that Mary had bought for him. His shoes were carefully polished. He felt happy.

'It's so much easier now I've made my decision. I know what I'm doing.'

He wandered from the station, along the main street of Goole, towards the Market Hall, until he reached Green's Fruit and Vegetables. The shop had buckets of flowers standing on the pavement outside.

'I'd like some flowers please.'

'At this time of year we've only got chrysanthemums, freesias and snowdrops.'

'That's OK. Can I have two bunches of chrysanthemums please? A bunch of the pink ones and another of those darker ones there.'

'Are they for somebody special?'

'Yes they're for my wife. Chrysanthemums are her favourites.'

'She will be pleased; the ones you've chosen are beautiful. They should last a while too.'

'And can I have a couple of bunches of snowdrops, they're for my son.'

'How lovely. I'm sure these flowers will make them both happy.'

'I'm know they will,' said Charlie, smiling at the assistant.

Charlie had a haircut, bought some Brylcreem and caught the midday train, back to Halthorpe. He devoted the afternoon to tidying up the flowers and arranging them in two vases; one large and one small.

The next morning Charlie, smart in his suit, walked to Normansly churchyard and spent half an hour tidying his mother's and father's graves. He told his parents, as he always did, that he loved them. He moved across the churchyard, to where Mary lay with their baby Matthew cradled in her arms.

'Hello you two,' said Charlie, as he knelt down next to the neat and tidy grave. 'I've brought you some flowers, chrysanthemums for you my darling because I know you love them. I've arranged them the way you like with the pale ones around the edge and the darker ones in the middle. I hope you like the colours I've chosen.' He fussed around with his arrangement until it looked perfect and added some water from a bottle.

'Matthew look! Daddy has brought you some snowdrops; they're pretty little white nodding flowers that grow each spring. The fairies love them. They wear the flowers as hats when they are dancing. If you listen very quietly, you can hear them singing.'

Charlie excavated two shallow holes, in the top of the grave and set his vases side by side, above Mary and Matthew. He used his knuckles to firm the ground around the vases, making sure they stood upright. Mary's vase was decorated with a fresco of swans, her favourite birds. Charlie had painted a ring of teddy bears around Matthew's vase. He kissed his finger tips and touched both vases.

'With these kisses and these flowers, I vow I will always be with you; I will always be your loving husband and loving daddy.' He paused, to compose himself before continuing, 'Matthew I have painted your vase with teddies, because I never had the chance to buy one for you.' He tucked a fold of paper down the side of the vase. 'I will join you both soon, so we can spend all time together, forever – the world's happiest family.'

Charlie stood up and walked towards the churchyard gate. He turned back to look at the grave and his flowers. They shone brightly in the sombreness of graveyard. 'I love you both, my darlings. It won't be long until I can hug you again.' Tears poured down his face, as he walked away from his loved ones. His chest was tight and aching. The weight of his heartbreak was almost unbearable, as he headed towards Halthorpe.

Reg Thomas looked out of the signal box window and watched Charlie walking slowly along the Duck Walk. He stopped at his favourite place and climbed onto the top rail of the fence. Then he sat looking out over the frozen surface.

'Same spot every day, whatever the weather,' said Reg sadly to himself, shaking his head with regret for Charlie's situation. He remembered how Charlie and Mary used to lean on the fence, laughing and chatting, with their arms around each other looking over the Delph when she was expecting. He felt for Charlie, he'd had a raw deal. 'Mary was such a lovely lass. They were such a loving couple and losing the baby as well. Poor bloke, life's not fair.'

The 'up line' bell rang and brought Reg out of his sad thoughts. He busied himself pulling his signals. 'Ah well, life goes on. I suppose.'

Charlie, sitting on the fence, was thinking about Mary and Matthew and the flowers he'd left for them. 'Chrysanths should last for a while Mary, snowdrops not so long perhaps. I hope our little boy hears the fairies sing.' He climbed over the fence and edged slowly down the bank towards the pond's frozen surface. *Looks thick enough to hold me to the middle*, he thought as he stepped carefully onto the ice. He avoided the cracked bits nearer to the margin of the pond. Walking slowly he edged towards the middle of the Delph, to where it was deepest. The ice creaked, groaned and cracked.

Reg Thomas had been busy and hadn't noticed Charlie climbing over the fence and walking onto the Delph. When he saw where Charlie was, he gasped in horror, dashed to the signal box window, slid it open and yelled at the top of his voice.

'Charlie, get off there you daft bugger, you know the ice isn't thick enough for walking on.'

Charlie heard Reg shout and looked towards the signal box. 'I'm fine, don't worry,' he shouted back, 'I know what I'm doing.'

Reg rang Mrs Potter in the ticket office at Halthorpe Station. 'Hello Nancy, it's Reg Thomas here.'

'Oh, hello Reg, it's not very often I get a call from you.'

'Nancy I think we've got a problem, an emergency! Charlie Wilson has just walked out onto the centre of the ice on the Delph.'

'Why's he done that? He's normally such a sensible bloke.'

'I don't know what he's up to. Nothing daft I hope. I've shouted to him to get off, but he says he's OK and he knows what he's doing. He's all dressed up, he's wearing a suit, hair all brushed. I'm going to leave the box and go down to him and see if I can make him see sense. Let everybody know that the box isn't manned for a bit will you?'

'Straight away Reg. I'll ring the Brough box. I'd better ring the police as well.'

'And the fire brigade, in case we need ladders. The surface is already cracked; he could fall in. Tell everyone it's really urgent. The ice is holding at the moment, but it could give at anytime.'

'Reg,' said Nancy pointedly.

'What?'

'Don't do anything daft yourself. I know what a big heart you've got. Take care. I don't want to have to tell your Edith about it, if you fall in the pond.'

'I won't.' Reg ran down the steps and crossed the lines. He climbed over both fences edging the Duck Walk and stood on the bank.

When Charlie noticed him he waved both arms and shouted, 'keep back Reg, the ice isn't safe. Go away.'

'What the hell do you think you're doing Charlie?' Reg yelled. 'Oh no, stop that.' Charlie had started walking around in a circle, looking down at the ice.

'Charlie lad,' said Reg, getting even more alarmed, 'come back over here. If you've got a problem, I'm sure we can talk about it.'

'I'm going to see Mary and Matthew.'

'They're not in the Delph.'

'I know they're not. I know where they are and I'm going to join them.'

'If you kill yourself they'll not put you in the churchyard,' said Reg, desperately thinking how he could persuade Charlie to abandon his increasingly obvious plan.

'I've not left a note. If I fall through the ice, it'll be recorded as accidental death. I've not been behaving strangely; I've kept myself neat and tidy, my house is immaculate, all the dishes are washed and put away. They'll say I was just having a foolish moment. The balance of my mind was temporarily disturbed.'

'Well I could tell them about this conversation.'

'I would be really grateful if you didn't, Reg. Please don't. I just want to lie next to Mary and Matthew. You know how much I miss them.'

'I know lad, but please don't do anything silly, you'll meet another lass,' pleaded Reg, as Charlie started to speed up his circling motion on the ice. Then he started skipping. Reg could see his lips moving as though he was muttering or chanting to himself.

'It's been a pleasure to know you Reg,' said Charlie, suddenly jumping into the middle of his circle.

'For Christ's sake Charlie,' screamed Reg, 'don't do it. Your Mary wouldn't want you to do this.'

'She knows. I've discussed it with her,' said Charlie jumping up and down. With a loud retort the surface cracked and then, with a crash, the ice folded and Charlie disappeared into the freezing depths.

'Oh, heaven help me,' muttered Reg, as he crept across the ice on his hands and knees, towards the watery hole into which Charlie had disappeared. Charlie's head popped up above the surface. He was spluttering.

'I'm here Charlie,' shouted Reg, crawling as quickly as he dared, towards him.

'Thanks all the same Reg, a nice thought, but I've made my mind up. See you later.' With that Charlie swam to the remaining ice sheet, flipped over on his back, pulled himself below the surface and hand walked under the ice dragging himself further and further away from the hole.

'Dear God, no!' Reg painfully crawled across the ice to the spot where he could see Charlie's body lying face up under the ice. It was terrible looking through the ice at him. Charlie was so far away from the break in the ice, that Reg had no chance of pulling him out. There were a few trapped bubbles, but no movement.

When Police Constable Thorne arrived on his push bike, he found Reg Thomas sitting on the pond bank, shivering.

'What's up here then?' he asked, as he wrapped his great coat around Reg's shaking body.

'Charlie Wilson's fallen through. I tried to get to him, but I couldn't reach.'

'Damn lucky you didn't fall through as well, if you ask me.'

'I suppose,' said Reg. 'He was a lovely bloke.'

'Deliberate? Do you think?' queried the policeman looking intently at Reg.

'No idea,' said Reg, 'he might just have been trying to take a short cut across the pond.'

'Damn silly whatever.'

'Yes it's a tragedy,' agreed Reg.

'Are you on duty?' asked the policeman, nodding towards the signal box?'

'Yes.'

'Well get yourself back in your cabin and get warmed up in front of the fire. Make yourself a cup of hot, sweet tea. I can't decide if you're shivering from the cold, the shock or both. I'll pop across and talk to you later, once the firemen have recovered the body. Not that I envy them that job, it looks hazardous. I'll need to get a statement from you. There's bound to be an inquest on this one. I'll see if I can get Doctor Frazer to call in to see you, just to check you're OK.'

***

'Mam, there's firemen at the far end of the Delph. They're laying ladders across the ice. Bernard says somebody must have fallen in and drowned. Can I go and watch?'

'No you can't, it's none of your beeswax. You don't want to be seeing things like that. Something terrible must have happened.'

'But Mam.'

'No buts. Into the living room with you. Your toys need putting away!'

***

That evening Tom overheard Mr Thomas and his Dad talking. 'When they pulled him out, the firemen said, he was smiling.'

'Who was smiling Dad?' said Tom, popping out of the lavvy.

Phil looked at him, startled by his son's sudden appearance. 'Oh hello Tom I didn't know you were in there. I'm sorry to tell you Charlie's had an accident, he's fallen in the pond and drowned.'

'Charlie! Is he dead?'

'Yes he is I'm afraid. I'm sorry lad, I know you liked him.'

The following morning Red Bess pulled up on the Duck Walk next to where Tom had last seen Charlie.

'See you later Alligator,' shouted Tom across the frozen surface. Charlie didn't answer.

'In a while Crocodile,' shouted Sitting Bull, as Red Bess galloped away.

***

Charlie was buried next to his wife and baby. The inquest decided it was accidental death, as there was no evidence to the contrary. The only note found was a poem tucked down the side of Matthew's flower vase.

> Round and round in circles the singing fairies go
> Dancing through the garden, wearing hats of snow
> They're having a special party for Daddy's boy Matthew
> And they're bringing lots of fairy cakes and cups of honeydew.

Chapter 9

STEPPING OUT

The 9.45am to Leeds puffed and wheezed into the station.

'Are we in the right spot for the guard?' asked Tom, laughing as he was enveloped in a cloud of steam.

'Should be. It'll be Mr Rawlings today,' said his dad as the train pulled to a stop in front of them.

'Hello Phil,' said Bryan Rawlings, smiling and jumping nimbly out of the guard's compartment door, 'Is this your lad?'

'Yes, this is Tom,' replied Phil, with his hand resting lightly on his son's shoulder.

'Hello Mr Rawlings,' said Tom.

'Hello Tom. Holidays is it?'

'Yes, I'm going to stay with my Aunt Dora and Uncle Jack in Rochdale.'

'Well that is a fine place to go for a holiday.'

'Where shall I sit?'

'Jump into that compartment there; next to the guard's van. I'll make sure you get on the right connecting train when you change in Leeds,' Bryan continued, nodding at Phil. 'I'll ask the guard to keep an eye on him.'

'Thanks. His ticket's in his jacket pocket if he needs it. His aunty will meet him at Rochdale.' Phil helped his son into the compartment, lodging his case and shopping bag on the seat next to him. 'Now have a nice time, be good, say hello to Aunty Dora and Uncle Jack from Mam and me.'

'I will Dad.'

'Don't forget your case when you get off the trains and for heaven's sake do not lose that shopping bag! It's got a letter and some baking in it from your mam to Aunty Dora.'

'And a cheese scone and a cherry bun for me to eat on the train,' chirped Tom.

Phil grinned, 'I'll see you in three weeks time and remember your mam will meet you in Leeds on your journey back.'

'OK Dad.'

'Don't forget to wave to your mam this morning, she'll be standing on the backs to give you a wave as you go past.'

'Will you blow your whistle Dad?'

Phil jumped off the train, checked all the doors were closed and, to Tom's delight, gave two long bursts on his whistle. Bryan gave Phil a 'thumbs up' as the train pulled out of the station. Tom pushed his nose hard against the window to watch for his mam as they approached the railway workers' cottages. The train was under the bridge and past the signal box in a few seconds and there was his mam standing on the backs, waving a tea towel. Tom waved back frantically, settled into his seat and fished out his cheese scone. His adventure had begun.

***

Tom loved going to his Aunty Dora's. She was short, round, cuddly and fun.

'Aunty Dora, there's a man on a bicycle in the street and he's ringing a hand bell. He looks as though he's got a smoking tea urn fastened in front of his handlebars.'

'That'll be the black pea[6] man. He comes every Thursday evening.'

'What are black peas?'

'Well they look like ordinary peas, but they're dark brown and they have a nuttier flavour. We eat them hot, from a tea cup, with a spoon. They're lovely. Would you like to try some?'

'Yes please.'

'Here are two cups and two shillings. Go out and ask him for a couple of helpings, with vinegar.'

Tom rushed out into the street and queued with other children. They were all holding empty tea cups. The children stared at him and didn't answer when he said 'Hello.'

The black pea man opened the lid of his urn and in exchange for their shillings, ladled a generous portion of steaming peas into each of the children's cups. Tom noticed the urn had a little charcoal fire under it, to keep it hot.

'Vinegar?' he asked, looking at Tom.

'Yes please.'

The black pea man smiled at him and sprinkled vinegar on the two cups of peas. Tom carried them carefully back to Aunt Dora's kitchen.

'Do you like them?' asked Aunt Dora, as she spooned peas into her mouth.'

'They're lovely,' said Tom, chasing his peas around the cup. 'Can we have them again next week?'

Another visitor to the street was a wrinkled old man, sitting on the side of a green and red trap, which was pulled by a scruffy black and white pony. He first caught Tom's attention by the cries he gave as he trotted slowly along. It sounded as if he was shouting 'Aagerown! Aagerown!'

Aunt Dora translated for him, 'he's shouting 'rag bone'. He's the rag and bone man. If you've got any unwanted clothes, or material, you can take them out to him and he may give you a couple of pence. He'll also take bits of furniture, broken bikes, old pots and pans, anything like that.'

'What bones does he take Aunty Dora?'

'I don't think he collects bones anymore. I think that's a left over from days gone by, when they used to collect bones for the glue works. They've always shouted 'rag bone' as they wandered up and down the streets. I think they keep up the tradition.'

'What do they do with the rags?'

'Sort them out I expect. Anything decent they'll try to sell second hand. The rest they'll bale up and sell to the shoddy mill. The mill chops and pulps all the rags and then turns them into a type of material called shoddy. They make new cloth from old.'

Whenever Tom stayed with his Aunt Dora and Uncle Jack he had a trip into the big cotton mill, where his uncle worked as warehouse foreman. It involved a bus journey from Rochdale, up the hill to Littleborough. Aunty Dora always called it 'going up the summit.'

In the mill warehouse Jack had to climb up a long wooden staircase to get to his little office, which was tucked under the high roof. He once told Tom, 'from here I can keep an eye on everything and everyone down on the warehouse floor.'

The light streamed in through the high windows of the warehouse, highlighting the dust particles hanging in the air. The floor of the warehouse was stacked with hundreds of bales of multi-coloured striped canvas material. Tom's uncle explained the mill's main business was supplying deck chair seats that were sent all over the world. 'We even make those used on big ocean liners like the Queen Mary. Of course they're 'specials'. They have to match the colours of the ship's décor and they have the ship's crest woven in.'

'Did you get us the material for our deckchairs at home?'

'Yes I did. Your dad bought two old chairs at an auction. They were in poor condition, so he did up the woodwork and I got him the canvas to make new seats.'

***

A trip to the cinema with his aunty was a real treat for Tom. They'd gone to see a war film accompanied by a B movie called *They Rode into the Sun*. Dora said that she knew nothing about it, but thought from its title that it was probably a cowboy film.

They settled down in their seats just as 'They Rode into the Sun' was starting. The first scene began with a lingering shot of a table on a beach. On the table lay a copy of *Health and Efficiency* magazine. Dora took a sharp intake of breath and went very quiet. To Tom's disappointment the film wasn't about cowboys, instead lots of men and women ran around playing games and rode through sand dunes on horses. Everyone was naked. All their naughty bits had smudgy clouds over them. Tom couldn't resist commenting, 'they've got no clothes on.'

'Shush!' Aunty Dora looked fixedly at the screen.

'But Aunty Dora, the men haven't got willies.'

'Shush!' Aunty Dora popped a Liquorice Allsort in her mouth and handed one to Tom. He thought the film was very boring and wished he'd brought his Beano.

Dora only started chatting again when the main feature came on.

***

'Thank you Ladies,' boomed Vera Venables, as she brought the room to order. The chattering faltered, and subsided. 'Opening waltz please Bella, when you're ready,' she continued. Mrs Venables firmed her grip on Tom. Her right hand rested on the back of his Fair Isle pullover, her left held his right hand at shoulder height.

Bella Figg, who had been chatting with Aunty Dora, leapt into action. Several of the ladies had to move rapidly out of her way as she swept with a clatter of heels and a scattering of 'excuse me's' towards the HMV. This essential stood on the card table in the corner of the room. Alongside it was a pile of 78rpm records.

With a loud scratching noise, followed by a mouthed 'sorry' from Bella, Victor Sylvester and his ballroom orchestra stumbled into their rendition of the 'Fascination Waltz'[29]. The stumbling start was caused by Bella, who had overbalanced after putting the needle in the grove, then rested her hand on the turntable just as it attempted Victor's introductory bars.

'Sorry' mouthed Bella again, looking aghast across the room towards Mrs Venables.

Vera smiled stoically, her grip tightening on Tom once more. The music recovered its rhythm and Vera counted the beats out loud. Her head swivelled, owl like, as she scanned the ladies around the room. Her brown felt and rabbit fur hat nodded as she counted. It reminded Tom of one of his mam's cottage loaves after a bad baking day. It was clearly riveted to her head by a huge hat pin. The top of the pin looked like a fox's foot holding a pheasant's tail feather. It pierced the hat and a few inches away its bayonet-like tip appeared.

Apart from a few laggards, the ladies all paired up and were hastily taking their positions. They were all dressed smartly in their best frocks. The regulars had changed into their dance shoes. Others wore their 'every days'. Tom was wearing his new short trousers, his red and blue elasticised belt with the double S buckle and his school shoes. To his amazement, many of the ladies had not taken their hats off when they arrived.

'So they don't spoil their hair,' Aunty Dora had whispered mysteriously, when questioned earlier by her baffled nephew.

'But Aunty,' he observed, 'the ladies who have taken their hats off have nice hair.'

'Shush!' said Aunt Dora, 'perhaps the ones with their hats still on have just finished their shift in the mill and haven't had time to do their hair.'

With a determined and well projected 'One…Two…Three…' Vera Venables launched herself across the dance floor, dragging the startled eight year old with her. The other paired-up ladies set off around the room with many false starts and much laughter, due to foot disputes over who should lead. There was no doubt about who was leading Tom.

Mrs Venables chanted 'One…Two…Three…, One…Two… Three…, One…Two…Three…,' whilst waltzing him around the room. Her momentum was such that his legs just followed wherever she wanted to go. His mind was into the rhythm, but his feet had to run to keep up.

Tom was the only male in the room, and only allowed admission because of his age. By default he became an honorary guest member of the 'Rochdale Ladies' Wednesday Afternoon Tea Dance Club'.

His partner for the first waltz around the Co-operative Function Hall was the club leader Vera Venables, who, along with Bella Figg (spelt with a double 'g' as Aunty Dora had clarified), were his aunty's two best friends.

'It is lovely to dance with a young man again,' said Mrs Venables, beaming at him and flinging him into a reverse turn. Her hat stayed firmly fixed in position and the feather waved in front of Tom's face, as she manoeuvred him into the corner ready for the next onslaught. Aunty Dora had told him that Mrs Venables had lost her son on Sword Beach at the time of the D-Day landings. He had been just eighteen years old and was buried with lots of other young men in Normandy. 'Can you do any other dances?' continued Mrs Venables.

'Yes Mrs Venables. I can do the 'Gay Gordons' and the 'Dashing White Sergeant',' gasped Tom. He was breathless, disorientated and out of balance as they advanced once more along the side of the room, all the time stopping, turning, dipping and swaying towards the next corner.

'Oh that is good,' laughed Mrs Venables, twirling him expertly through the dancing ladies.

Thanks to Connie, Tom had a limited knowledge of country dancing. He was a regular attendee, with his mam, at the Women's Institute Barn Dances. For these occasions the village hall in Normansly masqueraded as a barn. This transformation was brought about by the addition of three or four sheaves of wheat straw leaning against a milk churn placed at the edge of the small stage. The stage was just big enough to accommodate Mrs Rutland, playing an upright piano, and her husband Ron, on snare drum and symbol. Ron, a lovely smiling man, had the misfortune to have eyes that pointed East and West. The dancers were never sure if he was looking at them, so they all smiled at him every time they passed the stage, just in case.

Connie said it was a pity Phil always had a late shift on barn dance nights. Tom asked his dad why he never went to the dances.

'Because I've got a bone in my leg,' he'd reply.

Tom thought this puzzling and concluded it might be something to do with his dad's war injuries, although he reflected his dad could still run, play cricket and ride a bike.

The waltz ended and Tom, after thanking a glowing Mrs Venables, moved over to help Mrs Figg sort out the records. The ladies did several more dances and some practice sessions, before Mrs Venables declared it was time for afternoon tea. A tidal wave of women swept into action. Bags were unzipped, tin lids were removed and mountainous plates of potted meat sandwiches, freshly baked scones, biscuits, fairy cakes and butterfly buns were loaded onto a creaking table. Heading quickly across to the food table, Tom was overwhelmed by the generous women.

'The potted meat is lovely, just bought it in the market hall this morning.'

'Have a scone Tom, here's the butter.'

'You must try a fairy cake and my cherry buns were freshly baked today.'

'Load your plate up son. Don't be shy, you're a growing lad.'

Conversation and afternoon tea flowed in equal quantities, until Vera Venables once more called the room to order. 'That was excellent ladies. Thank you. I think we have time for a few more dances this afternoon, now we're replenished. I suggest we start with the 'Dashing White Sergeant'. Groups of six please.' She held her hand out. 'Tom, I would be honoured if you would partner me. I know it's a favourite of yours, as it was my son's.'

***

When Tom came home from his holidays with Aunty Dora, he would usually travel on the mid-morning train from Rochdale to Leeds, where Connie would be waiting for him. They would have a few hours looking around the shops and, as a special treat, they would have lunch in the restaurant in Schofield's Department store. Afterwards they would catch the late afternoon train home.

Chapter 10

WRITING CLUB

1956

'Can I borrow the little bag that hangs on the hook behind your bedroom door?'

'Have you been poking around in our bedroom?' Connie looked at her son and raised one eyebrow.

'No.'

'Hmm!' she said. 'Anyway you can't have it. It's very special. What do you want a handbag for?'

'Davy Crockett carried a leather bag to keep his shot dry and for his vittles.'

'Well I never knew that.' Connie was amused by Tom's words and her expression softened. 'I learn something new every day.'

'Mam! I really need a bag,' he pleaded, 'for when I'm Davy Crockett!'

'Oh I see.' She thought rapidly, trying to find a solution to his problem. 'Well I've got some bits of yellow coloured canvas in my sewing box, would you like me to make you, your very own Davy Crockett bag?'

'Yes please. That would be great. I can keep my Cisco Kid gun caps in it and a scone. Will you make it today? Please.'

'I suppose so. Now you've asked so nicely. I'll make it this evening, while we're listening to the wireless.'

'Why is your little handbag special?'

'Your dad made it for me when he was in hospital. He cut all the leather to shape and then hand stitched it.'

'You don't use it very much.'

'I know I don't. It's a bit small for all the stuff I carry around nowadays, so I keep my old letters in it.'

***

1943

Tantivy's hooves clipped briskly along the stony surface of the country lane. Connie's red hair ruffled in the breeze. Now her day's work was finished, she had time to put her plan into action.

Her hand had the lightest touch on the reins as the chestnut horse and the yellow-painted trap rattled along. Tantivy was always at this best when you let him have his head. Over the last four years, Connie's love of horses, and Tantivy in particular, had grown and she had become an accomplished horsewoman. The excitement and joy she felt when she and Tantivy were out exploring the lanes of East Yorkshire never diminished.

Today, however, was not just for pleasure – they were on a mission. They were heading for Widemarsh Village Hall; more specifically the battered old notice board that was nailed to two decaying wooden posts outside the green-painted front door.

Connie slowed Tantivy and walked him along the lane running between the scattered red brick houses of the hamlet. She yelled a cheery 'Good evening,' as they passed old Ted Trotter. He was busy in his front garden.

'Hello my beauty,' said Ted, looking up. 'Will we see you for tea this Sunday?'

'Wouldn't miss it for the world,' Connie shouted back. Ted always called her 'my beauty', she liked that. She noticed he was holding a large terracotta pot. 'What are you doing?'

'Trying to catch earwigs. The little blighters are nibbling holes in my dahlia tubers.'

'Good luck with that Ted.'

'I'll need it. They can run faster than Tantivy.' Ted laughed heartily, when he saw Tantivy's ears prick up, at the mention of his name. He loved the horse nearly as much as Connie.

Every two or three weeks Connie went for Sunday tea with Ted and his wife Daisy. They had taken to her since she'd arrived on Home Farm and treated her like the daughter they'd never had. Ted was a retired farm worker. He'd spent all his working life on Great Hall estate, as a groom and cow hand. Most week days he still pedaled sedately through the farm gateway on his old sit up and beg bicycle. He enjoyed a chat and loved to see how the beasts were doing. He shared his knowledge of good animal husbandry with Connie and frequently helped her with trickier tasks like horn and hoof trimming. Doing occasional odd jobs at the farm usually put a few shillings in his pocket each month.

Daisy and Ted lived a simple life. They had little money and relied on their chickens and home-grown vegetables to exist. They had bread and homemade jam for tea most days of the week. The exception was Sunday tea, when Connie was invited. Daisy would always keep back some of their meagre weekly butter ration so they could have butter on their bread as well as homemade jam.

Connie gently brought Tantivy to a halt outside the village hall. She thought 'hall' was a very grand name for the creosoted wooden shed, with its corrugated tin roof. However it fulfilled its purpose as a meeting place and focal point for the residents of the scattered rural community.

Tantivy stood patiently as Connie climbed down from the trap. He chewed happily on the half carrot she popped into his mouth. She headed through the wooden gate to the notice board. Reaching into her jacket pocket, she pulled out a carefully folded sheet of paper and four drawing pins. She unfolded her notice, pinned it centrally on the board and stood back to admire her handiwork.

WIDEMARSH LADIES' LETTER WRITING CIRCLE

I am convening a meeting at the village hall at 3.30pm on Saturday 5th June, with a view to starting the Widemarsh Ladies' Letter Writing Circle.

The purpose of our club will be to write letters to local men serving in the forces who are posted abroad, or billeted away from home, to give them local news and generally help to keep their spirits up.

Will all ladies who are interested in participating please come along so we can discuss how to proceed? Tea and jam tarts will be provided.

Thank you

Connie Aldridge, Land Girl,

Home Farm, Widemarsh.

The day of the meeting was sunny and warm. Connie arrived ten minutes early and was setting out chairs, when the two sisters from Wilson's farm arrived. Jane and Wendy were both in their early twenties. Connie had met them before at local events and she thought them both sensible and practical. Jane was wearing a sweater, jodhpurs and riding boots. She had a turban securing her hair. Her sister Wendy wore a cardigan, blouse, tweed skirt and polished brogues.

Next to arrive were Lucille Lamb, from the butcher's shop, and Martha Jones the school teacher's daughter. They were nineteen and seventeen years old respectively. Lucille looked pretty and confident in her bright floral dress and court shoes. Martha was quietly dressed in a white blouse and a plain blue skirt. She looked shy and nervous.

A bicycle clattered, as it was slung against the hut boarding. Marie Jacobson, the land girl from the nearby Norman House estate farm, hurried into the hall.

'Sorry if I'm late, our best sow is starting to farrow. I needed to give her some extra straw to make sure she's comfortable.' Connie had met her before and thought she was great fun. She was wearing her uniform and had knotted a bright pink paisley scarf at her neck. By 3.30 the five young women were sitting looking at Connie expectantly.

'Hello,' she kicked off, 'I'm Connie Aldridge. As some of you know I'm the land girl at Home Farm. Thank you all for coming.' She smiled at the women. 'I'm a bit nervous, so if I trip over my words you'll have to forgive me. This is the first time I've convened a meeting.' She paused, while she thought out her next words, 'To be honest I didn't know I was convening a meeting until Mr Wilkinson, my boss, told me that it was the correct terminology.' To her great relief the other girls laughed at her attempt at being light hearted. 'I tell you what,' she said, encouraged by this minor success, 'shall we start things off with tea and jam tarts?'

Connie opened her bag and took out the two large flasks of tea and the tin of tarts. Mrs Wilkinson had baked them that morning especially to support Connie's big event. She handed out freshly pressed napkins. Mrs Wilkinson had insisted. 'We should always follow the 'niceties' of life, whenever we can.'

Once they were all settled with refreshments, Connie continued. 'The reason I'm hoping to start this off, is because I'm aware that lots of young men from our area have either volunteered or been conscripted into the armed forces. They are stationed a long way from home, many are in danger. Some are bound to be lonely and pining for news.' She looked at the women, trying to guess what they were thinking. 'I wasn't brought up around here, I don't know everybody. I'm hoping you all have local knowledge to help us.'

All the women nodded, with the exception of Marie. 'I am in the same boat as you. I come from near Hull, so regrettably I don't know many young men around here.' She looked serious and paused theatrically, with her hand held to her brow, 'not that I knew many in Hull either! My parents are strict and sent me to an all-girls' convent school. I know what a nun is! What is a young man?' Everyone laughed and the ice was broken.

'So, do any of you know chaps from around here who are posted overseas, or billeted away from home?' Connie persisted. She was relieved the meeting seemed to be getting off to a good start.

'My brother is in the RAF,' said Lucille, 'and his best friend Tony Ward is in the Royal Navy.'

'I'll just write their names down.' Connie took out her notebook, 'I think it would be good for us to produce a list.' Within fifteen minutes the girls had contributed twenty one names to the list. 'If you think of any more we can add them later. Now what shall we do?' asked Connie.

'Well we'll need the addresses of where they are billeted if we're going to write to them,' said Jane.

'Maybe they won't want us writing to them,' said Martha, 'they may think we're interfering and being nosy.

'Well they don't have to write back if they don't want anything to do with us, do they?'

'No, I suppose not.'

'We could ask their parents for their addresses and tell them all about what we're proposing to do and why at the same time,' said Connie. 'I'm having tea with Ted and Daisy Trotter tomorrow. I could ask them about their son Cecil. I know he's in the army. I think he's billeted down south somewhere.'

'That's a good idea,' said Jane. 'That would get us started. Maybe in our letters, we could tell them how their parents are getting on and bring them up to date with local happenings.'

'So are we just writing letters to them?' queried Martha, looking a bit downcast. 'I'm not very good at writing letters, especially to people I don't know, I never know what to say.'

'Good point Martha,' agreed Connie, 'I'm sure we all feel like that at times.'

'We could also send the lads cards at Christmas and for their birthdays,' suggested Lucille.

'And we could raise some money, so we could send them a postal order or something, as a present,' said Marie.

'My spelling isn't very good,' said Wendy, her face reddening at her admission.

'Never mind about that, that's easily solved. We can draft out letters here when we meet, everybody can copy them out and then send them off to their allocated men.'

'I could do with an allocated man,' laughed Marie.

'Me too,' giggled Lucille, 'although I don't fancy writing to my brother, he gets a family letter, with snippets in from us all, every week.'

Martha's hand shot up in the air, 'Oh! I'll write to your brother.'

Jane winked at Connie.

'Can we allocate the men now?' asked Marie, 'I'm warming to this idea. How many can I have?'

The Widemarsh Ladies' Letter Writing Circle was born that afternoon. They worked hard on the wording of their first letters. If and when they got replies, they would read them out at the next meeting of WLLWC and then agree on the responses.

Connie was allocated Teddy Thomson, Alf Young, Phil York and Cecil Trotter. She knew some of their names, but had never met any of them. She visited all of their parents to tell them what the Widemarsh Ladies Letter Writing Circle intended to do. Everybody thought it was a grand idea and gave her their blessing, along with the addresses. She tried to tailor the basic letter to each young man.

Home Farm
Great Hall Estate,
Widemarsh
East Yorkshire
10th June 1943

Dear Phil

I am writing these few lines on behalf of all the folk in Widemarsh. I went to see your Mother to get your address. She and all at home look well. I do hope that you as well, are 'in the pink'.

My friend Marie is writing to your brothers, who I understand are posted overseas. Isn't it grand that they're together?

I remain

Yours sincerely

Connie Aldridge

(WLA 23969)

1956

Tom held the faded letter in his hand. 'Is this the first letter you ever wrote to Dad?'

'Yes and he kept it.'

'Did you write the same letter to all the men?'

'Yes more or less, with just a few variations if I had a bit of extra information.'

'Who wrote back to you first?'

'Your dad.'

'Had you ever met him?'

'No. His parents showed me a photograph of him and his brothers when I called on them to get his address and to see if they were happy with me writing to him.' She laughed aloud at the memory. 'He must have been quite young though; he was still wearing short trousers and a big pair of boots.'

'Dad, in short trousers! Did he have hairy legs?'

'No I don't think so. To be honest, I couldn't really see.' She giggled. 'His socks were so long they nearly came up to the hems of his shorts.' They laughed together at the mental image.

'Have you got dad's replies?'

'No regrettably, I was getting quite a lot of letters, so I didn't keep them all. He was probably asking questions, to find out a bit more about me.' Connie smiled as she remembered. 'Your dad kept all mine to him though. He was more organised than me at that time. Would you like to see my second letter to him?'

'Yes please Mam.'

The Railway Gatehouse

Burstthwaite

Near Hull

Dear Phil

Life is full of surprises isn't it? Your second letter was one, but not at all unpleasant. I have often wondered what the recipients of my letters are like, as quite a few of them, including you, had left before I came to Widemarsh. The day I came I never imagined that

I should be still among the cows, mud and wurzels in 1943, but I guess I could be among worse things; the snow and intense cold of Russia must be simply terrible for one.

Just at present I am at home, which, to me, is the finest place on earth. On Saturday I am going to Darlington to my Grandma's and then onto Newcastle to some friends I have up there, the following weekend. It seems a grand long spell to be away from work, doesn't it? But of course I have so many days' pay to lose, which doesn't bother me in the slightest (money being no object to me of course)!!!

I was born a 'Geordie', Darlington being three miles inside Durham, and aren't I proud of that same distance? We often have arguments at the farm over the subject Durham better than Yorkshire, but I guess your views will tally with the Wilkinsons.

My dad has always worked for the **LNER** I think, except of course when he was in the army, during the last war, and I think he'll stick it now till the end of his working days.

How long have you been in the army Phil? Do you fancy a military life or will you be home, sweet home, before the bells stop ringing?

By the way, I'm sorry not to oblige with the photo, as what freaks I do possess are at Widemarsh and in my usual rush for the train, I overlooked putting them in my case. Fair exchange is no robbery they say, so how about it? If you have one to spare don't forget to enclose it please. I've had a long day, so will sign off, I'm feeling a bit dozy.
Connie

'What happened after that?'
'Well we continued writing letters to each other and I started to look forward to receiving Phil's letter, more than anybody else's. After a few months he came home on leave and we saw each other for the first time. We must have liked what we saw, because he became my boyfriend. The rest, as they say, is history.'

***

November 1943

Phil stood beneath the Gossip Oak and watched nervously as the land girl cycled along the road. She dismounted before she got to the tree, dropped the bike on the verge and walked towards him. Phil realised he was standing almost to attention and forced himself to relax, into 'at ease'. He rubbed his clammy hands on his trouser legs. He'd been writing to her several times a week for months, but now he didn't know what to do. Writing to her was one thing, meeting her was quite another. *Will she shake hands? Will she still be my land girl after she's met me? She's stunning, much better than her photo. I didn't realise her hair was so red.*

He's very handsome, Connie thought, *although he does look as though he's on parade.* She looked at the soldier, standing rigidly to attention, waiting for her. *He's very smart, his uniform is immaculate, razor-blade creases in his trousers.* As she drew near she could see his eyes were blue. *Dark hair, what I can see of it under his beret.*

'Hello Phil,' she said holding her hand out for him to shake, 'delighted to meet you at last. I'm Connie.'

'Likewise. I'd have known you anywhere,' said Phil, shaking her hand vigorously before reluctantly letting it go.

He's got a lovely smile, she thought. Out loud she said, 'train on time?'

'Yes no problems. Got in a couple of hours ago, just had time to say hello to Ma and Pa and then pop along to meet you. What have you been doing today?'

'Oh glamorous things! Mucking out the stables, washing down the dairy and fixing a broken fence post.'

Phil pointed towards the bike lying in the grass. 'Is that the 'Tantivy' you're always going on about riding?'

'No you cheeky blighter,' she laughed, 'he's in his stable at the farm, probably sulking, because I didn't bring him with me.'

'Shall we go for a drink at the Royal Oak?'

'That would be lovely.'

'I thought we could sit and get to know each other a bit better.

I'll wheel your bike.'

As they strolled along the road towards the pub, two grinning young women, walked briskly past them. 'Hello Connie', they chorused over their shoulders, whilst looking with interest at Phil.

'Who are they?' asked Phil, amused by their obvious curiosity.

'Just Lucille and Martha, from the Letter Writing Circle They're having a nosy. That one is the butcher's daughter, the other is the head teacher's. Both nice girls.'

When they got to the pub, Lucille and Martha were sitting at the bar.

'What will you have, Connie?' said Phil.

'A beer please.'

'And you girls, what would you like?'

'Half of shandy please.'

'Same for me, thanks.'

Phil carried Connie's and his drinks across to a window seat. *He's generous and chivalrous*, Connie thought.

'So tell me about you,' she said, resting her chin on her hands. *I like his face.*

Phil looked shy and then thoughtful. 'Well, I like doing crosswords and I like playing cricket. I've just been selected to box for the regiment at welterweight.'

'What's welterweight?'

'You must weigh more than ten stones, but less than ten and a half.'

'Does boxing hurt?'

'Only if you let the other fellow hit you.'

Connie laughed. She thought she might be a welterweight too. Phil saved her from further thoughts by asking.

'What about you?'

'At the moment we're up to our eyeballs with work on the farm, because we're so short handed. I've had to resign from the Red Cross, because I could never get to the meetings. Not that I mind, I was finding it a bit boring because we kept going over the same things. Most evenings, after milking, I'm either writing letters or helping Maisie Wilkinson to pull the wool out of old jumpers and balling it up. She and her school pals are using it to knit blankets, for the war effort. They're going to give them to old folk to keep them warm in the winter.'

Phil laughed, 'We could do with some blankets where we are. We're bivouacked in drafty Bell tents, under camouflage netting, amongst trees, somewhere in Norfolk.' He winked and tapped the side of his nose. 'We're sworn to secrecy, so Fritz doesn't find our location and try to warm us up. We call our tent 'The Nest'. Fortunately it's at ground level, so if we fall out of it after we've been for a drink on Saturday nights, we don't have far to drop.'

The more they chatted, the more Connie was impressed with his humour, his twinkling eyes and his shy smile. She also liked the way he looked at her. She was enjoying her time with him, but there were duties calling.

'Come on, it's nearly milking time. I've got to get back.'

'Do you have to?'

'Unfortunately a land girl's work is never done.'

Chatting comfortably, they walked back together to the farm. Before they parted he nervously kissed her on the cheek and arranged to meet her again the following afternoon. She smiled to herself, as she crossed the muddy yard to the farm house. Propping her bike against a wall, she went inside and was met by a nosy Maisie.

'Come on then, spill the beans, what's your soldier like?'

'I'll tell you all about Phil after tea.'

Humming happily she changed into her working clothes, pulled on her boots and headed to the cow parlour.

Chapter 11

CONNIE'S WAR

'Mam?'

'Yes Tom.'

'Dad says you were very brave in the war and the Queen gave you a medal.'

'Well I did get a medal.'

'What did you do?'

'Nothing much, milked a few cows, ploughed a few fields and dug an awful lot of wurzels.'

'Can I see it?'

'No not now love, I'm a bit busy.'

'But Mam.'

'I'm not sure where it is. I'll show you it some other time.'

December 1941. Great Hall Estate, farmhouse kitchen.

'Hello Con,' said Maisie, looking up from her homework, as Connie came in from the yard and hung her greatcoat and hat on the pegs behind the door.

'Hi Maisie, what you up to?' she answered, before rolling up her sleeves, vigorously soaping her hands and washing them under the cold tap over the deep earthenware sink.

'Geography. American Plains. What about you?'

'Checking the heifers, feeding chopped turnips to the bullocks and giving Tantivy and the 'boys' some rolled oats.'

'How is he?'

'Tantivy? Beautiful as ever. Bit restless. Needs some exercise. Why don't you ask your Dad if you can take him for a gallop on Saturday?'

'Great idea,' replied Maisie enthusiastically. 'I could take him across the fields to the riverbank and home around the back lane. He always enjoys that.'

Phoebe, her mother, looked up from peeling potatoes and smiled knowingly. 'Not before you've done your chores.'

'No Mum,' said Maisie rolling her eyes at Connie. 'I'll rub him down and groom him, when I get back.'

'It's not the blooming horse I'm worried about, you're always fussing around him. It's you tidying up your room before you go galloping off that bothers me. When you've got that horse on your mind, nothing else seems to matter.'

'I'll do my room before I go. I promise.'

'OK then.'

'Postman's been,' Maisie said, moving the conversation to a more comfortable place. She looked towards Connie. 'He brought this month's *Land Girl*. Can I borrow it from you when you've finished reading it? I want to read the next chapter of 'Destination Unknown'.'

'Of course you can.'

'I had a quick flick through it,' continued Maisie, laughing as she waved the magazine above her head. 'I'm sure a letter from some Yorkshire land girl is on page 8. It's also got a snap of the same woman standing between two beautiful shire horses.'

'Pull the other one,' said Connie, excitedly snatching the magazine from Maisie.

Letter from the Land Girl *magazine, December 1941.*[27]

Dear Editor

I have been employed here for two years and have not regretted a single minute of it. Doing general farm work, one sees all sides of the job. First sowing corn and root crops, setting potatoes, hoeing from morning 'til night – then haymaking, hobbing thistles and mowing dykes as an interlude before harvest. Then stooking and forking on the stack, threshing, lifting sugar beet, turnips and mangel wurzels, sorting and carting potatoes. And so to winter, leading in straw and hay for bedding, chopping turnips and mangels, acting as assistant when one of the animals is sick or injured. A hundred and fifty animals need a good deal of attention, especially as between fifty and sixty of them are 'calvers'.

Let us cry shame on that section of city folk who think of the farmer as ignorant or a country bumpkin, for there is as much skill in tilling the soil as at the machines, desks and benches of our fellow workers in the town.

Finally the best of luck to the *Land Girl*, the best magazine ever. Yours sincerely,

Yorks. C. Aldridge. W.L.A. 23969.

***

August 1943

The girls met at the Gossip Oak. It was so old that its roots had pushed up the earth around its massive trunk into a gentle grass-covered mound. The tree's prominent location on the road verge in the centre of the village made it the ideal place to meet and have a chat.

They had leant their bikes against it and were sitting, shaded from the sun, below the wide canopy.

'We could organize a dance,' suggested Marie.

'What us? Here? In the hall?'

'Why not?'

'Well for a start it's an old hut pretending to be a village hall. It's in the back of beyond. It's not exactly the Floral Hall, Scarborough, is it?' said Martha

'I don't think it's too bad. The floor is reasonable. There are some card tables and loads of chairs,' reasoned Marie.

'I've never been to Scarborough,' said Lucille. 'Is it nice?'

'Picturesque, but cold; rains a lot,' laughed Connie. She was searching through the twigs and branches around her feet. 'The Floral Hall is very grand. A good place to shelter when it's wet on the beach.'

'The village hall's all right. The Women's Institute holds socials and parties there,' said Jane, backing Marie up.

'And whist drives,' added Wendy.

'We can soon smarten it up,' said Marie. 'It wouldn't take much doing.'

'My gran launders the tablecloths for the old folk's tea club. She'll let us borrow them,' said Lucille. 'Martha you're good at flower arranging,' she continued looking pointedly at her friend, 'you could put some in those little glass vases they keep in the cupboard.'

'Well I suppose so, but who would come to our dance? Everyone lives miles away.' Martha sounded wistful.

'I bet you're thinking about those American airmen we met when we were shopping in Howden, a couple of weeks ago,' laughed Connie. She was pretending to smoke an acorn pipe.

'No!' Martha protested and then smiled shyly, 'well maybe.'

'Everyone would come; the locals for a start,' said Lucille.

'Oh no! Not my mam and dad.' groaned Martha. 'That would put a bit of a damper on it. They might stop me from going.'

'No, they wouldn't if you told them we were raising money to send postal orders to the local lads who are stationed away, for their Christmas Boxes.'

'And they might not mind much if you had a couple of dances,' said Marie winking at Martha.

'You don't know my Dad! Anyway how would they get here?'

'Who? The Yanks?' joined in Connie, throwing her make believe pipe away and grinning, 'I expect they'll find a way. They borrow a jeep to come to the dances in Howden. They'd only have to drive an extra ten miles to get here.'

'Well that's all well and good but we can't have a dance without a band and there isn't a stage.'

'That's easy to fix,' said Jane. 'We can use the judges' podium from the agricultural show as a stage. Dad keeps it in the barn. We can organise our own band. Wendy plays violin, our cousin Jack plays piano and I'll talk Ben Partridge who leads the Boy's Brigade. He'll bring drums. I'll sing. I've always fancied being lead singer in a dance band. It'll make a change from the church choir, and I know lots of hit tunes. I've just got the music for 'Chatanooga Choo Choo',[30] we could do that, you could all join in on the chorus. It'll be fun. Come on let's have a go.'

'You leave the Pennsylvania Station 'bout a quarter to four,
Read a magazine and then you're in Baltimore.
Dinner in the diner, nothing could be finer,
Than to have your ham an' eggs in Carolina.'

'I'll start work on the posters,' said Connie. 'You'll definitely need more than 'Chatanooga Choo Choo' though. You'd better start practising. What will you call the band?'

October 1943

'Look out, here comes your handsome Yank,' said Marie, as the jeep pulled up outside the village hall.

'He's not my Yank, he's just a good friend,' Connie said smiling. 'I can't believe we've actually done it!' She turned to admire their notice.

A dance organized by the
Widemarsh Ladies Letter Writing Circle
in aid of funds to support our lads posted away.
Music by the WiLLoWs Dance Band.

The hall had been booked for a fee of five shillings. Connie and Marie were standing behind a card table taking the money on the door. Connie looked in the cash box and mentally added up the contents. *Great we've already covered our costs.*

Two paraffin lamps burned brightly in the raftered ceiling. The girls had knocked on every door in the locality and had asked the women to lend them cotton or lightweight scarves for the duration of the dance. Lucille and Martha had spent the day draping them across strings suspended from the ceiling, at a safe distance away from the lamps. The effect on the bare utilitarian hall was magical. The girls agreed the place had a carnival atmosphere, it felt warm and exciting. On each table was a small vase of wild hips and berries that Martha and Lucille had gathered from the hedgerows. On every table, next to the vase, a candle, donated by the local churches, burned brightly.

Members of the band were setting up their music stands on the improvised stage and Lucille and Martha were doing a roaring trade selling teas and lemonades from a table in the corner. There was a cheer from the men as Fred Burridge from the Wheatsheaf, brought in a barrel of bitter on his wheelbarrow.

Connie looked out of the doorway and saw him. She lifted her hand. Rusty Harcourt spotted her straight away. He smiled and waved back. Marie raised her eyebrows and laughed, 'Connie! What are you going to say to the lads that you're writing to?'

'They don't need to know. A girl needs some secrets.'

'Has your Yank kissed you yet?'

'Don't be nosy.'

'Well, has he?'

'Once or twice; but there's been no funny business. He's a gentleman. Anyway mind your own beeswax.'

'Is he a good kisser?' Marie asked, unfazed by her friend's resistance to her questioning.

'Pretty good,' said Connie laughing. She moved the conversation onto safer ground. 'He is nice to dance with, very light on his feet. I suppose he's not too bad to look at.' She paused. 'A girl's got to do what a girl's got to do, for the war effort you know!'

'I've heard that one before,' giggled Marie.

'Now shut up, they're coming in.' Connie gave her friend a warning glance.

The four Yanks strolling towards them, were seconded to the RAF station at Holme on Spalding Moor. They were all wearing leather flying jackets and neatly pressed flannel trousers. Rusty's 'bomber' had stripes on the shoulder. A line of bomb-shaped patches were sewn across the chest. Each symbol signified a successful mission.

They look so swish, a bit like film actors thought Connie as she admired their relaxed, neat appearance. *Plenty of money I suppose.* Her gaze drifted around the hall to the groups of locals chatting and waiting for the dance to start. She jumped involuntarily when she realized her eyes had settled on Eric Jenks and his cronies. Eric was leering at her and making thrusting movements with his hips. His pals were laughing. Disgusted, she turned away. *What a hateful man, I feel sorry for his wife having to put up with that.*

'Hi Con' said Rusty. He rested his hand lightly on her shoulder. Noticing her expression he followed her gaze. 'You OK? Is that idiot bothering you?'

'No, everything's fine,' said Connie, regaining her composure. 'He's just a pathetic pest, I can handle him.'

'Well if he bothers you, let me know and I'll have a word with him.'

'Thanks, but it's OK,' said Connie, guessing what sort of a 'word' Rusty would have. 'He's probably been in The Oak before he came here, topping himself up with Dutch courage.'

Eric Jenks, playing to his audience of drinking cronies, raised his voice, 'Bloody Yanks, over paid, over sexed and over here.' A ripple of raucous comments followed his remark.

'The booze sure makes him act foolishly,' said Rusty, ignoring the remark and deliberately turning his back on Eric. 'Can I get you a drink?' he asked Connie. He jiggled and clinked the contents of the bag in his hand, before placing it on the table.

Connie laughed, remembering the conversation she'd had with him about the glamorous lifestyles of film stars in Hollywood. 'You haven't! Have you?'

Rusty grinned at her. 'Go on then, ask me. You're always going on about it since you saw that movie.'

'OK then,' giggled Connie, 'Please can I have a Gin and It?'

'Ma'am, you surely can,' he said opening the bag with gusto. 'I anticipated your request and as if by magic I have a bottle of Gin, Dutch of course, and another of Italian Vermouth.'

'Can I have one too…?' asked Marie, as she showed the Americans to a table, '…if I go and find some glasses?'

'Sure thing. You grab the glasses Marie. Me and the boys will rustle up the drinks and get some extra chairs. 'Gin and Its all round, coming up.'

Ben Partridge gave a drum roll, followed by a series of reverberating notes on his symbol, to bring the room to order. Jane Wilson stepped onto the front of the make-shift stage and waited for the room to quieten. She was wearing a deep maroon knee-length dress. A wide belt pulled in her waist. Around her slender neck she wore a string of her mother's pearls. Her hair was set in victory rolls, a style she'd copied from a Rita Hayworth photograph. Her red lipstick accentuated the cupid's bow of her lips.

'She looks stunning,' whispered Martha to Lucille. 'I've never seen her legs before. Where did she get the stockings?'

'No, she's not wearing any! She's painted them with gravy mix. Wendy penciled a seam down the back with eyebrow pencil,' confided Lucille. Jane was worried in case it rained on the way here and made them run, but it stayed dry and she's got away with it.'

The crowd started to applaud Jane warmly. Encouraged she took a deep breath and launched in to her introduction. 'Ladies and Gentlemen welcome to the Widemarsh Ladies Letter Writing Circle Harvest Dance. Thank you all for coming. To get the evening going we'd like to start with that old favourite by Frank Loessor and Hoagy Carmichael. It is called 'Heart and Soul'.[31] So please take your partners.' She nodded to her three-piece band and counted them in. They struck up with the melody. The dancers took to the floor and Jane started to sing.

'Wow she's got a lovely voice,' said Marie.

'May I have the pleasure?' said Rusty, taking Connie's hand. She smiled and nodded. As he led her onto the floor Jane sang:-

'Heart and Soul, I fell in love with you
Lost control, the way a fool would do
Gladly
Because you held me tight,
And stole a kiss in the night.'

As Rusty waltzed Connie around the dance floor, she relaxed into his arms. He was a skilful dancer. Try as she might she couldn't stop the little thrill of excitement that rippled through her when his brown eyes looked directly into hers and he murmured the words with his mouth next to her cheek. She smiled up at him, then tore her eyes away and forced herself to look at all the happy people around her. Marie's dance idea was turning into a success.

'Now I see what one embrace can do
Look at me, it's got me loving you
Madly
The little kiss you stole
Held all my heart and soul.'

***

Three days later

'Not so fast Connie.' Eric Jenks stepped out of the field gateway and forced her bike to stop by grabbing hold of her handlebars. He leant towards her and she smelt his foul breath

'What do you think you're doing?' she snapped, trying to pull the handlebars from his grasp, without overbalancing. 'Let go of my bike you stupid man.'

'Not until you've shown me a bit of that affection you heap on those bloody Yanks.'

'Affection! Why should I show you affection? You're just a disgusting drunk. At least the Yanks behave like gentlemen. You could never be accused of that. Shouldn't you be at home with your wife?'

'I think it's time you spent a bit of time with a proper man.' He was fumbling with the buttons on his trouser fly.

'You must be joking. You a proper man! Now let go off my bike and let me get on my way.'

'Not before we've had a bit of fun,' leered Eric putting his other arm around Connie's waist and pulling her from the seat. The bicycle fell to the ground, spilling her groceries from the basket.

'Take your hands off me,' screamed Connie. 'Push off! You're starting to annoy me.' She regained her balance and tried to shove him away.

'First I'm going to have a look at those big tits of yours.'

'Go away and don't be so filthy, you horrible man.'

'You know what I want.' He reached forward and grabbed at her breasts. His fingers hooked the front of her blouse and tore it open.

'Well you're not going to get it,' shouted Connie. Taking him by surprise, she leaned towards him and punched him hard in the mouth. The blow was driven by fear, anger at her torn blouse and muscles that had been working the land for four years. It was delivered with such force that Eric fell, stunned, into the hedge bottom. He landed hard on the unforgiving ground among brambles and nettles. He lay on his back, holding his hand to his mouth. 'You've split my lip and loosened one of my teeth,' he whined, showing her the blood on his hand.

'Serves you right, you pig,' spat Connie, rubbing her skinned knuckles. 'You try anything like that with me again and I'll geld you.'

She picked up her groceries, flung them into the basket and gathered up her bike with shaking hands. Clutching her torn blouse to cover herself, she ran off a little way down the road before remounting and pedaling away as fast as she could.

'You ungrateful bitch,' snarled Eric, spitting blood as he struggled to untangle his jacket from the brambles.

***

Henry Wilkinson's expression was grim. He flexed his huge gnarled hands as he watched Phoebe and Maisie comforting the sobbing Connie when she returned to Home Farm after her ordeal with

Jenks. Henry had great affection for his land girl and had come to regard her as another daughter. The next morning he was missing from the breakfast table. Phoebe told the girls he had an early call to make. When he returned later, he made no mention of where he had been.

It was teatime, when Maisie burst into the house with village news. Apparently Eric Jenks had been in a fight and had a broken nose, two black eyes and a split lip. He'd also developed a limp. 'He won't tell anyone who he's been fighting with.'

Phoebe glanced across at Henry. He was busy reading his *Howdenshire Gazette*.

***

16th/17th December 1943

'You'd think we had a swarm of bees in the hayloft. The air is vibrating so much, it's upsetting the cows,' worried Henry, casting an anxious eye over their fidgeting milkers.

'Sounds like there are a lot of them,' said Connie, stroking Clover's neck to calm her. Clover, their Golden Guernsey, was prized for her rich creamy milk. Connie squatted on the milking stool, holding the bucket to try and protect the contents from Clover's restless legs.

Henry looked upwards out of the milking parlour door to the massed squadrons of bombers. The air was filled with their droning. They flew eastwards, low over the Humber towards Europe. 'A few hundred of them up there, I reckon. Going to hit old Adolph where it hurts with a bit of luck.' He rubbed the back of his neck and grimaced, before taking one last look heavenwards and hurrying back to his cows.

'I hope they get home safely,' said Connie. 'Rusty if you're up there, stay lucky.'

'Fred spoke to someone at Howden market, on the QT of course. They couldn't say for definite, but reckon we might be hitting Berlin[7]. If that's the case they'll have some flak to cope with, poor buggers.'

'I'd hate it. I'd be terrified to be up there with people firing at me.'

'It's likely we'll hear them coming back after midnight. I think I'll sit up a bit and sky watch.'

'I'll keep you company. I won't be able to sleep. We could have a game of doms.'

Hours later, they were sitting at the farmhouse table, when they heard the first planes returning. Henry opened the top half of the back door and peered into the dark. The clouds hung low; it was raining. He couldn't see them. The Rolls Royce Merlin engines throbbed reassuringly as aircraft headed for home.

'Well, that lot sound OK,' said Henry, returning to the table, 'but it'll be a bugger finding their way back to base in this weather.'

'Following the Humber, do you think?'

'They'll only see it if they dip below the clouds. Navigators will be earning their crust tonight. Fancy another game?' As the night wore on, the planes continued to drift over the house. Some of their engines were spluttering.

'Sounds like they're nursing them, running on fumes. God help them,' said Henry shaking his head and returning to his dominoes. *I bet Con's got the last two sixes. Hang on, that plane sounds very close and the engines are spluttering a bit.* Suddenly he shot to his feet, knocking over his dominoes, 'Christ almighty, he's coming our way!' Henry dashed into the yard, with Connie close behind. They ducked low as the aircraft swept over their heads. One engine was trailing smoke and sparks. The descending plane came so close to the barn roof that the drag scattered tiles and debris. It crashed onwards through the tops of the trees. Droplets of burning fuel splashed down all around them. The farm dogs started barking loudly and the cattle locked for the night in the cowshed, began bellowing and kicking at their stalls trying to escape. Tears filled Connie's eyes, and she tried to stop her uncontrollable shakes by clutching Henry's hand tightly. They listened, terrified about what they might hear, and knowing with certainty that they would. Somewhere at the far side of the barn the plane hit the ground with a massive bang. They felt the earth shake beneath their feet. Eerie screeches of tearing metal filled the air and reverberated in their ears. For a moment Henry and Connie were too shocked to react.

Connie held her hand to her mouth. 'Oh God help them!'

'Christ what do we do now?' shouted Henry, overwhelmed. He made a huge effort to calm his breathing. His heart pounded. He slowly gathered his wits and uncharacteristically hugged Connie to him. 'At least he missed us,' he gasped. He felt breathless and shocked at this rapid turn of events. He released Connie, turned and dashed towards the house. 'We'd better go and see if there's anything we can do,' he yelled over his shoulder.

Brushing the tears from her cheeks as she ran, Connie followed Henry into the house. He was pulling on his waterproofs and looking anxiously across the kitchen towards Phoebe and Maisie, who were standing in the kitchen with their arms around each other.

'You two OK?'

Phoebe nodded. 'We're fine. The noise woke us. Was it a bomber?'

'Lancaster I think. We were damned lucky. I'm going to see what's going on. Con will come with me.'

'I'll come too,' said Maisie, pulling on a pair of trousers and tucking her nightdress into the waistband, 'I'll bring the first aid kit.'

'Well if you're sure,' said Henry. 'It is bound to be a bit grim. There'll be things a young girl should never have to look at.'

'I'll be fine.'

'Put some socks on,' Phoebe instructed Maisie. Then to Connie, 'how are you?'

Connie was pulling on her working boots and determinedly lacing them up. 'A bit shocked, if I'm honest.' She grabbed her great coat from behind the kitchen door.

'Will we be able to help them?' Maisie asked.

'It didn't sound too good.' Henry replied. 'Will you hold the fort Phoebe?' He buttoned his jacket and grabbed a torch from the windowsill.

'Here put this in your pocket,' she said, thrusting a half bottle of brandy at her husband.

Alan Durham

'Maisie, get your coat on, quick! Torches everybody.'

'I'll make sandwiches. You'll be hungry when you get back!' shouted Phoebe, as they ran out of the door. 'Take care.'

They ran out of the house, across the yard and threw open the gate into the pasture. The clouds were clearing and by the moon's wintery light they could see that trees had been toppled and hedges ripped up as the Lancaster made its emergency landing. The plane had slithered across the sodden grass, scattering bits of fuselage and tearing off the landing wheels. It had chewed up the pasture and gouged out a deep and ragged furrow, before stopping nose down in a ditch at the far side of the field. One of the engines was ablaze and an acrid smell of burnt oil and rubber filled the freezing night air. When they got closer to the wreckage they could see the mangled remains of a young bullock crushed under the tail plane. The other bullocks were milling around in the far corner of the field and were bellowing pitifully.

'Bloody hellfire,' said Henry, expressing the horror they all felt as they stood in mud, peering through the freezing rain at the carnage.

Maisie sobbed aloud and Connie put her arm around her shoulders to comfort her. 'Those poor lads,' she said, hugging her young friend hard and taking a long slow deep breath to steady her own nerves.

A series of loud cracks came from the plane.

'Ammo exploding,' warned Henry, 'we'd better not get too close.'

'But somebody could be alive in there,' shouted Connie above the rattle of exploding bullets.

'Doubt it lass,' answered Henry, 'it's bad. That was a hell of a landing.' Out of the darkness a man ran towards them waving a torch.

'Stand back! Stand back! She could go up at any time,' he shouted. He shone his torch in their faces.

'Is that you Percy?' yelled Henry. Percy was the air warden for their area.

'Fine bloody mess this, ain't it?' I was on patrol and saw it come down. Stand back! Stand back!' he ordered, as he shoved them away from the blazing wreck. 'I don't think they'll have brought bombs back, but you never know.'

'Are you going to check the plane?' said Connie. 'They might still be alive.'

'Not me lass. Far too risky.'

'They could burn to death.'

'Fire brigade and the police will be here soon, I expect. They'll sort it.'

Flames were illuminating the cockpit. They could see the outline of the pilot's head. He wasn't moving.

'I can't stand here and do nothing,' screamed Connie, grabbing the first aid kit from Maisie and running towards the wreckage.

'Come back you bloody fool,' shouted Percy.

Henry held Maisie firmly to him. Connie edged her way around the plane. *What shall I do?* She held her arm in front of her face to protect her from the heat of the burning engine. There was a jagged hole on the other side of the plane where the wing had torn off. *Lot of smoke. Not so hot. Should be able to get in OK.* Tying her scarf around her mouth and nose, she shone her torch into the hole. *How do I get in?* Leaning over she grasped a spar and heaved herself inside. Her trousers ripped on a spike of metal and she felt it scratch her leg. *I'm in! Now what?* She edged her way carefully through the tangled mess of buckled wing struts. The flames flickered and lit up the fuselage. There was popping and cracking all around as metal bent and expanded. Fear made her gasp at every sound. Her stomach churned.

The mid upper gunner was trapped by his legs and dangling upside down from a canvas seat rigged in the top of the plane. His torso and arms were hanging down. Connie shuddered, gathered her wits together and checked him over. *Blood covering his chest and head. No pulse, skin cold. Dead! For a while?* As she left him her stomach heaved violently and she vomited between her feet. Leaning against the side of the plane to steady her dizziness, she fought hard to control her rising panic.

Bracing herself mentally, she moved towards the rear and looked for the tail gunner. He was lying very still in his cramped turret. She slid forward, reached through the entrance hatchway and pulled his arm back until she could feel his wrist, *no pulse*. His parachute hung on a peg outside his restricted fighting space. *Not enough room to wear it? Fat lot of use that is!*

Wiping tears from her face with her coat sleeve, she gritted her teeth and edged her way through the bomb bay. *Can't see any bombs. Racks empty. Thank the Lord!* Connie crawled and twisted her way through the tightly packed wing spars. *Ouch they're hot!* Grabbing a bandage from the first aid kit, she wound it around her right glove and pulled herself towards the front end. The wireless operator's body was still warm. He was slumped against the Marconi radio. He was wearing his head set. *Blood around nose. Eyes wide open. No pulse. Killed by the landing maybe? Poor soul.*

The navigator was lying over his chart table. *Head at an unnatural angle. Broken neck?* She checked his pulse. Nothing. *Oh God! Four dead. Seven in a Lanc? Three more?*

Her trembling was constant, her teeth were chattering and she sobbed and choked as she gasped for breath in the smoke and fumes. She had to rest for a moment. *Come on you can do this. You owe it to them.* Pulling herself together again, she scrambled into the cockpit. She looked at the pilot sitting on the left, in his raised seat. Another man lay in a pool of blood at her feet. *Co-pilot maybe? Severe wounds to head and face. No sign of life.* She lifted the pilot's arm. *Is that a faint pulse?* She checked his pulse again, looked into his face and took a sharp intake of breath, he was looking at her. Her heart thumped in her chest. His lips moved. She leant over him to hear. His voice was weak.

'The others?'

'Not good I'm afraid,' she said, 'I haven't checked the forward gunner yet.'

'Ronnie, killed Berlin.'

'I need to get you out of here.' She said fumbling with his harness.

'No, leave me,' he croaked, 'I'm done for.' He lifted his hand slightly and Connie grasped it. His grip was very weak. 'Scared,' he whispered, 'don't want to die.'

'You'll be OK,' she reassured him. 'What's your name?' She squeezed his hand and stroked his cheek with her other.

His eyes closed, his head fell forward and his throat rattled. Tears poured down Connie's cheeks, as she held his hand. *Please don't die. I don't want you to die.* She kept stroking his cheek. She didn't know what to do. *No pulse now. He's dead.* Connie released his hand and tenderly laid it in his lap. She felt she should say something. *I'm not up to this.* She gathered all her strength. 'May the Lord watch over you,' she said aloud, kissing him gently on the forehead.

Before making her way back through the fuselage she checked the forward gunner. His remains were crushed in the folded metal of the 'plane's nose. Eventually she managed to scramble out and fell face down in the wet grass and mud. Henry ran to her, helped her upright and half carried her away from the plane.

'You bloody idiot,' Percy yelled, shaking his fist at them, 'flames are getting worse, even empty fuel tanks blow. Get away, get away!'

They ran across the field to where Maisie was waiting. 'Couldn't you do anything?' she asked.

'Dead, I'm afraid, all seven of them.' Connie's head slumped forward and her shoulders shook uncontrollably as she sobbed, 'the pilot died while I held his hand.' Henry put his arm round her shoulders and gave her a swig of brandy. Maisie held her around her waist.

'Come on Con, it's time we went home, nothing more to be done here.' He hugged her to his side. 'Phoebe will have the kettle on. The authorities can sort this lot out.' As they walked away there was a huge explosion and the flames spread rapidly along the Lancaster.

Connie looked back at the blazing wreckage. 'At least we know they're not burning to death.'

'Thanks to you,' said Henry.

***

December 1945

Phoebe and Connie climbed down from the early morning train onto the platform and looked at the clock on Kings Cross Station.

'Good! We've three hours to spare. Enough time for a quick breakfast,' said Phoebe. 'And then we'll get you to Faringdon Street.' They hurried through a stone archway and caught a taxi.

I feel like a Hollywood star, thought Connie, *first trip in a taxi.* She was grateful for Phoebe's company. *It's not every day that you go to a party with the Queen, and now, thanks to Phoebe, I'm also going to achieve another ambition – a visit to Lyons Corner House.* Fifteen minutes later the taxi pulled up in Tottenham Court Road.

'Here you are ladies. Lyons Oxford Corner Tea Shop.'

'It's enormous,' exclaimed Connie excitedly, craning her neck as she looked upwards at the imposing building. There was large food shop at street level. High windows reached through the floors above it, to where a Union Jack flew on a flagpole over the huge CORNER HOUSE sign.

'There are different restaurants on each floor,' explained Phoebe. Henry and I had dinner here before the war. After that we went to the theatre and saw 'Me and My Girl'.' They walked through the entrance and were directed to the Brasserie by the doorman. A 'nippy' in her immaculate black and white uniform greeted them. Kiss curls peeped below her broad white headband.

'Good morning. Table for two?'

'Yes please. We'd like breakfast.'

'This way please.'

They followed the nippy through the lines of tables. She stopped at one, near the window.

'Here you are. Is this OK? Good. I'm Betty. I'll just get you some menus.' Connie smiled at the waitress when she noticed her studying her land girl uniform.

'You here for the parade?' Betty asked.

'Yes I am. There'll be quite a few like me in London today.'

'You girls are doing a wonderful job. When I've finished me shift,

I'll pop over and watch you going by.' Betty dashed off. Connie and Phoebe noticed a smartly dressed pianist playing a medley of favourites.

'It's the first time I've had breakfast while someone plays a grand piano.' Connie looked around admiring the room. 'I love the pillars with the big lights around the tops.'

'The music's lovely, but I think Art Deco style is a bit old fashioned now. In fact the whole place could do with a lick of paint. The war has aged it a bit since I was here last.'

'I like it. A bit faded, but very grand. Thank you for bringing me.'

Betty, handing out the menus, overheard. 'There hasn't been any paint available for years. We've been told they're going to put pictures on the walls next year to brighten us up a bit. The bosses have got some well known artists doing them.'

'It's still lovely,' said Connie.

They ordered poached eggs on toast and a pot of tea. The pianist played 'Tea for Two' and Connie felt it was just for her.

Later that morning Connie met up with the other Yorkshire land girls and they were allocated their position in the parade. The seven hundred and fifty women were led by a military band as they marched past cheering crowds, through the streets to the Lord Mayor's Mansion House. Sir Charles Davis, the Lord Mayor of London, had invited the land girls who had joined the service in 1939, to a Christmas Party with the Queen. Her Majesty was to present them with their long service armlets. Their party was held in the Egyptian Banqueting Hall.

Years later Connie recalled one incident which amused her. 'You'll never believe it Tom,' she said laughing, 'it was very posh. The Egyptian Hall has really high ceilings and gold trimmed Corinthian columns. We were allocated tables and served by liveried footmen. We used gold teaspoons. The footmen counted them out in front of us before we started the party and then counted them back in at the end before anyone left the building. It was ever so funny.'

'Why did they do that?'

'So we didn't keep them as mementoes.'

In her speech the Queen praised the land girls…

'You came here six years ago, with your great gifts of youth and strength and with high purpose to serve your country in her hour of need. Never have British women shown more capacity and pluck. On the farms and in the fields, gardens and forests, you took your place in the battle for freedom and through your endurance and toil, supplied the needs of this island and sustained the life of the nation…and I pray that the harvest of victory which you have helped to reap may bring you one and all, an abundance of peace, prosperity and happiness.'

When Connie's name was called, she walked with pride to the front of the hall and curtsied before the Queen, who presented her armband to her.

Later that month a letter arrived at Widemarsh, stating that she had been awarded the British Empire Medal in the New Year's Honours List 1946, for services to her country. She was always modest about her medal and never spoke about it, unless pressed. Phil 'annoyed' her twice a year by sending her a Christmas card and a Birthday card addressed to Connie York BEM. Although she protested embarrassment when these came through the post, Tom always thought she was secretly pleased.

14

Chapter 12

THE ROAD TO AMERIKA

Spring 1944 Shuker's Camp, Thetford. Norfolk

'What's this all about then?' Taff pointed to the notice on the orders board.

'Doesn't read like good news to me,' Phil shook his head.

> 'A' squadron 15th/19th (1st and 2nd troop)
> report to Mess tent at 15.00 hours today.
> Briefing with General Hobart.
> 15th/19th C.O. will be in attendance.

'Better watch out. Hobo's[8] about! The bugger's always here nowadays.'

'Pip Roberts as well. Top brass everywhere,' added Chalky. He looked worried. 'What are they up to?'

'Don't know,' said Phil, 'but it'll be a best bib and tucker job, Hobo's a bugger for correct dress.'

'Hell, polishing boots and bloody buttons again!' Chalky sounded fed up.

Taff ignored Chalky's moan. 'Did you two see the Sherman arrive on that low loader yesterday? It had a bloody great tarpaulin draped over it. Very hush-hush!'

'Do you think it could be one of Hobo's funnies?

The penny dropped. 'That's it Chalky! Hobo's coming here to tell us about his latest mad idea. God help us all!' Phil took a sharp breath. 'Oh Christ! I hope he's forgotten that ride I gave him in the jeep the other week.'

Taff grinned. 'Would that be when you floored the accelerator and tore across the parade square, with him hanging on for dear life? He may have forgotten, but I don't think I ever will. My ribs still hurt from laughing. I keep trying to remember what the charge is for frightening a General to death.'

'Well I might have been a bit heavy footed. What could he expect after two years of driving tanks?' laughed Phil. 'He didn't say anything. Maybe he was OK about it.'

'You hope,' said Taff. 'All I can say is that when you off loaded him, his beret looked a bit askew and his expression was set like concrete. He doesn't look the type to forgive and forget, so don't be surprised if he pulls your name out of his hat and you find yourself volunteering for something.'

'Thanks a lot for that Taff! Now I'm really looking forward to this afternoon!'

15.00 hours, the same day.

'Good afternoon men. Major General Hobart will conduct this briefing.'

'Attention!'

Major General Percy 'Hobo' Hobart strode briskly to the front of the assembled men. 'At ease men, please sit down. Before I start I must thank General Roberts for allowing me the opportunity to talk to you this afternoon.' His eyes flicked briefly to the officers seated at a table. Hobo Hobart spoke rapidly. His energy filled the room. His presence and personality demanded attention. 'What I am about to tell you is top secret. It is absolutely vital to the war effort and relies heavily on your skills, courage and abilities.' He paused; his hawk-like face, furnished with a bristling moustache and exuberant eyebrows, glowered at the troops. 'If our tanks are to overcome the obstacles the enemy has created for us we must fit them with diverse equipment.'

The Major General paced as he addressed the men. 'Recent innovations[8] have proved useful. These include the canal defence searchlight, chain flails that help us to clear mines and tank bridges that speed the movement of our convoys over difficult terrain.' He scanned the nodding heads in front of him. 'Today I'm here to talk to you about a new challenge. The enemy is dug in at the other side of the English Channel. They have fortified the sea walls stretching through France, Belgium and Holland. They know that when we go back into Europe our biggest challenges will be their fortifications and massed guns.

So how will you men get ashore with minimum casualties? Success depends upon the element of surprise. The enemy will expect boats and landing craft carrying our troops to shore. They will not anticipate little boats, with tanks beneath them. When our tanks land, they will give the enemy defences a battering and give our infantry the opportunity to win the day.' Hobo finished his speech with a triumphant flourish. 'Gentlemen we are about to trial swimming tanks.' There were sharp intakes of breath from the men. 'Sergeant Major, if you please.'

CSM Humphries marched smartly to the front of the room, and unveiled a display board. Pinned to it was a large photograph of a tank. He handed Hobo a pointer.

'Thank you Sergeant Major.' Hobo stepped to the side of the board and tapped the photograph. 'One of our top engineers, Mr Nicholas Straussler, has developed a Duplex Drive Sherman tank. 'A' squadron and its highly trained, enthusiastic crews will assist in the testing of this new weapon. You are all familiar with the Sherman. This one has been fitted with inflatable rubber flotation skirts.' Hobo tapped the loops of material that hung around the top of the tank in the photograph. 'These will provide enough buoyancy to enable the Sherman to float. When the duplex drive mechanism is engaged, the engine will no longer power the tracks, it will drive twin propellers.' He smiled at the men. 'We anticipate these tanks will be able to swim through the water at about four knots. When you approach the shoreline, the propellers are disengaged and the tracks re-engaged. Tests begin next week. I wish you every success. In the meantime I know your officers will afford you every opportunity to familiarise yourselves with this new weapon. I will be there to observe your trials. Thank you.'

One week later. Fritton Decoy Lake.

Their Sherman Tank was sitting at the top of a soil and stone ramp, facing downwards towards the peaty waters of the lake. Toby was carrying out the final inflation checks on the rubber flotation skirt and throwing the used oxygen bottles onto the grass alongside. The skirt was fastened, box like, on top of the tank. The boffins anticipated that when the tank was in deep water, only three feet of the flotation screen would show above the surface.

'No boffins on board for our first voyage,' observed Taff drily.

'Maybe they get seasick, or they forgot to bring their wellies,' Phil looked cynical. 'You would think they'd be desperate to come for a swim with us.' His laughter didn't hide his nervousness.

The tank's exhaust pipe had been trunked upwards, above the anticipated water level, to vent inside the flotation skirt. The fumes were accumulating and Toby, their tank officer, was coughing badly. He leant over the side of the skirt to find some fresh air.

'Who'd be a tank Skip?' mused Taff. 'If he doesn't drown when we sink to the bottom, the fumes will finish him off.'

'Please don't mention sinking,' Phil groaned. 'Have you seen the size of the waves on this lake?'

'They're only ripples. She can cope with them. Designed to handle a twelve-inch wave, apparently.'

'Only if she bloody well floats and doesn't dive straight down!'

The 600 horsepower Rolls Royce Meteor engine roared as Phil applied a few more revs.

'I'd be obliged if you can take her across without stalling.' Toby shouted, between coughs, from his perch in the turret.

'I'll do my very best Skip. I don't think any of us fancy being fish food.' Phil noticed his hands were shaking.

'Jolly good. We're trying her in coastal waters next week. Wind and waves permitting.'

'Oh good,' muttered Taff, 'I've been fancying a day out at the seaside.'

A klaxon sounded from the observation platform, where Major General Percy 'Hobo' Hobart and his land-lubber boffins were watching.

'OK Phil, here we go. Brace positions everyone. The very best of luck to us all. Advance!'

Phil put the revs up, engaged forward gear and the thirty-five ton tank clanked down the ramp into the lake. The crew were thrown violently about as they entered the water. The Sherman was enveloped in the wash. Water flooded the turret, pouring into the driver's space and soaking Phil. He could see nothing. He felt the tracks slithering and slipping as they left the ramp. Sweat stood out on his forehead as he fought the controls. The tracks churned the water, the engine screamed and the tank swayed alarmingly from side to side. Feeling claustrophobic, Phil steeled himself to stay calm. *Bloody hell, I feel like Captain flaming Nemo under the sea, struggling with this huge metal beast.*

'Anybody got a lifebuoy?' Taff shook water from his beret.

'She's floating. Engage the props Phil,' shouted Toby. Phil disengaged the drive to the tracks and then pulled the lever to allow the twin propellers to drop into place. When he heard them clunk into position, he re-engaged the engine. They cruised slowly forward, edging their way towards the far bank of the lake. Everyone was quiet. All focus was on the engine noise and the trickles of water seeping into the hull. Troop Officer Toby, in his turret, was the only man who could see where they were going. All the others were below water.

'Keep her steady on that line Phil. We're getting there.'

Thank god for that.

After what seemed an age to the nervous crew, the tank started to drag on the bottom.

'OK Phil, disengage the props and re-engage the tracks. Let's have her back on dry land pronto. Bath time is over.'

The tank emerged from the lake, a grumbling undersea monster, slithering, slurping and dripping mud and water as it struggled up the bank.

***

One month later

'I reckon something is definitely going on. We are doing loads of practising at the coast,' said Chalky. 'I have a nasty feeling we'll be going for a swim in French water shortly.'

'I'm not looking forward to that.' Phil said. 'Taking a tank for a bath over here is bad enough. I can't imagine what it'll be like in hostile waters.'

***

13th August 1944

'Port Winston ahoy.' Taff leant against the rusty bulwark of the scruffy coaster. It chugged and surged through the swell.

'Not before time,' groaned Chalky clutching his stomach, 'I'm fed up with feeding the fishes.'

'I'm surprised you've got anything left. You've been chucking up since we left Tilbury.'

'Don't remind me.' Chalky hung limply over the bulwark rail, 'I still feel greener than grass.'

'Doesn't look much of a place.' Phil peered through the misty, early morning light towards the Mulberry Harbour[9], off the coast at Arromanches.

'I don't care what it's like, as long as I'm soon on good solid earth and nothing's moving up and down.'

'Anyway, look on the bright side; we're arriving in style in this old tub. It's better than us trying to come ashore, in one of those bloody swimming tanks, with Fritz throwing everything he's got at us.' Taff pointed towards a buoy with a red flag flying from the top. 'At least we haven't hit a mine like those poor devils last week.'

'Something hit a mine? How do you know that?' whispered Phil, looking around and checking they weren't being overheard. 'What was it?'

'Not supposed to know; war office censorship; keeping mum and all that. I was in the bogs and some of the crew were chatting. I don't think they knew I was there. It was one of our hospital ships; she'd just left here, then hit a floating mine apparently. Six days ago.'

'Christ, that's terrible. Is that what the buoy is marking?'

'Aye it is. The ship went down very quickly, quite a few drowned. They haven't recovered all the bodies yet. The blokes that sail around the harbour collecting corpses for burial pulled out a couple of girls a few days ago. Nurses, I guess.'

'Oh bloody hell. Do they know what ship it was?'

'Yes, the SS Amsterdam. Apparently she used to be a LNER passenger ferry, on the Harwich to Hook of Holland run.'

'She was,' said Phil sadly, 'I have a cigarette card with her picture on it.'

'One of the blokes I overheard was really worried because his cousin was in the medical squad. He doesn't know if she's survived.'

This bloody war! Poor souls! Phil thought, as the troopers peered across the grey water towards the lonely marker flag.

'All right men! Gather your kit up. We'll be coming alongside any minute now,' shouted Paul, their new troop leader, from the upper deck. 'Apparently that floating chunk of concrete over there is where we're mooring. It's called a Spud. Once we have disembarked, there'll be a lorry waiting to drive us along the harbour side.'

Chalky looked at the swaying metal roadway suspended from floating pontoons, which ran from the Spud to the shore. He shuddered and gritted his teeth for the next part of the journey. *Oh God!*

'All right men, get formed up ready to disembark. We've got an appointment with the 2nd Armoured Reinforcement Group. They've got a Cromwell waiting for us to play with. Welcome to France.'

***

The Cromwell rattled through the French countryside. On its front was a picture of a charging bull[10]. They were on rapid advance from the coast to the front. The roads were bordered by battle-shattered villages, burned-out military vehicles, orchards of broken and burnt fruit trees and churned-up fields scattered with bomb craters and decaying cattle carcasses.

'Brenda always fancied coming over to France for a few days. She has an aunty here, married a frog sailor. I could never face the sea voyage.' Chalky looked sadly at the desolation. 'What a bloody mess. I don't suppose we'll ever come now.'

'I feel sorry for the poor people who have to live here.' Phil had seen dejected locals salvaging possessions from piles of rubble. 'How will they ever recover from this?'

'Well I suppose now we're here, they've got some hope. Many of them wave and cheer as we pass.'

'I expect you're right Taff,' agreed Phil. 'At least they can see a future, without Fritz bossing them around.'

'Another couple of days at this rate and we'll be at Argentan,' said Jock. 'We'll be meeting him then.'

'Who?'

'Fritz! We'll be face to face with the bugger.'

'I can't say I'm looking forward to that pleasure,' said Taff.

'Me neither.'

Argentan/Falaise Pocket.

'What's that over there Taff?' Paul pointed in to the distance. He was standing in the turret, looking with his field glasses across the battle fields towards Argentan[11]. Their squadron was part of a combined operations action. They were working with British, Polish, Canadian and American infantry, pushing the enemy army back. The Germans, trapped by the allied forces' rapid advance, were mounting a determined resistance. The air was filled with the rattle of machine guns, the crack of small arms and the explosions of hand grenades. British tanks were using their big guns to attack the heavy armaments of the enemy. Their hull-mounted machine guns were used to assist the troops in their advance against German infantry.

Taff, who was operating the gimble-mounted gun, peered through his periscope but couldn't see where Paul was pointing. 'Where are you looking?'

'Sorry Taff, I forgot you can't see me. Three o'clock from your position, in the gap between those houses. Is it a tank?'

Taff swung his periscope around. 'Could be, I can't really see, there's too much smoke and dust between us and him. It looks pretty big. If it's a Tiger we might want to pull back a bit, we're a sitting duck on top of this ridge. He'll have no trouble brewing us up from that distance.'

'Quite agree Taff; however I don't think he's seen us yet. I can't see a gun facing our way. Phil why don't you see if you can drop one on him, before he spots us and we have to move back into cover?'

'OK, Skip,' replied Phil, hastily working out angles and distances.

'Fire when you're ready Phil. I'll watch to see if we get any reaction.'

Their tank rebounded as Phil fired the high explosive shell.

'Good shot Phil, you hit the blighter.' Paul gasped. 'Bloody hell! The shell bounced off. It is a sodding Tiger.'

'Bounced off!' exclaimed Phil in disbelief, 'I hit him smack on.'

'Unbelievable isn't it? Their armour's a lot thicker than ours.'

'Let's hope we made the bugger's ears ring at least,' said Taff.

'Their gun is swinging our way.' Paul watched the Tiger tank calmly. 'Chalky, pull back into the gully behind us, then head right at full revs' he ordered. 'Let's find some cover. There's no way we can match him for fire power.' The shell from the Tiger, ploughed into the ridge they'd just left and exploded.

'Top speed Chalky.' Paul ducked as soil and debris flew over their tank. 'I think we may have annoyed him. Well done lads.' They kept in the shelter of the ridge and eventually met up with two more tanks from their squadron. They were escorting a handful of British and American soldiers, who were shepherding a couple of dozen captured German troops towards the allied lines. The prisoners of war walked, dejected, with their hands held high.

An American soldier, strolling behind the POWs, eyed the motif on the front of their tank. 'Swell Bison you've got there.'

'Yeh, mate. It's great isn't it?' Paul felt he should explain further. 'It's the Charging Bull symbolising…' Out of corner of his eye, he saw movement on the top of the ridge. Suddenly, out of the dust and smoke, appeared two SS personnel carriers with roof-mounted machine guns. The vehicles were driving at high speed towards them. 'Enemy alert lads,' he shouted.

The vehicles skidded to a halt and their gunners opened fire. The allied troops fell to the ground and immediately retaliated. The prisoners hesitated, ready to run now their captors were under threat. Taff swung his machine gun preparing to fire at the SS. 'Crap, can't get it high enough. Christ…'

'Bloody evil bastards,' shouted Phil.

'What is it? What the hell's going on?' Jock, squatting in the radio ops seat, could see nothing.

'They are mowing down their own men.'

'Fucking hell. Why are they doing that?'

'God alone knows. Probably because they've surrendered.'

'As Phil says, they are evil bastards.'

'They're off. Back over the ridge,' Paul yelled down to his men.

'Shall I go after them, Skip?' asked Chalky.

Paul looked towards the top of the ridge and considered their options. 'No, it could be a trap. Swing her around, ready for the buggers if they come back.' He shouted towards a sergeant on the ground, 'Can we help? We can ferry the wounded if you need us to.'

'We're still checking for signs of life. I've not got much hope. I'll give you a shout if we do need you.'

***

The road to Amerika

'Phil, point 'Gertie' towards that haystack,' ordered Paul. 'I can't see any meadows around here.' The stack was on the edge of dense woodland, that was surrounded by marshy land. 'Taff, on my command, put a high explosive shell into it.'

Taff raised his eyebrows. 'OK Skip.'

The shell hit the centre of the haystack. It immediately collapsed, caught fire and began to explode. It was a wooden structure with hay bundles fastened to its walls. German troops spilled out of their hide and from bolt holes around its perimeter and ran away in panic. Paul's well-directed shell had just destroyed a disguised field artillery anti-tank gun.

The following day Phil's squadron fought to gain ground beyond the 'Pimple House', near the village of St Petrus Hoeve. The farmhouse had been renamed by the soldiers due to the large moss-covered lump seemingly growing out of its roof. It was mid October. The weather was cold and wet and the Germans were in retreat. Their latest line of resistance was thrown across Holland's inaccessible wetlands, an area known as the Peel Country. The Germans had heavy defences in place around the little impoverished villages that dotted the area. The only access for tanks was to approach in single file along unstable muddy tracks. The tracks were planted with land mines and were further protected by camouflaged German tanks and artillery guns, dug into ditches and hedge bottoms.

'A' squadron's objective for the day was to push forward, through rain-drenched orchards, towards the little village of Amerika. Occupation of this village was of strategic importance to both the German and Allied forces, as its position gave vital access to the roads and railways across the southwest of the marshlands. The tall church spire in Amerika towered above the woodlands. This gave the German spotters located within it, and the gunners they were directing, deadly advantage over the allied troops.

The team's tank 'Gertie', was fume-filled, freezing cold and dripping wet. Phil was shaking with fear as he listened to the constant, terrifying swish and screams of armour piercing shells and tracers all around them. *I'm fed up with those bloody 'Moaning Minnies'. They're really getting on my nerves.* 'Moaning Minnies', proper name Nebelwerfers, were 36-barrel batteries that fired all their blast bombs at the same time. Each bomb was fitted with fins. These made blood curdling screams as they hurtled through the air.

Phil was sitting in the driver's seat on the right of the tank, in the front of the hull. He peered through his letter box sized visor slit, desperately trying to see where they were going. *To make things even worse, it's always pissing down here. If there is a God, he has certainly forsaken this dreadful place.*

Taff, the hull gunner today, was alongside him, separated by a bulkhead. A rear bulkhead with access holes divided them from the central fighting compartment, where Chalky, Jock and Paul were located. They were firing at the German guns.

Phil never heard the high explosive shell that hit them. A blinding flash, instant searing pain and he passed out.

Gertie's fuel tank ruptured and she caught fire. The explosion shook the tank and the men were temporarily disorientated by the noise and blast. They were all concussed and had blood pouring from their ears and noses. The heat was intense and the hull rapidly filled with dense black smoke and the acrid smells of cordite and burning fuel. Jock recovered first and threw open the turret lid. 'Bale out! Bale out! We're on fire.' He located Chalky, and pushed him up the turret ladder. Jock scrambled after him.

Paul shouted frantically, 'Phil, Taff get out now!' Paul followed Chalky and Jock, who helped him out of the red hot turret. All three burned their hands badly. Paul bellowed down the turret, 'she's red hot lads, be careful, but get out now.' Although he was covered in lacerations, had a bleeding nose and ringing in his ears, Taff was still functioning. 'I'm on my way Paul,' he yelled back. He crawled out of the gunner's seat and followed his mates up the ladder and out of the smoke filled tank. He pulled the sleeves of his sweater over his hands, to insulate them from the heat of the metal turret. The four hussars threw themselves onto the marshy ground, ducking the machine gun bullets and bazooka shells that crisscrossed over their tank.

Taff looked around at his terrified friends. 'Where the hell's Phil?' he shrieked above the rattles, explosions, screams and boom of the big guns. Chalky's ears were in excruciating pain. He couldn't hear what Taff was shouting, but guessed it was about Phil. He pointed at the tank, shook his head and held his hands palm up, signifying he thought Phil was probably still in there.

'Christ almighty! He's still inside Gertie?' Taff yelled, jumping to his feet and immediately crouching low, as bullets whistled around him. He looked at Gertie. *She's well ablaze.* Petrol fumes had ignited into a cloud of fire, which was billowing low around the turret. *Oh bloody hell.* He pulled his balaclava out of his pocket and pulled it on, tucking it well in. With his burned hands, Paul fumbled his scarf from around his neck and thrust it at Taff, who wrapped and knotted it around his mouth and nose. Taff nodded his thanks to his young tank officer and put his thumb up.

'Good luck old man,' said Paul.

'For God's sake take care, Taff. Gertie's well brewed up,' shouted Jock, leaning close to his pal's ear.

'Breath in before you get there, and for Christ's sake blow out when you're near the flames,' yelled Chalky. Ignoring the pain, he bent down, cupped his blistered hands and hoisted Taff towards the top of the burning tank. Taff jumped through the flames towards the turret, He grabbed the scorching hot top fleetingly, with his sweater covered hands, then dropped into the fighting compartment of the Cromwell.

'Phil! Phil! For Christ's sake can you hear me?' he shouted, his voice catching, as he took a breath. He coughed as the choking fumes stuck in his airway. He felt his way through the access hatch into the driver's compartment. Finding Phil's sleeve he pulled it hard and shouted 'Phil! Phil! It's Taff here boyo, I've got you now.'

'Taff I'm on fire,' croaked Phil. He sounded weak, barely conscious.

'Not so bad,' shouted Taff, pulling Phil towards him and patting the flames out around the neck and collar of his one-piece pixie suit, *Christ his face is badly burned.* Looking at his mate he said, 'just singed your pixie a bit, a bit like last night's hen.' He hauled Phil out of his seat and dragged him into the fighting compartment. Phil groaned loudly, as Taff slapped out the flames on his gloves.

'I'm burning up Taff.'

'Not anymore boyo,' gasped Taff, between racking coughs. Acrid fumes were scorching his lungs. 'It was just your gloves; they're only smoking a bit now. I think you'll have to ask your mam to knit you another pair, these ones are knackered.' He dragged Phil to the bottom of the turret ladder and then grasping his friend's arm he climbed upwards, hauling his mate with him. He fell exhausted out of the turret, but never released his grip on Phil. Gasping in precious air, he raged impotently at the Germans troops who were still firing at them with machine guns. 'Will you stop that you bastards, haven't you done enough to us?'

'I don't think they're listening.' Paul had crawled back onto the tank, amid a hail of bullets to help Taff. 'Is he still alive?' he said.

'Yes, but he was on fire when I got to him, he's badly burned.' With a huge effort Taff hauled Phil half way out of the turret. Paul thrust his blistered hands under Phil's armpits and lifted him the rest of the way. Dragging Phil with him, Taff slid off the tank, onto the marshy ground where Chalky and Jock were crouched. Phil groaned with pain. He was barely conscious.

'Jock, splash some water onto Phil to cool him down a bit,' shouted Taff, scrambling onto his knees and rushing to help. He shouted back to Paul. 'Thanks Skip, I don't think I could have managed without you. I was about done in.'

Paul didn't reply. He slid slowly over the side of the tank and plunged to the ground alongside Phil. His chest was soaked in blood.

'Oh Christ, no!' Taff crawled across to him and cradled him in his arms. Paul's eyes opened briefly and he looked at Taff. Blood spilled from his mouth.

'You'll be alright boyo,' lied Taff.

'I think the lad's a goner,' said Chalky, his was voice shaking with emotion as he felt Paul's wrist for a sign of a pulse.

'He's just nineteen! What a bloody senseless war!' Taff cried. He hugged Paul to him.

Chalky gathered his thoughts and said, 'we'll be done for as well, if we don't get out of here. These bastards seem to throwing everything they've got at us. The field ambulances are stuck miles back. We might have to leave the Skip here.'

'No, never! He's one of ours.' Taff's tone was fierce and his eyes swam with tears. Gently he laid Paul on the sodden ground. 'He's our Skip. We can't leave him here with these murderous bastards.' He hoisted Phil over his shoulder in a fireman's lift. 'I'll carry Phil. Can you and Jock manage Paul between you?'

'Yeh, no problem.' Together the men tenderly lifted Paul's body.

Their journey, carrying the dead and injured men, to the field hospital at St. Petrus Hoeve, was hazardous. They ran most of the way, dodging behind trees, jumping over ditches, running low behind hedges to confuse the German infantry, who pursued and fired at them for most of their two-mile struggle through the marshes.

The road to Amerika, although only four miles long, continued to be a challenge. It was another month before the allies finally occupied the strategically positioned village.

Chapter 13

THE VISIT

Early November 1944

What is the matter with me? Connie was watching steam billowing alongside the train window.

Why am I crying? This is silly! She fumbled her handkerchief from her bag and dabbed her eyes self consciously, before risking a quick glance around the compartment. *Just soldiers playing cards and two women having a natter. They're not interested in me. Why should they be? I don't know why I'm being so negative. Fretting like this, it won't do anyone any good.*

Thinking back over the last few days, she hardly noticed the scenery flashing past the window. The truth was she still felt angry and upset at the way John, Phil's dad, had spoken to her. *Blooming man! Marching down the blessed field towards me, waving that bloody envelope! Giving me that dressing down! In front of the Italians too!* Connie immediately regretted her bitter thoughts. She wasn't being fair. *John must have been shocked and frightened too. Bloody hell!*

It had been a sunny autumn day and she'd been working in the top field, with the Italian POWs assigned to the farm. They were forking potatoes and loading them into hessian sacks. Guido, handsome and charming, was leading the singing of "Oh Sole Mio".[41] The other Italians were joining in with the chorus. They sang in Italian but Guido had translated the words for her.

'What a beautiful thing is a sunny day!
The air is serene after a storm,
The air is so fresh that it already feels like a celebration.
What a beautiful thing is a sunny day!

But another sun that's brighter still,
It's my own sun that's upon your face!
The sun, my own sun is upon your face!
It's upon...'

Their joyful singing had suddenly faltered and stopped, so Connie turned and followed their gaze. Phil's father was tramping down the potato furrows, towards them, an envelope clutched in his hand. Connie's heart pounded, blood drained from her face. *A telegram!* She felt she was going to faint. Guido stepped across the rows, reached for her arm and steadied her. It wasn't a telegram that John held – it was a War Office letter.

'It says Phil's been injured.' His voice cracked, as he read "...severe burns to the face, hands and left leg.' They're transferring him back here, to a hospital somewhere in England.'

'Oh, thank goodness!' Connie clapped her hands together and laughed nervously.

'It's no laughing matter.' John snapped.

She blushed hotly and to her shame, burst in to tears.

'I'm just so relieved he's not dead,' she sobbed.

'Hmm! Well alright then,' John said gruffly. 'When we find out which hospital he's in, Ma wants you to take him some soap, talc and pyjamas.'

There had been no more communications for eight days, and then Connie received a letter from Phil, written in another hand. Those few lines had been poured over by Connie and by Phil's family, as they tried to glean any scrap of information about his condition.

As the train rattled on, Connie dug to the bottom of her bag and found the simple note, written in shaky pencil on a scrap of paper torn from a notebook. She thought about the injured soldier who had written the letter on Phil's behalf. She smoothed it out and read:

'Dear Con. Just thought I'd drop you a line to let you know I'm thinking about you. I'm OK but can't hold a pencil. Geoff in the next bed is writing this for me. I expect you'll have heard from my Pa that I'm back from my holiday in Holland. I'm sorry I forgot your tulips. I'll get you some in the spring. I'm now enjoying another vacation, in the Birmingham Accident Hospital and Rehabilitation Centre[12], Bath Row, Birmingham and would love to see you if you happen to be passing Ward C.
Love Phil.

'2pm until 4pm every day' had been added in bold letters at the foot of the note.

Connie carefully folded it and put it away. *Phil writes such good letters. It's one of the reasons I fell for him in the first place. Now he's got to ask someone else to write for him.* Thinking about him lying horribly injured, managing to joke about tulips tore her emotions to shreds. As she struggled with more tears, she turned her face to the window, no longer seeing the fields as they gave way to grimy buildings and terraces of smoke-stained houses. The train was huffing and puffing, slowing as it entered the Birmingham suburbs before approaching New Street Station. Connie peered at her reflection in the mirror of her powder compact. *I'll have to stop blubbing! I don't want Phil to see me with puffy eyes.* She sighed and pinched colour into her cheeks.

What will he think? She ran a comb through her red hair and fluffed it up with her fingertips. She felt a little thrill of decadence as she took out her new lipstick. Such luxuries were normally out of reach, but this was a gift from her kind and attentive American friend, Air Force Flight Lieutenant Rusty Harcourt. She enjoyed dancing with him and had sometimes fantasised about life in America as an air force wife. That was before her relationship had blossomed with Phil. *Ah well! I've made my choice.*

Anyway Rusty was engaged to Evaline, a girl from his home town in Illinois. He longed to be with her. Rusty and Connie enjoyed swapping stories about their sweethearts and they'd become good friends, but never lovers. *Well not really, but nearly.* She smiled at her memories. When Rusty had heard about Phil's injuries, he'd presented Connie with the lipstick. She hadn't wanted to accept it at first.

'Shouldn't you be sending this to Evaline?'

'Nope, she's got plenty of this stuff. She'd want you to have it. You'll feel like a million dollars when you visit that guy of yours. It'll certainly cheer him up when he sees you looking beautiful and brave. Plus it's another one in the eye for that nasty little Nazi, Aiy-dolph.'

Rusty is right. I owe it to Phil to keep a stiff upper lip. He doesn't want me blubbing over him, after everything he's gone through. The lipstick looked expensive in its gilt case. She slipped off the cap and wound up the red tube of bright colour. *Patriot Red! The perfect colour for war paint,* she thought as she applied it carefully to her full lips. *Hitler would never be able to ban British women from wearing makeup, as he'd tried to in Germany. Mind you he didn't have much success over there either. According to the newspapers, the frauleins refused to go to work without makeup when he'd tried it in '39!*

Pleased with the result and feeling much cheerier, she collected her bag and got ready to leave the train. Catching sight of herself in the train window, she allowed herself a moment of pride in her appearance. *Quite smart! I'm pleased I wore my uniform.* She took a deep breath. *Come on girl. Head up! You can do it!*

New Street Station bore the scars of war. As Connie walked along the platform, she looked up and saw great gaping holes in the Victorian roof canopy. The metalwork was twisted and the glass was either missing or fractured. She grimaced. *What a mess! The roof is ruined! It's as bad as Paragon Station in Hull.* From the platform,

Alan Durham

she walked into New Street and was shocked to see the extent of the bomb damage. *Now where do I go?*

'Excuse me,' she said to a policeman, who was standing near the station exit. 'Can you tell me where I can catch a bus to Birmingham Accident Hospital? It's in Bath Row.'

'Walk up there and on the right you'll find the bus waiting,' he said, pointing up the road. 'Just check with the conductor, before you get on 'im.'

Connie found the right bus. The friendly conductor agreed to let her know when to get off. They chatted while she ate her sandwich lunch.

'Land girl are you? Not much for you to be doing in these parts.'

'I don't work here. I've just found out that my boyfriend is in the Accident Hospital.'

'Armed forces is he?'

'Kings Royal Hussars.'

'They're tanks aren't they? In the thick of it I expect?'

'Yes. He's been injured. This is my first visit. I'm feeling very nervous. I've no idea where to go or what to expect.'

'Don't you worry, me love. They'll look after him in there. I've overheard passengers on me bus. Everybody says good things about the hospital. I'll let you know when we're there.' Connie found the warmth of his words reassuring. It wasn't long before she heard him yell down the bus, 'stop for the Accident Hospital.' He smiled at her as he helped her down the steps, with her parcel of nightwear and toiletries for Phil. 'Bus stop on the other side of the road when you come back. Chin up beautiful!'

Several other women got off at the same time. Like Connie, most carried packages. They all appeared to know where they were going. Connie followed them. They walked around the side of a large Victorian building. To Connie's relief they soon reached a door marked 'Reception'. Connie walked to a desk. A woman was hammering on a typewriter. Suddenly aware of a visitor, she stopped typing and peered over the top of her glasses.

'Yes?' she barked.

'I'm here to see Phil York. He's in Ward C,' said Connie, stammering nervously.

'That's Plastic Surgery,' said the receptionist in a more kindly tone. 'First time is it? Travelled far?'

'Yes, from near Hull.'

'Well the ladies lavatory is over there, and that lady near the table is Gladys. She'll get you a cup of tea, if you want one, now or later. When you're ready, go up to the first floor. The Plastic Surgery ward is through second door on the right. It's got a big C painted on it. Go straight in. Matron or one of her nurses will sort you out.'

'Thank you,' said Connie 'I think I'll go straight up.'

'Don't be put off by what you see. It looks worse than it is. Pretend not to notice the smell. Some of the poor souls smell a bit singed. It takes a while to wear off.'

'Thank you.' Connie's heart sank. She felt her alarm growing.

'Nice uniform. Land girl, are you? Very smart! Lucky man!'

Connie smiled gratefully at the woman and headed for the stairs. The hospital walls were dingy green and in need of a coat of paint, but everywhere looked spotless. At the top of the stairs she turned right along polished wooden floors and soon stood in front of double doors leading to ward C. She took a deep breath, straightened her back, lifted her chin, fixed a smile to her face and pushed open the doors.

Looking down the ward, she was aware of tightly packed metal-framed beds. Between each bed there was a wooden chair and a single cupboard, each with a jug and glass on top. Most beds were occupied.

Oh no. I can't see him. She looked down the rows of patients. Many of them were heavily bandaged. A smiling nurse saw her hesitate and walked towards her.

'Hello, can I help you? I'm Ward Sister Miller.'

'I'm Connie Aldridge. I've come to visit Phil York. He's my boyfriend.'

'Oh good! He will be pleased. He's always talking about you. Is this your first visit?'

'Yes. I only found out where he'd been sent two days ago.'

'Have you come far?'

'East Yorkshire, near Hull.'

'That is a long way. I'll take you along to see Phil in a minute. However there are a couple of things I need to tell you first.' She smiled to reassure Connie before continuing. 'He's been quite badly burned. He's had quite a rough time, poor love, so I'm afraid he looks a bit like an Egyptian mummy. He's bandaged around his face, hands and his leg. He's very sore, so you won't be able to hug him. We're giving him morphine. Movement, even talking, is painful for him. You can hold his elbow, but you can't touch his hands.' She gave Connie's shoulder a reassuring pat. 'He can't see you, which is a pity, because you look lovely. He can hear you and there is a slit in his bandages for him to speak through. His voice is quite hoarse because he's been burned down his throat. He has a tube to drink through, so if he's thirsty give one of my nurses a wave and they'll soon sort him out. The doctors are wonderful and he's being well looked after, but he's going to be with us for a while.' She looked anxiously at Connie's pale face. 'Don't worry he's safe now, no more war for him.'

Connie's anxiety was building. Her hand went to her throat and she felt her chest tighten. *Get control, you cannot fall at the first hurdle.*

'Are you OK?'

'Yes I'm fine,' replied Connie, 'can I see him now? Please?'

'Yes of course, I'll take you. Follow me. You coming to visit will do him a power of good.'

'I've brought him some pyjamas and soap from his mam,' she said, tapping the parcel clutched to her chest.

'Just put them in his locker and we'll sort them out, and don't worry, our doctors are experts with burns. They've had lots of practice over the past few years.' Sister Miller walked down the ward with Connie. Curious faces turned to watch them. Those who could, whistled appreciatively.

'Don't mind them. I think the sight of you has cheered up quite a few of our lads.' Sister Miller stopped at a small side ward. 'We've got him parked here where we can keep a good eye on him, just in case he gives us any cheek,' she said, speaking loudly towards a bed. 'Phil,' she continued, 'you've got a visitor, a beautiful land army girl, all the way from East Yorkshire.'

Connie stared, shocked at the sight of the figure trussed up in bed, unrecognizable as her Phil. He was lying on his back. His left leg, both arms and hands were encased in bandages and suspended in slings. His fingers were held apart by corks. *God! He looks terrible! He's covered in bandages. Sister Miller did warn me, but...it's a shock.* Phil's head was completely swathed from the neck up. The bandages across his face had a greasy sheen. Connie wondered if it was ointment.

'Hello Phil,' she said gently. Phil didn't react.

'You'll have to speak up because the bandaging reduces his hearing. Why don't you sit on this chair next to him? Bend close so you can hear him if he answers.'

'Thanks Sister.'

'Hello darling, it's Connie,' she said loudly, towards Phil's head.

'Hel..lo Sweet..heart,' croaked Phil, his voice barely louder than a whisper. He struggled with every syllable. Connie leant over him and listened hard.

'How are you darling?' Her heart was pounding. *He can hardly speak.* She gently stroked his elbow.

'Bit bet..ter now,' Phil gasped, 'ask Geoff?' Connie strained to hear every word. It was obvious the effort of speaking was too much for Phil.

'Who's Geoff?'

'That'll be me,' said a voice, from the other side of the bed.

Connie looked across her boyfriend's prone form and realised for the first time that a man was sitting on a chair between Phil's bed and the one next to it. She had been so focused on Phil, she hadn't noticed him.

'Oh I am sorry! I didn't see you there,' Connie said, feeling flustered; her face and neck flushed. *How rude of me!* The man's face was bandaged too, but his left eye and most of his mouth were uncovered.

'Hello I'm Geoff,' he said, reaching over with his left hand to shake Connie's.

She grasped it awkwardly 'Hello, pleased to meet you.'

'Sorry about the shake; Fritz kept my other arm, as a souvenir of my visit to Holland,' he laughed. 'Phil's told me all about you.'

'Did you write the letter for Phil?'

'I did. Sorry about the poor writing, I'm not used to writing with my left hand yet. Phil was desperate to send you a letter. Took us a while mind; me writing cack-handed and Phil with barely a whisper. I must have read it back to him half a dozen times before he was happy with it.'

'Your writing was fine. Thank you for doing it. It was a godsend. His ma, pa, sisters, cousin and me have been worried sick. His brothers are in Africa, they don't know yet.' Connie looked down at Phil. *Oh Lord. The effort Phil and Geoff must have expended to send me that blooming letter.* 'Thank you,' she said again looking at Geoff, as she rubbed Phil's elbow.

'He'll be delighted you're here. Aren't you Phil?' said Geoff in a loud voice.

'I am,' croaked Phil. Geoff reached across the bed and gently rubbed Phil's other elbow with the back of his hand.

'You'll feel a lot better now, my old mate, now your girl has come to visit.'

'Al..read..y do.'

'Has Phil told you what happened?'

'I don't think he knows for certain,' replied Geoff. 'They were fighting in the marshes in Holland, pushing Jerry hard and well inside the enemy lines. They were up against a line of entrenched field artillery guns. He thinks they may have been hit by a high explosive shell. Am I right Phil?'

'Yes.'

'We've heard his doctors discussing his injuries. Blast burns they think. That certainly links in with an HE attack. From what I can make out he had a hell of a journey travelling back home, nearly two days, just field dressings, he didn't get anything for the pain until he arrived here. He must have been in agony.'

Connie leant towards Phil to hear him mumble 'Fritz near..ly had me.'

She gulped and fought hard to hold back her tears. 'But he didn't thank goodness; he only managed to singe you a bit. Sister tells me your doctors are experts at treating burns, so you're in good hands.'

'Sore thro..at, dry.'

Connie looked around and caught the eye of a nurse. She smiled and came straight across. 'Phil says he's thirsty.'

'Anything for our Phil, he's one of our best behaved patients.'

'Hello Phil, it's Nurse Wilson here, I'm just getting your drink off the locker. Can you ease your mouth open very gently, so I can feed in your straw. I don't want to catch any of your blisters or sore bits. There. Can you feel the straw with your tongue?'

'Yeh.' Phil raised his head a fraction and struggled to suck in and then swallow the water. He lay back on his pillow exhausted.

'Well done Phil,' said Nurse Wilson, 'you've had a third of a pint this time.

'Tha..nk you.'

'You OK Geoff?'

'Champion thanks.'

'Matron says only five more minutes.' The Nurse looked sympathetically at Connie. 'I know it's only a short time this visit, we're sorry. You've come a long way, but we don't want to tire Phil too much. He probably hasn't told you, but he's having some work done on his face in the morning.'

'No, he hasn't told me about that yet.' Connie stroked Phil's elbow again. Nurse Wilson smiled at her.

'I think the surgeons are going to start tidying up his burns a bit.

Hopefully it should be a bit easier for him when you see him next. Just needs a bit of time. When will you be able to visit him again?'

'In about a week or so, if I can get time off.'

'Good, you'll help him no end,' the nurse said, moving on to another patient.

'She's a good one,' said Geoff, 'ever so caring, even though they're rushed off their feet in here.'

'She seems nice,' Connie said. 'Do you like her Phil?'

'I do, she's kind.'

'Phil darling, they say I'm going to have to go in a minute. I don't want to, but you need your rest. It will help you recover.'

'Don't want you to go.'

'I'll try to get back next week if Henry Wilkinson can wangle it.'

'Good, talk better then, lips might not be so sore.'

'I hope so. I expect your ma will try to arrange a visit as well, and I know my mam said she would like to come and see you, if that's OK?'

'Give them my love.'

'I will.' Connie leaned over and kissed Phil's elbow. 'I love you darling and I thank God that you're alive and being looked after. I'll come back to see you soon.' Her tears ran uncontrollably and she fought hard not to sob.

'Don't cry. I'll be fine. Love you too.'

'Shall I walk out with you?' asked Geoff.

'Yes please.' Connie blew her nose hard, and steeled herself for the walk down the ward, with her red, tear streaked face. 'God I must look a mess!'

'You look just fine,' said Geoff.

She turned back. 'See you soon Phil.'

'OK.'

Geoff tucked a crutch under his good arm and hobbled slowly around the bed. 'I could do with a stretch.'

Connie looked back over her shoulder to the figure lying helpless in the bed. 'Bye for now darling,' she said, trying to keep her voice even. They walked slowly down the ward. Connie wanted to cry and was grateful Geoff was with her. When they got to the ward door they stopped and shook hands, left hand to left hand this time. It felt awkward but she was pleased for Geoff's sake that she had remembered.

'What happened to you?' she asked.

'Grenade attack! Got me down the right side.'

'Is your face badly injured?'

'Could be worse,' said Geoff. 'Lost me right eye and its socket. That's why I'm in this ward. They're building me a new socket with grafted bone and skin and they'll eventually fit me with a glass eye.'

She squeezed Geoff's hand. 'I'm so sorry. Do you have a girlfriend?'

'Nah! I used to know a girl before the war, but she married a Yank. I've got two great sisters though and they're in and out of here all the time, fussing around me. I'll tell them about Phil's land girl, when I see them next.'

'Thank you so much for looking after Phil.' She reached up and kissed his cheek. Wolf whistles echoed down the ward.

'Ignore those daft devils,' said Geoff, blushing bright pink. 'Connie is Phil's girl, not mine, more's the pity!' he shouted towards the beds.

'Phil's a lucky bugger,' a voice shouted back.

Connie turned smiling towards the men in the beds. 'Thank you,' she said. 'You know how to cheer a girl up.' She left Geoff at the ward door and walked slowly down the stairs.

'I bet you're ready for a cup of tea now?' said Gladys, the W.V.S. lady. She waved her teapot.

'Thank you that would be wonderful,' said Connie, settling gratefully onto one of the hard wooden chairs near the table. 'I'm feeling a bit shaky.'

'I'll pop one of me special biscuits on your saucer,' said Gladys, smiling at her and opening a small metal box with a picture of King George VI's head on the lid. 'They always brighten up me first timers.'

Chapter 14

SEEING

Two weeks later, Connie was back at the hospital. She headed towards the stairs, only deviating to hand Gladys a bag of oat and honey biscuits. 'Just to say thank you for your kindness to me the last time I was here. My boss's daughter makes them on the farm where I work.'

'Thank you dear. That's very thoughtful of you. I'll keep them for my visitors. Cheers them up you know.' Gladys peered in the bag. 'Maybe I'll try one, just so I can tell them what they're like.'

'I would,' laughed Connie. 'They're very good. Let me know what you think of them. Maisie will be pleased to hear.' As she climbed the stairs, she wondered what was awaiting her. She'd had a strange letter from Phil. That, combined with the sniping she was getting from Phil's blooming cousin, had put her nerves on edge.

The train journey had been horrible. She couldn't stop fretting about Phil's last letter. Again it was written by Geoff on Phil's behalf. It instructed her not to waste her time and money visiting him. 'I'm a lost cause. You're too good to be bothering with me.' Geoff had written an extra note at the bottom. 'Connie, ignore all of the above. Phil is just a bit down in the dumps.'

Then there was bloody Hilary, Phil's catty cousin, who seemed to get endless pleasure from unsettling and annoying her. Ever since Connie had met Phil, she'd had to contend with bitchy little remarks from Hilary. There was only a year difference in age between Phil and his cousin. Hilary was irritatingly over-protective of him. *Maybe she's jealous? It wouldn't be the first time that a girl mooned over her good looking, older male cousin.*

Apart from anything else Hilary was bad mannered. She'd interrupted Connie when she was telling Phil's parents about her first hospital visit and the extent of their oldest son's injuries.

'Pretty girl like you will soon get fed up with our Phil now he's lost his looks,' she'd sneered. Connie had wanted to tell Ma and Pa about Phil in the most caring way to minimize their upset. But Hilary's jibe meant she had to fight hard to control her temper. Her eyes had filled with tears of frustration.

'How can you say that Hilary?' she snapped. 'Anyway, no one knows how he'll look until he gets his bandages off. Whatever he looks like, I'll still love him, he'll still be my Phil.'

'Time will tell,' Hilary countered.

'Shut up Hilary,' Pa growled, 'you can see Connie's upset.'

'That's because she's going to dump him.'

'I am not!' Connie yelled.

'We'll see,' smirked Hilary.

Connie had managed to suppress her urge to slap the young woman's smug face. She resorted to glaring and muttering 'drop dead' under her breath.

'There!' said Hilary triumphantly, 'I told you she was a nasty piece of work.'

Now, opening the ward door, Connie forced herself to push the unpleasant memories away. *Oh! God give me strength.* Sister Miller spotted her standing hesitantly in the entrance.

'Hello again. You're Phil's girl, aren't you?'

'Yes I am, but he didn't sound too sure in his last letter.'

'Don't worry yourself about that. Lads in here often get the blues in the early stage of their recovery. They are still coming to terms with what's happened to them. Coping with the shock can be hard.'

'How is he really?'

'On the mend, he's propped up in bed now. We've relaxed his bandages so he can talk and hear better. He's been into theatre three or four times since you were here. They've started to tidy up his burns. The scarring around his mouth has been eased, so he can drink more comfortably. He's a bit low in spirits, but I'm sure talking to you will help. Come on I'll take you down. See if you can cheer him up.'

As Connie approached Phil's bed she said in her cheeriest voice 'Hello Phil, you are looking so much better.'

'Oh, you've come,' he answered. His voice was stronger, but sounded sad. 'Why have you come?'

Connie pretended she hadn't heard. 'Hello Geoff, how are you doing?'

Phil's friend grinned at her and gave her a thumbs-up. 'Just fine. It's good to see you.'

Settling down on the chair next to the bed, Connie said, 'Your pa and ma send their best, as does Hilary.'

'How is she?'

'Same as usual! You know what she's like. Worrying about you.'

'I can imagine.'

'So how are you getting on? Sister Miller tells me you've seen the surgeons a few times.'

'Yes I seem to be a regular visitor to the operating theatre. I just get over one lot of anaesthetic and they give me another dose. I'm permanently groggy.'

'I'm sorry, it must be very tiring.'

'It is.'

'You are talking a lot better and you seem to be hearing well now.'

'I suppose.'

'I see they've taken the bandages off your hands,' she continued cheerfully. 'That's a big step forward.' She stared, horrified, at the raw, vivid pink flesh of his hands and fingers. He had lost several finger nails. *I hope they grow back.*

'Geoff tells me, they've trimmed all the blistered skin from my hands, to help them heal. It's a relief not to have the corks anymore.'

'I'm sure it must be. That must have been very uncomfortable. Your hands look as though they're healing and well on the way to getting back to normal. You'll soon be playing cricket again.' She hoped she sounded as if she believed it was the truth. Phil sighed and didn't answer.

'You don't sound like your normal cheery self. What's up?'

'Oh, this and that.'

'I'm sorry you're not feeling on top form darling. It's probably the shock of your injuries and all the ops and the anaesthetic you keep having. Being permanently stuck in bed can't help either.'

'No, it's not that.'

'Well what is it?'

'I don't think we should carry on.'

'I don't understand. What are you saying?'

'I think we should split up.'

'Split up! Why? I thought you loved me.'

'I do, but…'

'But what? I love you too! So what's going on?'

'You don't want to be saddled with a blind man. You're too good for that.'

'Don't talk such rubbish. Have the doctors told you you're blind? Anyway surely it's up to me who I get saddled with.'

Phil groaned. He didn't speak. Connie rubbed his elbow and he started to sob. She looked desperately at Geoff. 'What's he on about? Has anyone told him he's going to be blind?'

Geoff shook his head and smiled reassuringly at Connie. 'No. They've told him there is a fifty/fifty chance the explosion may have blinded him. But they've emphasised they can never be sure until things have settled and healed a bit more. They've packed his eyes with lanolin to soothe the inflammation. He's having an eyesight test in a couple of days. I've got my fingers crossed for him. He's worrying himself to bits about it.' Geoff reached over and stroked Phil's other elbow. 'Aren't you mate?'

Without touching him, Connie floated her hand over the top of Phil's. She desperately wanted to hold him and comfort him. His sobbing increased.

'I'm sorry Con! I don't want your life ruined, just because mine is.'

'I tell you what Phil, your life is not ruined. Let's cross the bridges in our life when we get to them. Nothing is certain until it happens.'

'Time will tell.'

Connie felt herself bristle as she remembered her last conversation with Hilary and how she had trotted out the same remark. *It's as though the blasted woman is here with us! Get control!*

'Yes it will.'

Phil continued, unaware of Connie's strained expression. 'I've lost my eyelids Con. Even if I get my sight back, I'm going to look strange. The docs tell me I've lost most of the flesh on my ears, on the sides of my nose and my lips. They can't replace flesh, just tidy up and reshape what's left. My face will be patched with bits of skin from my arms and they say they can fit me with new eyelids. I'm going to look like Frankenstein's monster.'

'Rubbish! Have faith in your doctors, they're very clever. You'll be OK. Anyway, whatever; you'll still be my Phil.'

'I love you Connie and I don't want to lose you.' His sobbing grew worse. 'But you'll find someone else, someone who still has his face.

'You won't lose me and I don't want anyone else. I only want you.' She squeezed his elbow reassuringly. For a few minutes she sat quietly next to him, hoping her steady breathing would calm him. Gradually his sobbing slowed.

After a while he said, 'well, only if you're sure.'

'I'm sure.'

***

Ten days later an envelope addressed by Geoff arrived. The letter inside was written in an almost indecipherable hand. Connie read the signature – Phil. *Phil's written me a letter!*

Hello Darling,

This is my first attempt at writing. My eyesight has been given the all clear. I am very relieved. Yes, I can also hold a stub of pencil, once Geoff has wedged it between my fingers. The nurses have made a big slit in the bandages around my eyes so I can peer out. It's a bit like a knight's helmet.

I regret my fit of the miseries the last time you came to visit. I'M SO SORRY.

Things are a bit of a blur and I'm still having bouts of double vision. The docs hope my sight should continue to improve. I might get back to normal over the next few weeks.

To help my recovery, speed my dexterity and stop me from dying with utter boredom, the hospital has started me on felt toy making. My first one is going to be a rabbit with a blue jacket holding an orange carrot. It's for you, xxx (although you may need to tidy my haphazard needlework). It could take a while, because I'm very slow and keep dropping everything. Geoff is up and down all the time, picking stuff up for me.

I look forward to <u>seeing</u> you soon,

All my love, Phil. xxx

Christmas 1954

'Mam?'

'Yes Tom.'

'Did Dad make the little rabbits and the donkey we put under the Christmas tree when he was in hospital?'

'You know he did.'

'Did he have lots of operations?'

'Yes. He had fifty three to rebuild his face.'

'Was it sore?'

'Very.'

'He's alright now?'

'Yes he's fine.'

Chapter 15

NIGHT TERROR

Pain! Why?

Flames, bloody flames, scorching hot. Nooo! My eyes! Melting. Burning fumes in my throat, cough them out. Poison! Poison on my lips. Oh God help me! Agony!

Run, run from hellfire. Can't run. I'm trapped. Something's holding me down.

Searing, agonising pain! No! Nooo! Someone screaming? Me? Bubbling, pain, blistering skin. My eyes!

Must close my eyes. Why can't I close my eyes? Cover them. Protect them. Pain won't go away. Won't go away…

My hands hurt…fingers on fire! Gloves Ma knitted…smoldering. Wool stinks when it burns.

Oh bloody hell! Incoming! Moaning Minnies! Horrible whining bastards. Explosions everywhere. Must keep low, Bullets. Snipers! Too much noise, I can't think, my ears hurt.

I'm crying. Tears flooding my eyes, bubbling hot. I can't see. I can't see. Why can't I see?

Smoke all around, acrid. Cordite, diesel, cooking meat, scorched wool, burning hair.

What a stink! Bloody cordite, it stinks. No…it's not that!

What is it? Gather your wits for Christ's sake!

Something's burning. Meat? My hands are on fire. It's me! I'm burning! I'm the meat. It's me! Christ I'm on fire!

Taff's voice…'I've got you boyo.'

'Taff?'

'I've got you boyo.'

'Taff I'm on fire!'

'Nah! Just a bit singed, like last night's hen.'

Taff's laughter drifts away. It's gone quiet. Where's Taff? Nothing!

I'm in a fog. I can hear Fred laughing. Our Fred? Christ I'm cold. Why am I naked? My hands. Must look at my hands. They're OK? No gloves?

Where's my kit? Mustn't panic! Where am I? Widemarshe pond? Why?

'Come on Phil, stop pratting about,' yells Fred, 'jump in, cool off.' Our Fred's in the pond, pretending to swim.

I'm nervous. Why? Nettles! Mustn't step in them. I hate nettles… once had a fight and was pushed face down into a bunch by that big bastard, Trevor Evison…good cricketer though. I broke his nose.

I look down! My best black boots. In the mud! My best black boots! Where's my old pair? The pair I should have been wearing? They're too small, they hurt, curl my toes. They let in water, they're split. Is Pa at work? Christ! Why have I brought my best boots to the pond…Pa will fill my ear.

Moor hens and a bad tempered coot fighting in the reeds at the far side of the pond. Probably got a nest? Good eggs with a bit of bacon. Hungry. I hate bloody eel!

Wish I'd never caught that bugger when I was twelve, like a bloody great slimy snake in the grass. Clonked it with a stick and chopped its head off with my 'Green River' knife. 'Conger' Pa says, cutting it into big round slices. Slithered in from the Humber? Lucky it didn't bite you. Wrap em' in newspaper…best way to carry them. I never carry newspaper!

I can taste it! Horrible. Chew harder and swallow. All bone, gristle and slime.

'Eat up.' says Pa. Them Cockneys are always eating eels. Food is food, you never know where your next meal's coming from.

I wish I'd never killed the bloody thing. Thank God I'm not a Cockney.

'Can we have a scone before we go to bed?' asks our Fred.

'That's enough cheek from you,' says Pa, chewing stoically at the eel. 'Bedtime scones can be cancelled.'

I scream 'where's Taff?' at my brother.

'Taff who?' Fred shouts back. 'For Christ's sake Phil. Stop pratting about'.

'Taff,' I scream, 'you know Taff!' Foggy now, why? There's noise, explosions. Incoming! Lifting me? Hurts. Paul? Mate – are you there? Taff?

'I'm here Phil,' says Taff, 'and for Christ's sake stop wriggling. I bloody near dropped you back then. Now lie still for a minute while Jock pours a drop of water on you to cool you down.'

Water trickles down my face, into my mouth. No! Nooh! Fucking hell. Stop it! Too much. Let go, slipping away...swirling mists, black, deep water.

My lips feel salty. I never liked the seaside. I hate it. Frightened. Shivering. Soaking wet. It's freezing. Brrhh! I hate it.

Where's all this bloody seawater coming from? I'm pissing wet through, my foot's slipping. Gertie's coughing.

'Don't let her stall Phil, or we're all going to see Davy Jones,' shouts Toby. 'That last wave nearly took me with it.'

At least you can go for a swim, if we sink. No chance for me down here. I'm first in the queue to meet old Davy.

Can someone stop that water from pouring on me? My hands are slipping on the controls. I feel like a bloody octopus trying to control this bastard under water. How much further?

Heart hammering. Are we nearly there?

Toby yells 'I can see the beach, we seem to be heading in the right direction. It looks like fun.'

Fun? What surprises are we in for – if we get there?

'Any fish down there with you?' asks Taff. 'I could fancy a bit of cod.'

'My father was the keeper of the Eddystone light,[42]
and he slept with a mermaid one fine night.
Out of this union there came three,
a porpoise and a porgy and the other was me!'

Taff has a good strong voice. 'Mind you Phil, If we're near the
Eddystone Light, we're very lost!'

'Only a Welshman could think of singing in this situation', I
shout, 'or an idiot! Or maybe an Eytie! Connie says they sing opera
while they hoe.'

'Just trying to keep your spirits up boyo.'

'Well there are no bloody mermaids down here. For God's sake,
sing about solid ground. Something dry and warm and a long way
from the sea...'

I shiver. I'm outside. Shaking. Oh! Christ! I think I'm going to
puke again. What's that horrible smell? I look around. The woodland
is quiet. Just leaves rustling, others silently falling to the ground,
covering the clearing in a mosaic of autumn colours. Pretty. No bird
song. Funny! Quiet as the grave. I feel tense. Mustn't move, could be
a trap. Don't move!

Something's not right. High alert! Stand still, next to this tree.
A young oak? Not looking its best! Lower branches torn off, bark
scraped away down one side. It's leaning, pushed over, root bole
exposed...Why am I looking at the tree? I don't care about the
bloody tree! Just something to hide behind.

I scan the clearing and clutch the aerial. It's my only weapon. Can't
use my pistol...Fritz has big ears.

God I hate that smell. Smelly cheese? Nothing like it. This is
different.

Not like that stinking stuff the Colonel used to eat at the Hall. It
had tiny white maggots crawling through it. Wouldn't have had it, if
the old 'b' had offered me some. Not that he ever would! The old 'b'.

I know this smell. Not ripe Stilton. It's death! Where's the body? I
scan the clearing. There!

I can see it now! Face down in the leaves, legs twisted. Khaki merging with the leaves, already becoming one with the earth. One of ours! Poor sod. Dog tags still in place. Better report the location, when I get back. Where am I?

What's that? Over there. Movement? Fowl or Foe? Watch! Don't breathe! Yes – again. Fritz?'

Look! A bicycle leant against that tree.

Where is he? I'm frightened. Hitler youth sniper? Nasty little bastards are everywhere! I hate them. Him or me? Him! Where are you? There! Jump on the bastard and throttle him!

Got him! Good! Hands around his throat. Squeeze hard.

Fritz screams and he's managed to wriggle out of my grip.

'For Christ's sake Phil stop it, you're hurting me. Phil! Phil wake up!'

Fritz pummels my back. He pushes me aside. How does the bastard know my name?

I open my eyes.

Oh Christ! It's Connie! What is she doing here? What's going on? I'm trying to strangle Connie!

'What are you doing here?' I ask, releasing her throat. I'm very confused. What's happening to me?

***

Connie pushes Phil away and rubs her neck. 'I'm your wife! Where else would I be? You've been having that nightmare again, haven't you? I think you've bruised me. My neck really hurts. What the hell did you think you were doing? You could have killed me. I'll have to wear a scarf. The neighbours will think you've been bashing me.'

'I thought you were Fritz,' Phil mumbles. He can't think straight. *How could I do that, to Connie?* He fights back tears. 'I'm so sorry Con, it was so real. I didn't know I was dreaming.' His horrified eyes focus on the red marks, where his fingers had pressed into her neck. 'Your poor neck, oh darling, I'm so sorry.'

'Do I look like Fritz? Does Fritz wear a nighty? Does he sleep with you? Is Fritz having your baby?' She rubs her neck again. As she remonstrates she notices his distressed face. Her anger and fear subside. *Shell shock, no one tells you how to deal with this, do they?* Connie pats his arm. 'Oh well! Never mind! Worse things happen at sea, I suppose. What's done is done. I'll heal. I'll dab some witch hazel on it. Shall we get up and have a cup of tea? I don't think I'll be able to sleep again tonight.'

Phil nods, smiles gratefully at his wife and follows her downstairs. *Will it ever get better? Connie shouldn't have to put up with this.* He looks lovingly at his courageous, forgiving wife. *Please God, don't let anything like this ever happen again.*

Chapter 16

ALL CHANGE

'Hello love, have you had a good day at school?'

'Yes thank you. Can I have something to eat?'

'Sure, look in the blue tin and then you can tell me what you've been doing.'

Tom rushed into the pantry and emerged clutching a rock bun, before he searched through his jacket pockets and pulled out a crumpled drawing. He dropped it on the table and Connie helped him smooth out the creases.

'That is lovely. What is it?' Connie concentrated and looked with interest at the pencil and crayon drawing. She tried to work out what her son had drawn.

'Stephenson's *Rocket* and *Locomotion No 1*,' Tom answered taking a bite of his cake.

'Oh I see now.' Connie ignored the crumbs falling on the table and pointed at an orange coloured barrel shape, to one side of her son's artwork. It had wheels and a black pipe sticking up at one end. 'Is this Stephenson's *Rocket*?'

'No, silly. That's *Locomotion No 1*,' answered Tom scornfully, 'it's got little wheels at the front and big ones at the back.' He pointed to another barrel shape, which was coloured yellow with a matching pipe sticking up at the front. 'This is the *Rocket*, it's got big wheels at the front and little ones at the back.'

'Oh yes, now I understand. I didn't know that. So what's this?' she circled her finger around lots of curved red and yellow lines that were sweeping to the top of the page. A one-legged matchstick man was suspended upside down among the lines.

'That was when *Locomotion*'s boiler blew up and the driver was killed.'

'Poor man. That must have been terrible.'

'1828,' said Tom.

Connie smiled. Her son had a good memory for the dates of gruesome events. 'Steam engines have changed a lot since those days, haven't they?'

'They have, they're a lot bigger and a lot faster. Mr Burton says they keep the *Rocket* in a museum in London. *Locomotion* is kept on the platform at Darlington.'

'I know, I've seen it. It stands on some railway lines that go nowhere. I used to go and see it with Grandma when we went to visit her sisters in Darlington. It's not very big and it has a little open-topped wagon behind it. The first passengers had to stand up, with no protection from the weather.'

'What? It didn't have any seats?'

'Don't think so.'

'Do they still take *Locomotion* out for rides?'

'No it's been retired for a long while.'

'Can I go and see it?'

'We could organise a day out with your dad. He may have a spare free travel pass. Why don't you ask him when he comes home from work?'

'I will.'

'By the way, your dad says there's an article in the NUR magazine that says they're going to get rid of all the steam engines because of all the smoke they create.'

'What's wrong with the smoke? I like it.'

'I know you do, but in some places, like London, there's so much smoke that people are becoming ill and dying. The government's decided they have to do something[23], before the situation becomes even more dangerous.'

'If they get rid of the engines, what will pull the trains?'
'I don't know, I think they're still working it out. Your dad says they're trying out engines that use oil instead of coal.'

***

Halthorpe children grew up listening to, and enjoying, the huffs, rattles, puffs and smells of the steam engines. They laughed every time they were enveloped in clouds of smoke and steam. Tom and his friends would hang on the fences, like ragged washing, and wave at the drivers and the passengers as the trains went by. There was particular excitement when one of the 'A4 class' engines tore through, pulling an express train. They were beautifully designed and had a sloping front. They were built for speed. These were known by the children as 'streaks'. Whenever one was spotted, a rush of children would run excitedly along the inside of the fences, yelling 'Streak! Streak!,' at the tops of their voices.

'Is it the *Mallard?*'
'Don't know, can you see its number?'[24]
'60007 I think'
'It's the *Seagull!*'
'No it's not, *Seagull* is 60033...60007 is *Sir Nigel Gresley*'.
'Wow!'

Connie was not as excited as Tom when one of these smoking giants hurtled through Halthorpe. 'Just look at that,' she would grumble, with a resigned acceptance, 'black specks all over the clean washing again! It's always the same when the wind's coming from the west.'

Tom was eleven years old when Phil took him to Halthorpe Station to see the first ever diesel-powered train pass through. A small crowd had gathered on the platform to witness this event. When the two-coach diesel pulled in, it was greeted with complete silence from the onlookers. Their disappointment was obvious.

'It looks like a bus, dad!'
'I know. I'm not keen.'

The despondent audience wandered away, no doubt thinking the same as Tom and Phil, that the past may have been smoky and noisy, but at least it had personality and thrills. If this was the future, huh!

Chapter 17

FRIENDS IN NEED

1958

'Mam?'

'Yes love.'

'Mrs Pugh at chapel says all nations on earth should live together in peace and that we should love each other.'

'Mrs Pugh is right.'

'But Mam, I think the Germans hate us.'

'Do you Tom? Why do you think that?'

'Because we won the war.' Tom rushed on before Connie could answer. 'And it wasn't right, them killing and injuring people just so they could rule Europe. They wanted to capture our country too.'

'Terrible things happen in war time Tom. Germany's leader was a horrible dictator.'

'I hate them.'

'What makes you say that?'

'Because of what they did to Dad.'

'Yes. Fighting the Germans did cause your dad's injuries. Surprisingly he doesn't hate all Germans, just the really nasty ones, the Nazis and the SS.'

'Dad never talks about them.'

'I know he doesn't, but in the past he has spoken to me about them.'

'Does he like some Germans?'

'I wouldn't go that far, but he thinks a lot of the ordinary German army blokes were just like him; obliged to fight for their country. They were ordered to do it. He suspects many would rather have stayed at home with their families.'

'Well I still hate them all.'

'I understand why you should think that. I used to hate them too, but I changed my mind. I used to be so angry about what they did to my handsome man; still am I suppose! I was furious with them because of all the suffering they caused him and the months he had to spend in hospital and then in nursing homes while he recovered but I don't hate them now.'

'What made you change your mind?'

'When I was on honeymoon with your dad someone told me a story that made me think that perhaps all Germans aren't bad.'

'Tell me Mam, please.'

'When your dad was injured fighting the Germans in Holland in 1944, his troop leader Paul, was killed.'

'Was he? On the same day?'

'Yes, in the same action'

'How was he killed?'

'Shot, I think.'

'That's terrible, poor man.'

'Yes it was. Anyway your dad was lying injured in hospital when he found out that Paul had died. He was very upset. We agreed I would write, on your dad's behalf, to Paul's parents – Mr and Mrs Cavendish, to tell them how sad he was to hear about his death. Paul was only nineteen.'

'He was only ten years older than me.'

'Yes he was. He was very young.'

'Anyway, to cut a long story short, Sophia Cavendish wrote back to us, thanking us for the letter and enquiring about your dad's injuries.'

'That was kind of her. She's got a nice name hasn't she?.'

'Yes, it is lovely. Had you been a little girl we may have called you Sophia.'

'I like Tom best.'

Connie laughed and continued, 'we kept in touch throughout your dad's recovery and then Sophia did a remarkable thing. When she found out that we were getting married, she paid for us to have a fortnight's holiday on the Isle of Wight as a wedding present.'

'She paid for your honeymoon?'

'Yes she did. We stayed in a small hotel in Ryde. We were amazed at her generosity. We had no money, so without her we wouldn't have had a honeymoon.'

'Why did she do that?'

'Because she was kind and generous, but also perhaps because Paul spent the last two months of his life fighting alongside your dad. Maybe she wanted to do it in memory of her son. After all she would never be able to see him wed.'

'Did you ever meet her?'

'Yes, while we were on honeymoon. She lives on the Isle of Wight, in a big house on a cliff top overlooking a sandy bay. It has really wonderful sea views.'

'So you've been to her house?'

'Yes, she invited us for afternoon tea.'

'Was it nice?'

'Yes it was. Very grand! We'd only ever been in such a big house when we worked in them before the war. It was bigger than the doctor's house where I worked as housemaid, but smaller than Widemarsh Hall where your dad was under footman. Mrs Cavendish's world was very different to ours. We were both very nervous. Your dad was really shy and self conscious about his appearance. His skin grafts hadn't had time to settle in, so his face was still all red, white and purple blotches. Dad didn't want to draw attention to himself, so I had to do most of the talking.'

'Was she stuck up?'

'No, not at all,' laughed Connie. 'She was lovely.'

'Did she have a maid?'

'Yes she did. She helped Sophia serve at tea time.'

'What did you have for tea?'

'Earl Grey tea, we drank it from bone china cups. We ate dainty cucumber sandwiches made with brown bread. We had homemade scones with clotted cream and strawberry jam. There was carrot cake too. She gave me the recipe.'

Tom was impressed. 'They must be really posh.'

'Yes they're very well off. You can tell Sophia is well educated. She speaks properly. A really nice, well brought up lady. She was very concerned about your dad.'

'Do you still keep in touch?'

'We exchange Christmas cards.'

'Does she know about me?'

'Yes she does. She was delighted for us when you were born. You know the blue blanket you have on your bed?'

'Yes.'

'Well she sent that for you as a Christening present.'

'What did you talk about when you met her?'

'Well, as you would expect, we talked about her son, Paul. She was very keen to know what those last two months had been like for him.'

'She must have been very sad.'

'Yes she was. Anyway your dad told her about their time fighting across France, Belgium and Holland while Paul was the leader of their hussar troop. He told her how brave Paul was and how all the men tried to look out for him, because being troop leader was very dangerous. They had to stand in the turret of a tank so they could see to direct manoeuvres. They were easy targets and German troops deliberately tried to kill our officers.'

'Why did they do that?'

'So we didn't have as many men in command. Officers had to remove all their badges and stripes from their uniforms, so they looked like ordinary hussars. It didn't do to let the enemy know you were an officer.' Connie paused to recall Phil's conversation with Sophia. 'Oh yes, and dad told her about how Paul would sit writing letters home in the evening, after they'd stopped for the day. Apparently he would whistle quietly to himself while he wrote. The men nicknamed him Ever Whistling Paul.'

'Did he mind having a nickname?'

'No, they did it because they liked him, he knew that. Sophia laughed and said that ever since Paul was a little boy he had whistled when he concentrated. She was very pleased the men had cared for him. Her son's last letter home had described the great bunch of lads he had in his troop. Sophia was very upset when she talked about him.' Connie paused and dabbed at her own eyes. 'She went on to say how sorry she was when she found out that your dad had been so badly injured and that he was having such a tough time recovering. She said that Paul would have been pleased your dad had survived.' Connie smiled at Tom. 'Later on we chatted about the war years in general and what made the Germans start the war and Hitler's ambition to create the master race.'

'You were going to tell me what made you change your mind about hating them,' prompted Tom.

'Patience child, I'm just getting to that bit.' Connie reflected for a minute or two. 'I remember saying that the Jewish doctors I had worked for had been so worried about Hitler invading Great Britain that they'd closed their practice and gone to live in the wilds of Cumberland. I'm ashamed to say I got onto my soapbox. I got angry that another nation caused such fear, also that I'd lost my job because of it. I said I hated the Germans, they had no right to cause such terror or kill people en masse, just because they had a different religion. I said I was furious with them for causing Paul's death and your father's terrible injuries and that I would never forgive them.

Sophia agreed. She said after Paul's death she had been very angry. She and her husband had lost their only son, who had been a lovely, clever young man. Paul would never have the chance to fulfill his potential or to have the happy life he deserved. Then she surprised me by telling me she had a German friend, Beatrix, who lived in Berlin. I asked how they knew each other.

Sophia said that when she was seventeen and in the sixth form at her ladies' college, her languages teacher suggested it would be good for her to develop her written German skills by corresponding with a pen pal. The teacher said she was in contact with a family in Berlin who had a daughter about Sophia's age. It turned out that Beatrix was as keen to develop her English as Sophia was to improve her German.'

'Mrs Cavendish wrote to a German?' queried Tom, amazed. 'Was she a spy?'

'No, Sophia and Beatrix were just two educated girls, of different nationalities, sending letters to each other.'

'Oh, is that all?' said Tom, disappointed by the answer.

'Listen, and I'll tell you the rest. It gets better.'

Tom settled with his head resting on his hands and gave the story his full attention.

'Sophia and her friend soon agreed a way of working. Sophia would write a letter to Beatrix in English and Beatrix would reply in German, then Sophia would write her reply in German and Beatrix would reply in English. This gave them both practice at translating and writing each other's language.'

'Wow that was clever.' said Tom.

'The girls stayed friends after they left school. They wrote to each other regularly until the troubles in Germany made it difficult. During the war years Sophia never heard from Beatrix. She wondered if Beatrix had been killed. To her great relief she received a letter a few months after the war ended. They quickly renewed their correspondence.'

'Do they still write to each other?'

'They might. I don't really know. Anyway, I'm getting to the bit that changed my mind. Sophia read us part of one of her friend's letters that she sent after the war. In it Beatrix talks about her time in Berlin during the war and the terrible sufferings of the Jewish Berliners. The letter was written in German, so Sophia translated it into English for us. Everything in that letter made me question my belief that German people were all tarred with the same evil brush. After our honeymoon I wrote to Sophia to thank her for being so kind to us. I also told her how much thought I'd given to Beatrix's letter and asked her if she would translate it into English and send me a copy.'

'Did she send it to you?'

'Yes eventually, but only after she had written to Beatrix, to ask her permission, because the letter was private between them. When Beatrix wrote back she said it was important that others understood that not all German people were Nazi sympathizers, so it was fine for Sophia to share it. It's quite a long letter. I've still got it tucked in the back of my old handbag upstairs. I'll go and get it if you like.'

Beatrix's Letter. Extract. May 1946.

As you know I live in Berlin. It is the city where I was born. I expect I will always love living here. It is home. It saddens me to tell you that much of my beloved city is now in ruins. By 1943 we were being bombed by the Americans during the day and by the British, throughout the night. It was said that Hitler would only travel through Berlin during the hours of darkness, so he didn't have to look at the destruction.

Surviving here before and during the war was hard. We had many troubles. Before the outbreak of war, Hitler's government began persecuting our Jewish people. I had many friends who were of that faith.

I remember a terrible night in November 1938, which we call Kristallnacht, the night of broken glass, when nearly all the synagogues were burned down and many Jewish-owned stores and homes were looted and vandalised. Many Jews were killed and thousands more were sent to concentration camps. It was a very sad time.

By 1941 our Jewish population had been halved, although the city was still home to thousands. Many of them were clever, educated people with government and business occupations, but regrettably by the end of that year, deportations recommenced. The Nazi strategy was to remove all Jews from Europe. Many Jews took their own lives rather than submit to deportation. They were all very frightened and worried for their families, homes and jobs.

We other Berliners were actively, sometimes brutally, discouraged from helping and supporting Jewish people. Those who did, would be punished by the thuggish 'brown shirts' of the Nazi party.

This was an era of blind fanaticism, a time of distrust and treachery, a time when a son could turn against his mother, or a wife betray her husband. I heard of one woman[25], who, upon becoming a 'brown shirt', promptly betrayed her Jewish husband and watched as he was beaten and then shot dead in front of her in their own apartment. I shudder when I think of it.

This was a time when a knock at your front door, after ten o'clock at night, was not welcome. To open your door cautiously and find two terrified Germans of the Jewish faith shaking with fear on your doorstep caused a massive dilemma.

This happened to me in November 1941. I have never known such a confusion of feelings.

I was already very upset because my son Erik, who had not yet reached his nineteenth birthday, had just been killed in Libya. He was part of the Deutsches Afrika Korps and had been sent to Africa in early 1941, with Erwin Rommel to bolster the crumbling Italian Army. The Italians were on the brink of total collapse and after discussion with Mussolini, Hitler ordered the new joint offensive called Operation Sonnenblume (Sunflower)[13] to push back the British and their Commonwealth allies. Erik died in this fighting, I miss him so much. I am looking at his photograph as I write this letter; he was such a handsome young man.

Anyway to continue, I was terrified. Opening my door and speaking to Jews could bring trouble, yet at the same time I found it impossible not to hold out the hand of friendship to my fellow Berliners.

These two poor frightened souls stood at my door. The man

said, 'Man hat uns zugeflüstert dass Sie ein guter Mensch sind und dass Sie uns helfen würden.' We have been told you are a good person and that you will help us.

The woman said, 'Wir sind jüdisch und haben grosse Angst.' We are Jewish and we are very frightened.

What could I do? I knew I would risk everything if I invited them in. I was risking my husband's and daughter's lives. I was risking my husband's career in the army. I could have lost my house. I could have lost everything including my life. I looked up and down the street but thankfully could see no observers.

'Come in,' I said. 'Quickly.'

Once they were in the house, I locked all the doors and drew all the curtains tightly so no one could see in. They told me that their family and friends had been rounded up and taken to one of the Jew Assembly Centres at the Jewish cemetery in Gross Hamburger Street. My couple had managed to run away from the SS troops, even though they had been shot at. They hid behind the tombstones and on the streets, without food or water for three days before they came to me.

I found out later that men, women, children, even the old and infirm, were collected at these 'centres' throughout Berlin, until they numbered one thousand people. This was deemed to be a train load. They were forcibly loaded into railway carriages, sometimes freight wagons, at the Grunewald Freight yards before being taken away to the Lodz ghetto in Poland or the Aushwitz-Birkenau concentration camps.

I decided to hide my Jewish couple in my home until I could think of a way to help them escape. I made them a bed in my cellar and only let them upstairs into my living space when it was dark.

They had escaped with no possessions, no change of clothing and no money. They were called Joseph and Heidi Schultz. Yes they had German names! They had been born, educated, married and worked in Berlin; as had their parents. They could not understand why people in their own city, their own country, hated them so much.

I certainly didn't hate them, I had huge sympathy for the danger they were in and I felt a true German responsibility for them. I wanted to protect and care for them.

However caring for them was very difficult. Food supplies were sparse in the city and I could only buy the ration of food we were allowed. The allowance was for my daughter and me. I had the income my husband sent each month, but money means nothing when you can only buy a certain amount of food.

Every day I would wander the poorly stocked street markets, which hung on in these austere times, in the hopes that I could persuade some trader to part with something edible to add to my soup pot. Soup was our salvation and we lived on it. Trying to add something nourishing to the pot was my challenge.

It was during one of my foraging trips that a small miracle occurred. I was jostled in the street by a neighbour whom I barely knew. She apologised and walked briskly away. It was only later that I realised she had slipped one of her precious potatoes into my coat pocket. When I found it I nearly cried. An additional potato was like a gift from God.

The next day when I went out, I felt something drop into my shopping basket. It was a small turnip, I was astonished. I was in a crowded part of the street and the donor did not make themselves known to me.

During the months I kept my Jewish friends hidden in my home I received many small gifts of vegetables, all of them were passed to me in the street, without a word spoken.

I came to the conclusion that the people around me, many of whom I didn't really know, were sharing their rations with me and helping to feed my Jewish lodgers. How kind of them, how brave they were to risk their lives to help us.

I eventually managed to get my first set of friends – yes, more Jews came to my door late at night – onto a train bound for France. During those terrible years I shared my home with four families of

Jews, ten people in all. I have never heard from any of them since. I pray daily for their safety.

***

'That is amazing' said Tom, 'Beatrix is a brave woman.'

'Yes she is. She took some terrible risks,' said Connie, 'and there were many more like her throughout Germany and Europe.'

'Does she still live in Berlin with her husband?'

'I think she still lives there, but not with her husband. He was killed towards the end of the war.'

'So she lost both her son and her husband?'

'Yes, poor woman. Her husband was regular army and he didn't approve of the way things were being carried out by Hitler, the Nazis and the SS. I don't know all the details, but he was part of a resistance movement in the Wehrmacht, dedicated to removing the Nazis from power. Anyway, there was an attempt to assassinate Hitler in 1944. Something went wrong and the resistance movement was discovered. Beatrix's husband was rounded up, along with others, and was executed by firing squad.'

'By the nasty Germans?'

'Yes I'm afraid so.'

'Both the English and the German lady lost their sons in the war then.'

'Many sons on both sides were killed, and a lot of daughters too,' reflected Connie, with sadness in her voice. She changed the subject. 'Did you know your Uncle Fred and Uncle Bert were in Africa fighting when they were in the Infantry?'

'Where they fighting in the same part of Africa where Erik died?'

'Yes. Thankfully they came through it without injury.'

'Did they ride on camels?'

'No I don't think so,' laughed Connie. 'They told me that all they saw was thousands of square miles of sand. Why don't you ask them about it, the next time you see them?'

'OK, I will.'

'Do you remember I told you about Guido and the other Italian prisoners of war I worked with on the farm?'

'When you were a land girl?'

'That's right. Guido and several of the other POWs I knew were captured by our lads in Libya.'

'They were fighting alongside the Germans?'

'Yes they were, but I don't think their hearts were in it. They weren't really warriors, so they surrendered rather than be killed.'

'They were happier working and singing in the fields?'

'Yes they were much happier. They were lovely chaps, not at all aggressive. Guido used to flirt with me and say he was a lover not a fighter.'

Chapter 18

MOVING ON

As Tom grew up his life in Halthorpe changed and broadened. From five years of age, he walked a mile and a half to and from Normansly School each day. On his way he frequently called into Taylor's shop. The loud clang of the shop bell alerted the slightly deaf owner to the arrival of customers. The shop, with its scrubbed plank floor, half-empty shelves and simple whitewood counter, on which the shop cat snoozed, had never changed in fifty years. Tom liked to spend his pocket money on arrowroot sticks, wagon wheels, flying saucers and sherbet dips. If he had wanted, he could also have bought a packet of two Wills Woodbine cigarettes. These were displayed alongside the children's sweets.

'Hello Mr Taylor,' Tom bawled, 'can I have a packet of sweet cigarettes and a stick of liquorice please?'

'What was that?'

'Sweet cigarettes and liquorice,' he yelled again, holding out his threepenny bit.

'That'll be tuppence ha'penny. Do you want your ha'penny change, or would you rather have a gobstopper?'

'Gobstopper.'

Tom took the huge sweet from Mr Taylor's fingers and forced it into his mouth. It's almost too big to suck. He stuffed his sweet cigarettes and his liquorice stick into his trouser pocket, spluttered, 'Fank you,' to the smiling shopkeeper and hurried to school. All the way he alternated between sucking the gobstopper and spitting it out into his hand. Cor! It's changed colour five times. Tom still hadn't finished it when he got to school, so he wrapped it in his clean white hanky and stowed it for later in his other pocket.

Sometimes on Saturdays Tom went to Taylor's with his mam. He watched fascinated as the old shop keeper, with his twisted, arthritic fingers, managed to deftly cut slabs of butter and cheese, and then wrap them in waxed paper sheets. Flour and sugar would be scooped from big sacks kept behind his counter and weighed into blue paper bags. Wafer-thin slices of bacon and ham would be carved with a dangerous looking razor-sharp knife and folded neatly into greaseproof paper parcels. If he had been good, his mother might buy him a quarter of sweets, perhaps wine gums or jelly babies, that Mr Taylor weighed, then slid into a cone of twisted paper.

***

Normansly Primary school had three teachers, about seventy pupils, two dinner ladies and a caretaker who worked in the evening. When Tom first started the school, other than a couple of boys from Sunday School, he knew very few of the children in Normansly.

Classes always had at least two year groups, sometimes three if a teacher was ill. Classrooms were usually divided, with one age group on the right and the other on the left. Older groups were usually given a task at the start of the lesson, perhaps reading or writing practice, while the teacher concentrated on setting up the younger group with work. Tom was always more interested in what the other group was doing than getting on with his own work. He was convinced that his teachers had eyes in the backs of their heads and ears that missed nothing.

'Tom, are you getting on with what you should be doing?'

'Yes Miss Sutton.'

'How can you do that when you're looking over here? Perhaps it would be more worthwhile if you concentrated on the work on your desk, rather than what's going on with year 1. Do you agree?'

'Yes Miss Sutton.'

'Tom, please stop whispering to Bernard, I can hear you.'

'Yes Miss Sutton.'

'Bernard, don't encourage Tom.'

'Yes Miss Sutton.'

While the children were attending morning assembly or doing exercises in the hall, they were always aware of the rattle of dishes, busy chopping noises and alluring smells that drifted through the closed hatch doors of the adjacent kitchen, where the dinner ladies were preparing and cooking lunch. The meals were invariably meat and two vegetables, with a hot pudding to follow.

'What do you think we're getting today?'

'It's Wednesday, it'll be cottage pie or mince and onions.'

'What about pudding?'

'Treacle sponge or spotted dick.'

'Spotted dick's my favourite.'

Tom enjoyed his lessons, but the highlight of his day always came when he and the other children were lined up in queues so they could collect their lunches. The dinner ladies went to the same Women's Institute as his mam, so he knew them well. This was because Tom was a regular attendee at WI social functions. He found that being an 'honorary' member worked to his advantage.

'Hello Mrs Sharrett, Mrs Hancock,' said Tom, standing on his toes and peering through the wooden hatch into the school kitchen.

'Hello Tom,' said Mrs Sharrett, beaming at him, 'Meat and potato pie today. Did you enjoy the 'Beetle Drive' the other night?'

'Yes it was good fun. I kept getting all the legs but I couldn't get a head.'

'That was bad luck. My beetle had only one eye and three legs. I've got a bit of extra crust here, would you like that?'

'Yes please.'

'Another spoon of gravy?'

'Yes please Mrs Hancock. What's for pud today?'

'Suet pudding and custard. Do you like it?'

'I do.'

'With extra custard?'

'Yes please.'

When Tom was nine he and his pal George, had the honour of being made milk monitors. This sought-after position gave them control of milk distribution. At ten o'clock every morning, each school child was given a one third of a pint bottle of milk to drink. Tom and George would collect the crates from outside the cloakroom door and take the correct number of bottles to each classroom. An hour later they would gather up the empties and stack them ready for the milkman to collect. There were always more bottles than children, so Tom always managed to drink one spare bottle while working out the allocation, his own bottle in his class and then another when they collected the empties.

***

'Come on Tom, hurry up, or we'll be late. Also be a love and put some air into the back wheel of my bike, it feels a bit soft. I haven't got time to do it. I'm putting the joint in the oven. Don't dilly-dally, I don't want us to be late. You know how I hate going into morning service when it has started. Mrs Pugh will not thank you for turning up late for Sunday School either. The last time I arrived late for a Chapel service, I clattered through the door and put Mr Clarke, the organist, right off. He played the first verse of the hymn twice. I thought the preacher was going to explode, his face was so purple. And the congregation! Well, they were all mixed up because they didn't know which verse to sing.'

'OK Mam, I'm nearly ready. I'll go and pump your bike wheel up now.'

'And I've just remembered, isn't it today you do your poem from the pulpit?'

Oh lawks!

'I hope you've learned it, I know you were practising a poem with Mrs Pugh.'

'Yes Mam,' answered Tom thinking frantically. *I can't remember the poem…what was it? Gentle Jesus meek and mild…something, something…Oh yes…look upon…something, something…Oh lawks! I've forgotten.*

'For goodness sake stop mooching about and hurry up Tom, we're going to be late. Do you know what you're going to recite?'

It was that moment when inspiration hit Tom. *I do know a poem!* 'Yes Mam,' he answered confidently.

'Good. I'll look forward to hearing it.'

At the allotted time during the service, the Sunday School children filed into the chapel and sat in the front pew, directly in front of the pulpit. Mr Jones the preacher welcomed them with a friendly smile.

'I'm delighted that Mrs Pugh and our Sunday School children have joined us for this morning's service. They will be sharing some of their poems with us. I am very much looking forward to hearing them. Tom would you like to be first to come up here and recite your poem?'

Tom clomped up the pulpit steps and stood next to Mr Jones. He looked at the expectant expressions of the congregation. His mam smiled encouragingly at him as Mr Jones said, 'When you're ready Tom.'

Tom took a deep breath and recited his poem.

'Little fly upon the wall
Ain't you got no clothes at all
Ain't you got no togs for rugger
Oh you silly little bugger.'

He stood back and waited for the applause. None came. Mr Jones was momentarily lost for words, but eventually managed to smile at the startled congregation and then pat Tom encouragingly on the shoulder. 'Well thank you for that Tom; that was…that was unexpected.'

As Tom clomped back down the pulpit steps, he looked towards his mam. She was staring unblinkingly at the vase of flowers on the table in front of the pulpit.

***

Tom and the other railway children sat along the top of the fence, chatting like a line of cheerful, garrulous sparrows. Farmer Wilson's big blue Fordson Major Tractor, with the red wheels, towed the little red baling machine up and down his thirty acre hay field. It was pushing rectangular bales out of its back end. It reminded Tom of a chicken laying eggs. Every now and then, Mr Wilson stopped to stack his bales into neat little columns. He would test the tightness of the strings around his bales, and then fiddle with the tensioner on his new piece of equipment.

At the far side of the field, two of his farm hands were working with a pair of carthorses and a binding machine, turning cut hay into sheaves. Another farmhand was working his way along the field behind them, gathering up the sheaves into little stooks.

Tom didn't realise at the time that he was witnessing the end of one farming era and the birth of another. He was more interested in what Russell was saying. Russell was ten and usually took the lead. Tom and the other younger children were happy to follow.

'After tea when Mr Wilson's gone home, we'll build a fort.'

***

'Mam,' said Tom, between mouthfuls of sardines on toast, 'we're going to build a fort from the hay bales this evening.'

'No Tom, you're not, it's very dangerous. Some children have been crushed to death doing that. It was in the paper last week,' answered his dad, peering over the top of the Hull Daily Mail.

'But Dad, all the other children are going.'

'Well that may be, but you're not to go, do you understand?'

'Oh Da-ad.' Tom folded his arms and looked sulky. He saw the warning expression on Phil's face. 'Okay. I suppose so.'

***

The fort was three bales high. Tom was deep inside when he felt a firm hand grip his arm. He looked up horrified as Phil dragged him out and across to the edge of the field. Phil sat down on a bale and pushed Tom face down over his knee.

'Didn't I tell you not to play with the bales because you could get hurt?'

'Yes.'

'Well this is what happens to little boys who disobey their fathers and risk their lives by playing stupid, dangerous games.' With that Phil whacked him hard across the backside with the pig mash stick. The pain was intense and Tom immediately started bawling.

Bernard ran over to them and shouted at Phil, 'you bloody bastard.' Phil continued to whack his son's bottom. 'Any more of that Bernard and you'll get some of this as well.'

'You'll never catch me,' said Bernard waving a V sign and preparing to run. 'Anyway you're still a bastard.'

Tom ran home, sobbing, with both hands clasped to his stinging bottom and was immediately sent to his room by Connie. 'You'd better get to bed quick, before your dad catches up with you.'

He scrambled up the stairs, only pausing in front of the landing mirror to pull his trousers carefully down so he could admire the vivid red, throbbing stripes criss-crossing his buttocks.

Tom was later to reflect that although he was well pleased with Bernard's support, his intervention did nothing to lessen his dad's fury or the intensity of the blows on his backside.

***

'Mam is Robert Louis Stevenson related to George Stephenson who built the first railway?'

'I don't know. I think their names may be spelt differently, even though they sound the same. Why do you ask?'

'We are reading Treasure Island at school.'

'With Miss Sutton?'

'Yes.'

'Why don't you ask her? If she knows the answer, tell me.'

'Yes OK, I will.'

'When I was at school I learned a poem by Robert Louis Stevenson.

Would you like to hear it?'
  'Yes please.'
  'Well sit next to your dad and I'll recite it, if I can remember. It's called "From a Railway Carriage". It's about a railway journey. Listen and tell me what you think.'

> 'Faster than fairies, faster than witches,
> Bridges and houses, hedges and ditches;
> And charging along like troops in a battle
> All through the meadows the horses and cattle:
> All of the sights of the hill and the plain
> Fly as thick as driving rain;
> And ever again in the wink of an eye,
> Painted stations whistle by.
>
> Here is a child who clambers and scrambles,
> All by himself and gathering brambles;
> Here is a tramp who stands and gazes;
> And here is the green for stringing the daisies!
> Here is a cart runaway in the road
> Lumping along with man and load;
> And here is a mill and there is a river:
> Each a glimpse and gone forever!'[28]

  'That's good. It sounds as if it's about here.'
  'Funny you should say that,' she smiled. 'I like it because it makes me think of us, but it was written in the last century.'
  'That reminds me Tom,' said Phil, giving his son a hug, 'there are loads of brambles ready along the side of the Duck Walk; it would be a shame to let them go to waste.'
  'We'll all go together. I'll find some basins to put them in,' said Connie. 'If we can find enough I'll make some jam.'
  'And an apple and bramble pie.'
  'I suppose!'

***

'Pay attention children, please,' boomed Mr Burton, the head teacher. His black brows bristled, the gravity defying glob of spit that was permanently suspended between his top and bottom lips stretched as he spoke. He glowered at his class.

'That's right, settle down. Hurry up! Thank you!' He sighed, and then forced his severe face into a more pleasant expression.

'I'm delighted to tell you that four of our pupils have passed their eleven plus examinations. Rodney O'Driscoll is one of them. His parents tell me he will be continuing his education at the private school at Dunbridge. My best wishes to Rodney.' Mr Burton beamed at Rodney before continuing. 'The other three successful pupils are Sandra Forbes, Robin Bartholomew and Tom York. They will be going to Goole Grammar School. On behalf of their teachers at Normansly Junior School, I wish them every success.'

Tom's teacher looked his way and smiled. Somehow he managed to return the smile, as he knew he should. The announcement wasn't a surprise to him. He had kept the secret for a week since his mam and dad received the letter. His mother had been thrilled, his father quietly proud. All Tom felt was a sinking sensation in the pit of his stomach.

'But Mam, all my friends will be going to the Secondary Modern School. I won't know anyone.'

'I'm really pleased you've passed for Grammar School, it's a wonderful opportunity. I had to give up my chance because my parents couldn't afford for me to go.'

'The Grammar School uniform will be very expensive, I'll need spare shirts and trousers, rugger kit and a tie and a…'

'That's not your worry, I'll get myself some extra work at Wilson's farm. I'll soon earn enough to pay for it.'

So that's that then.

***

Tom felt too sick to notice the train pulling into the station. For the first time ever he ignored the steam engine, not even bothering to read the number as it chugged past. He wanted to hold his Dad's hand but couldn't because the other boys would see. He didn't want to get on the train.

'I hope you have a good first day. You look very smart in your new uniform,' Phil said, 'I'll put you in with Robert and Michael. They'll look after you. They have been travelling to school on the train for three years.' His dad pointed to boys standing just along the platform from them. They looked very big and old to Tom.

He didn't like them. Every time his dad looked away, Robert pointed at him and made a fist.

Why is he doing that? I've never met him before.

Michael just grinned at him and nodded. Although Tom had never spoken to Michael, he recognised him as the son of his dad's boss.

When the train stopped the two older boys ran along the platform until they found an empty compartment, then piled in. Phil walked along after them and held the compartment door open for Tom to follow them in.

'In you go lad. Have a good time, work hard and don't forget to wave to your mam.' Phil slammed the door shut, waved to the guard and blew his whistle.

Tom sat on the end of the bench seat next to the window, so he could look out.

As the train pulled out of the station, Robert heaved Tom up by the lapels of his new jacket.

'Why are you sitting in my seat?' he demanded, his voice and accent harsh.

'I'm sorry,' said Tom, blushing bright pink, 'I didn't know it was your seat.'

Robert pushed Tom roughly across the compartment so that his back fell hard against the opposite seat. 'You sit where I tell you to sit.'

'I promised I'd wave to my mam.'

'Well you can't. You didn't ask my permission.'

As the train picked up speed, Tom saw his mam standing on the backs, holding her tea towel ready. He felt so shaken by what had happened, he didn't wave to her.

Suddenly he found his cap being snatched from his head. Robert dropped it on the unswept floor of the carriage, then scrunched it under his foot in the dirt, before picking it up and throwing it onto the netting luggage rack.

Tom tried to reach it, but it was too far away. 'Can I have my cap back please?'

'No, you can't,' said Robert thrusting his open hand into Tom's face and pushing him back onto the seat again. 'I've thrown it up there because it's dirty. When we cross the Ouse Bridge, I'm going to throw your mucky old cap out of the window and into the river to give it a wash.'

'My mam only bought it last week. Give it back or I'll tell my dad.'

'Tell your dad if you like, I couldn't care less. Anyway Michael's dad is your dad's boss, so if you tell, your dad will get the sack.' Tom looked at Michael. He was nodding and smiling.

Tom didn't know what to do. He slumped miserably in the corner of the carriage looking away from the older boys. *I hate going to Grammar School.*

'Look,' said Robert, 'little mammy's boy is sulking.'

When the train stopped at Widemarsh an old lady chose their compartment and settled herself next to Tom. The older boys resorted to glowering at him for the rest of the journey. Tom decided to ignore them. The cap stayed on the luggage rack and wasn't thrown into the river.

When the train arrived at Goole, both boys thumped Tom on the back of the head as they alighted. After they had gone he stood on the seat and frantically hit the underside of the net rack until his new cap flew off onto the floor.

Throughout Tom's first two terms the bullying continued, becoming more violent as the older boys dreamed up worse tortures. To avoid them he would delay getting on to the train until the whistle blew and then he would climb into a compartment as far from theirs as possible. Soon they got wise to this and jumped off the train at Widemarsh, running down the platform looking through the compartment windows until they found him. Then they would start again. They would tip out his sports kit, tear up his exercise books, give him Chinese burns, twist his ears, bend his fingers back, kick his shins and stamp repeatedly on his toes. Tom bravely bore it, because to tell meant his dad might lose his job. It seemed he couldn't escape them.

It was in the third term that things became slightly better after a bad incident. Tom was standing on the platform at Goole Station, next to a porter's barrow, waiting to catch his train home when he heard them.

'Look there's mammy's boy,' shouted Robert running along the platform. He grasped Tom by his jacket lapels, lifted him off his feet, swung him around and then thrust him away. Michael meanwhile had got down on his hands and knees behind Tom, causing Tom to fall backwards over him towards the concrete floor. As he fell, Tom's head struck the metal corner of the porter's barrow. He screamed in pain. Struggling to his feet, he rubbed the back of his head. It was sticky. His hand was covered in blood. A woman rushed over to him.

'Are you alright son?' She rounded on the older boys.

'You horrible boys,' she shouted.

'Wasn't anything to do with us missus.' said Robert defiantly. 'He fell over 'cos he's clumsy and stupid.'

'I saw exactly what you did, you big bullies.'

Robert and Michael skulked away as she mopped Tom's head with her handkerchief and checked him over.

'We'll get you later, mammy's boy,' shouted Robert waving his fist at Tom.

'You can sit next to me,' the helpful woman continued as she tried to stem the bleeding from the wound. She frowned at the other boys, as the train pulled in.

'You've got blood all over your shirt collar and down the back of your jacket but I think the bleeding has stopped now. Are you OK?'

'Yes I'm fine thank you.'

When Tom got home Connie saw the mess he was in. 'What on earth happened to you?' she asked examining the back of his head.

'Robert and Michael pushed me over and I hit my head on the metal corner of a porter's barrow.'

'Why did they do that?'

'They're always doing things like that.'

'Why haven't you told me before?'

'Because I don't want dad to lose his job.'

'What do you mean?'

'Robert said if I told, Michael's dad would sack my dad.'

'What nonsense. Wait till your dad comes home and I tell him.'

'Aw Mam, you can't say anything, things will just get worse, and I don't want to get dad sacked.'

Connie stayed silent while she dabbed the wound with iodine. Her son wriggling under her ministrations suddenly burst out 'They're horrible. I hate them. I wish they were dead.'

'I know you must feel terribly angry, but you know what I've always told you, it's better to turn the other cheek.'

'But there are two of them. It's not fair. I wish I was bigger and stronger so I could fight them.'

'Don't you worry about that. Your dad and me will sort this out. How about a buttered scone to keep you going until you have your tea?'

Early October 1944

Their little group of reconnaissance tanks were hidden in a densely tree-covered area of the wetlands of Holland. They couldn't see the enemy, but they knew they were all around. Today's push had taken them miles ahead of their division and their supply convoys, such as they were. They were out on a limb, deep inside enemy-occupied territory. Not only were they constantly at risk from retaliatory attack by enemy heavy weapons, but also from the ever-present threat of Hitler youth and SS snipers. To make matters worse, they were hungry.

'Unscrew the whip aerial Chalky,' said Phil, 'it's time I went hunting.'

Chalky looked across to Paul. 'What do you think, Skip?'

Paul was sitting on a tree stump, whistling quietly to himself, while he wrote a letter to his mother. He licked his pencil, looked at Chalky, smiled at Phil and shrugged his shoulders.

'It'll bugger up the radio. What if we get a call?' said Chalky.

'Oh, to hell with it! We're so far ahead of division, we probably can't get a signal anyway.' Phil saw Chalky's doubtful expression, so continued persuasively, 'we can always say it was on the blink. What would you prefer, meat or biscuit crumbs? We're no bloody use to anybody if we're starving. I think I saw some hens around that old farm we passed.'

Charlie gave in and handed over the aerial. 'Do you think you can nab one? I could murder a drum stick.'

'Don't know. I can try. They're probably pretty flighty after everything they've been through recently. I'll have a go.'

Phil looked carefully around, choosing his route.

'Watch out for those nasty buggers on bicycles, lurking behind trees and hedges,' warned Taff. 'They seem to be everywhere.'

The unofficial recommendation from their officers on the sighting of one of the members of the Hitler Youth movement or an SS sniper was straightforward. 'They may only be fourteen or fifteen years old but they're deadly. Don't mess about being polite, just shoot the little buggers. If you don't get the first shot in, they'll have you.'

Phil took the aerial and worked his way along the line of trees towards the old farm. His progress was slow because he constantly watched for signs of the enemy while trying to keep well hidden. He loosed his side arm in its holster and trod very carefully to avoid snapping twigs. When he reached the remains of the war-blasted farm, he could see a few chickens pecking around in the rubble. He paused and scanned the buildings and yard for signs of Fritz. He studied the ground to check for Schu 42 landmines. Fritz had a nasty habit of burying 200 grams of TNT in wooden boxes connected to tripwires. Phil had no ambition to end up like the hungry infantryman who'd lost an arm when he'd inadvertently pulled up a booby trapped beetroot.

Phil spent a further ten minutes watching the ruins of the buildings before he felt confident about making his move. All seemed quiet. His hands were trembling. His heart was racing. He tried to calm his breathing. *Seems OK* he thought, as he edged slowly towards the chickens. He made little clucking noises in the hopes of keeping them calm. He was very wary. Danger was all around. Not knowing which direction attack might come from increased his fear.

I hope Dutch chickens understand English clucking, he thought laughing internally to try and reduce his tension. Silently, he crept slowly towards the birds. When he got near them he took a deep breath, had another quick look around and suddenly lunged forward, flapping his arms and running straight at the birds to confuse them. The chickens scattered around the farmyard, squawking loudly. Phil identified the fattest looking one and, brandishing the whip aerial, chased it round the yard. As he caught up with the panicking bird he whipped the aerial back and forth until he managed to hit it in its throat and knock it off its feet. He jumped on the stunned bird and wrung its neck. Clutching the bird to his body, he ran back to the relative safety of the forest and breathed deeply to calm his thumping heart. He daren't risk trying for another bird, he wasn't out of danger yet, all the noise could have alerted Fritz.

Carrying his prize, he carefully made his way back to the tank and to his relieved mates. While he plucked and gutted the chicken, Chalky and Taff siphoned some petrol from the tank into Taff's upside-down helmet. The helmet was set on the ground and an improvised spit using forked branches, was made over it. Once the chicken was threaded onto the spit, the petrol was set alight and Taff and Chalky took turns revolving the spit to roast the bird slowly and evenly.

'Chicken a la Holland for dinner tonight, lads,' said Taff, 'just like dear old mum makes.'

'No spuds or carrots though,' grumbled Chalky, 'and no gravy.'

'You can always sprinkle some biscuit crumbs on your drumstick,' joked Phil.

'Now that I would like to see,' laughed Taff.

***

England 1995

Tom picked up the letters from the mat behind the door. He steeled himself before he could open them. He still felt raw and emotionally spent following his father's death.

Tom slit open an envelope with a Swansea postmark. Inside was a handwritten letter. The letter expressed sorrow at Phil's death and to Tom's astonishment it continued:

'...did your Dad ever tell you about Hen Racing?...'

No he never did.

'...In the war we had this big push across Belgium and Holland to retake Amsterdam. It was a hell of a fight. We were frequently miles ahead of our supply trucks and we were permanently short of food. Your father kept most of our squadron fed because of his prowess at capturing the semi-wild chickens that were roaming around bombed-out farms and houses. Without him we would have starved. Phil was voted the Squadron Champion at Hen Racing.'

The letter was signed 'Taff' Evans.

Memories of forty years ago and an overheard conversation, flooded back. Suddenly an old family saying made sense. Tom understood why the first purchases Phil made, in preparation for married life, were two hen huts. Chickens represented survival.

15

***

1959

Connie and Tom swung their bikes onto the gravel driveway and stopped.

'Do you like it Tom?' she asked as they looked at the little red brick bungalow standing in its own grounds. 'Dad and I have bought it. I've got the keys to the back door. Shall we have a look inside?'

'Is it really ours now, Mam?'

'Yes, we went through to Howden and signed the papers at the solicitors yesterday. It's a bit run down but we'll soon do it up.'

'Did it cost a lot?'

'Yes it did. It was eleven hundred pounds, which was all the money we managed to save since we got married. We never spent a penny of your dad's war pension.'

'Wow, that's a lot. I like it up here. Robin Bartholomew, lives up this road, he's in my year at school. He goes to school on the bus. Will I still have to go on the train?'

'No, you'll be able to go on the bus with Robin now.'

'That's good. It's got a huge front lawn Mam,' yelled Tom excitedly, turning his bike onto it from the drive and pedalling around the grass in circles.

He started singing his latest favourite song at the top of his voice. Connie's heart lifted when she saw how happy her son was.

'Into the ring to a shout of a great **Olé**!
Came the parade, all prepared for a mighty fray.
Matadors and **picadors** and **toreadors**,
And who do you think as well?
Trotting right behind them came the little white bull…'[43]

'Come on Little White Bull, I'm dying to have a look.'

'Me too.' Tom threw his bike onto the lawn and ran after her.

A little ramshackle wood and glass verandah was attached to the back of the bungalow. The paint was peeling from it and several panes of glass were broken.

'The solicitor says to give the verandah door a good pull because it sticks a bit,' said Connie. She grasped the handle and pulled hard. The door didn't budge. She gave an almighty heave. Suddenly it came free from its frame. Connie staggered backwards across the yard. To her amazement she was still holding the door in her arms. They looked at each other and burst out laughing.

'The daft devil forgot to mention it doesn't have any hinges.'

Tom rushed forward to help his mum lean it against the verandah wall.

'Oh lawks!' giggled Tom.

END

Acknowledgements

My sincere and grateful thanks to my friends and relatives who have helped me with the production of this book, in particular:

Vanessa Histon for her talent as an editor, for her valuable suggestions and for her professional skills in helping me to get 'The Hen Race' into a publishable form. Her support, knowledge and encouragement have been invaluable. My thanks also go to her for suggesting the titles for chapters 9 (Stepping Out) and 14 (Seeing) and for producing the excellent blurb on the outer rear cover of this book.

Agnes Chilton for sharing her knowledge and experience of women's work in the nineteen fifties, and for her constant support, unfailing enthusiasm and endurance whilst listening to extracts from 'The Hen Race'.

Gunter Helft, for sharing his experiences of life in Berlin prior to the Second World War, and for the German translation in Beatrix's letter, chapter 17 (Friends in Need).

Polly Robinson our dear friend for her incredible help with producing The Hen Race website. https://henracepress.com

The members of 'Worcester Writers Circle' for being a constant source of inspiration and for their warmth, friendship and sharing of their many and diverse literary talents.

The directors and committee members of Worcestershire Literary Festival for their support for, and promotion of, literature and literary events, also for their friendship and help.

Heather Wastie and other talented participants of 'Mouth and Music' in Kidderminster, Worcestershire, for inspiring me to use the Frank Loessor/ Haogy Carmichael classic 'Heart and Soul', for the dance sequence in chapter 11 (Connie's War).

Historical Notes

1... German Bombing of Eindhoven

On the night of 19 September 1944, Luftwaffe Dornier Do 17 night fighters dropped bright phosphorus flares to light up the Netherlands town of Eindhoven. The Junkers Ju 87 "Stukas" accompanying them bombed the target, giving the civilian population very little time to take shelter, and British forces no time to mount air defence. No German planes were shot down during the bombing.

The supply chain of allied troops was hit hard. Drivers heroically drove many of the ammunition trucks to safety, but much of the food supplies were lost.

Sources...Wikipedia, 15th/19th Regimental History.

2... Women's Land Army

Extract from Lady Denman's foreword in the Land Army Manual 1940

"Germany is attempting to starve the British people into submission. To win the war our country must beat the blockade. This is the joint task of the British Navy and of Britain's great field force of agricultural workers.

The Women's Land Army was organized in readiness three months before the outbreak of hostilities. The calling up of men from the land had been slow and the growth of the Land Army correspondingly gradual. Farmers' memories are short, and in spite of the good work done on the land by women during the last war, the Land Army has had to encounter prejudice against the employment of women's labour. This prejudice has now almost everywhere been overcome through the really magnificent service, given by the first few thousand employed volunteers, who worked though the bitter winter of 1939, under conditions of great difficulty and loneliness and have stuck to their jobs ever since. To these volunteers and the many others with the same fine spirit now working in the Land Army the country owes a great deal."

Source...*LAND GIRL A Manual for Volunteers in the Women's Land Army*

3... *Railway Evolution and the LNER*

Richard Trevithick, a Cornish mining engineer, started the railway's evolutionary process, when he built the first steam powered travelling engine. It was designed to run 10 miles from the Penydarren ironworks to Abercynon in Wales pulling a 10 ton load of pig iron. On 21 February 1804, it took just over four hours to complete this distance. Trevithick's engine had problems because the cast iron track it was running on wasn't up to the job. The flanged rails cracked and fractured. Seventy men were employed to hold the train and its truck onto the tracks throughout this first ever steam engine journey. The ironworks went back to hauling pig iron with horses and mules. Steam locomotives weren't used again by the ironworks for another thirty years.

A mere twenty one years after Trevithick's engine made its journey, the first public steam powered railway between Stockton and Darlington, was opened. *Locomotion* the steam engine which pulled the simple open topped wagons, was built by George Stephenson.

After this entrepreneurs and engineers built railways, embankments, tunnels, bridges, viaducts and stations throughout Britain. By the start of the First World War there were circa 120 railway companies. Each company had its own tracks and route, engines and rolling stock, directors, engineers and workers. Britain had an incredibly diverse, complicated and uneconomic goods and passenger transport system. The government of the time had little interest in, or involvement with the railways.

The First World War was a major catalyst for change. Over a third of the men working for the railways signed up to fight. Consequently the railway companies had to engage women to work as porters, signal women and clerks.

When war broke out in August 1914 the railways of Britain were taken into government control. They served the country's needs throughout the war years, but after the war ended, much of the rail infrastructure was run down and in need of investment. The government praised the service provided by the railway companies during the war, but were lax in paying for it. Consequently many were on the brink of collapse.

In 1921 the government passed the Railways Act to amalgamate the railway companies in order to increase efficiency. This enforced 'bringing together' of the one hundred and twenty privately owned and managed railway companies, into four big national rail companies, caused much dissent. The 'big four', as they were known, were the Great Western Railway, the London, Midland and Scottish Railway, the Southern Railway and the London and North Eastern Railway (**LNER**). Bitter resentment and rivalry erupted as people were forced to work and co-operate together. It took three years of arbitration, to resolve some of the differences between the directors, managers and workforce.

From 1929 until 1937 the 'Great Depression' had a disastrous impact on traditional rail traffic in coal, iron ore and steel. Revenues dropped and poorly paid railway workers had their wages further reduced by two and a half percent. Many were made redundant, poverty was common.

From the late 1930s, the industrial recovery was focused on light industry which favoured road transport. However the Second World War put business back on the railways for a few more years.

When nationalisation of the railways took place on 1 January 1948, the big four became regions of the national rail network,

The **LNER**, ran north from London along the eastern side of the country. It covered 6590 miles (10,610 km) of tracks and reached as far as Elgin and Banff in the east of Scotland. It also travelled west to pick up Glasgow, Fort William and Mallaig.

Sir Nigel Gresley was the **LNER**'s chief mechanical engineer for most of company's existence. He was hugely influential in driving forward innovative steam engine design. Iconic engines like the *Flying Scotsman* and the *Mallard* are attributed to him. The *Flying Scotsman* was the first steam engine to travel at one hundred miles per hour and to travel from London to Edinburgh nonstop. the *Mallard* still holds the world steam traction speed record, having maintained 126mph for five miles on 3 July 1938, pulling a seven coach train.

Another major player in the rise of the **LNER** was inspirational advertising manager Cecil Dandridge. In 1929 he commissioned artist Eric Gill to produce the Gill Sans typeface. This was used on all of the **LNER**'s publicity material and posters. He allowed artists free reign to produce posters that would modernise the image of the railway.

At its peak the **LNER** owned 7,700 steam locomotives, 20,000 coaches, nearly 30,000 rail freight vehicles, a fleet of ships and several ports. It also held major shareholdings in related companies such as the Forth Rail Bridge Railway Company.

Major changes on British railways were driven by:-

Widespread concern about pollution in the nineteen fifties. Yorkshire coal used by the **LNER** was flaky and soft and produced more smoke and soot than others. Transporting coal to use on the railways was expensive, so rail companies tended to use their local collieries, irrespective of emissions.

During the great London smog of 1952, four thousand people died and many more were made ill. This gave momentum to the Clean Air Act which was passed by parliament in 1956. Whilst the Act didn't refer to steam engines directly, it created a greater awareness of pollution caused by smoke emissions. From 1956 smoke free zones were introduced, and there were moves towards cleaner fuels, such as low emission coal, electricity and gas, in industry and homes.

In 1955 the British Transport Commission unveiled their modernisation plan for Britain's railways. This plan had two main objectives. The first was the reduction in size of the railway network; the second was the abandonment of steam traction. Factors driving the abandonment of steam propulsion included the growing shortage of suitable coal to fire locomotives, reduction in air pollution and the need for greater acceleration. Electrification and dieselisation were encouraged

In 1958 there were over 16,100 steam engines on British railways. Five years later, in 1963, there were around 7,000. Change continued rapidly. On 8 August 1968 all steam locomotives were withdrawn.

Halthorpe Railway Station is a figment of the author's imagination based loosely on his memories of Staddlethorpe Railway Station when he was a boy. On 7 January 1975 Staddlethorpe Station was renamed Gilberdyke Station. It is now an unmanned halt.

Sources include...Wikipedia, British Steam Railways.

4... *The Foundations of Blitzkreig.*

In 1929 Heinz Wilhelm Guderian wrote:-

'My historical studies, the exercises carried out in England and our own experience with mock ups, had persuaded me, that tanks would never be able to produce their full effect, until weapons on whose support they must inevitably rely were brought up to their standard of speed and cross country performance. In such formation of all arms the tanks must play the primary role. It would be wrong to include tanks in infantry divisions. What was needed were armoured divisions. These would include all the supporting arms needed to fight with full effect.'

In 1937 Guderian published his book 'Achtung-Panzer'. The German Panzer forces were created and followed the recommendations of this book.

On the 10 May 1940 the Battle of France began in earnest. 'German Army Corps B' invaded and subdued the Netherlands and rapidly advanced into Belgium.

On the same day Winston Churchill became Prime Minister of Britain

On the 14 May 1940 'German Army Group A' burst through the

Ardenne, advanced westward and turned towards the English Channel. During the period 27 May to 4 June 1940 there was a huge drive to evacuate British forces trapped on Dunkirk's beaches. As well as enduring constant bombing by the Luftwaffe the troops had to suffer the indignity of propaganda leaflets being dropped upon them. The leaflets read "British Soldiers. Look at the map. It gives you your true situation. Your troops are entirely surrounded. Put down your arms!" The Allied soldiers used the leaflets as toilet paper.

After the Dunkirk evacuations and the abandonment of military equipment, the British Army had only one hundred tanks left.

Source...Wikipedia and Armoured Crusader.

5... The Burma Railway

The Burma Railway was also known as the Death Railway. It was 415 kilometres (258 miles) long and ran between Bangkok Thailand and Rangoon, Burma (now Yangon, Myanmar). It was built by the Empire of Japan during World War II, to support its forces in their Burma campaign.

The Japanese military made extensive use of forced labour during the railway's construction in 1942-43. About 180,000 Asian labourers and 60,000 allied prisoners of war were involved in the building. As a result around 90,000 Asians (or Romuska) and 16,000 allied POWs died before it was completed. The dead POWs included 6,318 British, 2,815 Australians, 2,490 Dutch, 356 Americans and a smaller number of Canadians and New Zealanders.

Hellfire Pass, in the Tenassirim Hills, was a particularly difficult section of the line to build. It was extremely remote. Much of the line had to be cut through solid rock with insufficient and ineffective tools. In the six weeks it took to build, sixty nine men were beaten to death by the Japanese guards. More died from cholera, dysentery, starvation and exhaustion.

The Burma Railway was brought to worldwide attention by Pierre

Boule in his book 'The Bridge over the River Kwai' (Khwae Yai). A film of the same name was criticised as unrealistic, because it did not show the realities of the terrible hardships the men suffered.

The U.S. Library of Congress estimates that in Java, between four to ten million Romusha were forced to work by the Japanese military. About 270,000 Javanese labourers were sent to other Japanese-held areas in South East Asia. However, only 52,000 were repatriated to Java.

Source...Wikipedia

6... Black Peas

Black peas are produced from the purple podded pea. They are also called parched peas. Parching being a term meaning long, slow boiling.

Source... Wikipedia

They are still sold and enjoyed in Lancashire today. In 2010 the author visited Bury Market and was delighted to find a stall selling black peas. They were steaming hot, served in a polystyrene cup and eaten with a plastic spoon. They were delicious.

7... Bombing of Berlin

During the period November 1943 to March 1944 British Bomber Command carried out 16 massed attacks on Berlin. As a result of these raids 4,000 Berliners were killed and 450,000 people were made homeless. Bomber Command lost 2,690 men over Berlin and over 1,000 more were taken as prisoners of war. Over 500 aircraft were lost.

The raid on the 17 December sent 494 planes, mainly Lancasters, from the airfield at Linton on Ouse, near York, to attack the Berlin railways. Their outward route across Holland and Northern Germany was accurately anticipated and tracked by German air control, consequently many German fighter planes were waiting at the coast of Holland. There were many combats and twenty five Lancasters were lost on the approach to the enemy capital.

The returning bomber squadrons shook off many of the fighters, by flying over Denmark. Weather conditions were bad and fog obscured many of the home airfields. A further twenty nine bombers crashed over the UK, several of those due to running out of fuel. An additional 131 lives were lost.

The main bomber was the Avro Lancaster (affectionately known as the Lanc) built at Chadderton near Oldham and tested at Woodford Aerodrome in Cheshire. They had a crew of seven; Bomb Aimer doubling as Forward Gunner, Pilot, Flight Engineer, Navigator, Wireless Operator, Mid Upper Gunner and Rear Gunner. Due to the tight construction, baling out in emergency situations was very tricky so the Lancaster crews only achieved a 15% success rate.

7,377 Lancaster bombers were built during the war. In 1943 these cost £45-£50,000 each.

Source... Wikipedia

8... Major General Sir Percy 'Hobo' Hobart

'The pages of history are adorned in plenty by the names of those whose convictions have sprung from a deep understanding of matters beyond the vision of their contemporaries, and who have willingly fought the entrenched hosts of vested interests in order that their convictions might prevail.'

Extract taken from *'Armoured Crusader'* by Kenneth Macksey.

This described the character of Major General Sir Percy Hobart who challenged the entrenched views of the military 'old boy' network. So much so that in 1940 when he was fifty five years old, he was forcibly retired from the army. He was living in Oxford and joined the newly formed Local Defence Volunteers as a Corporal. An article in the press highlighted the waste of Hobart's talent. This brought him to the attention of Churchill who immediately reinstated him and held back those who would have opposed him.

Despite this, Hobart still had to overcome massive resistance to drive forward his ideas on modern tank and combined forces warfare. He continued to be unpopular with his superiors because he challenged their traditional approaches. He was the visionary and the driving force behind the creation of the 11th Armoured Division and also the 29th Armoured Division. The German forces learned from Hobart's visionary approach, in fact, it is alleged that following successful evaluation of pre-war manoeuvres in 1939, Germany's General Guderian, (known as Hurrying Heinz to his men), Commander of the 2nd Panzer Division and of the 16th Army Corps proposed a champagne toast 'To Hobart.'

NB: This is an unsubstantiated claim and may have been made for propaganda purposes by the Allied forces

Hobart recognized that to overcome challenging war situations, the equipment had to meet the task. The 29th Armoured Division developed diverse uses for tanks. These unusual war machines became known as Hobart's Funnies.

Duplex Drive tanks were used on all five of the landing beaches on D-Day. Most landings were successful with a high percentage of the tanks reaching the shore. The American landings on Omaha beach were the exception. The sea off Omaha beach, was much choppier than the other landing zones, with waves up to six feet high. The American Duplex Drive Sherman tanks were launched from landing craft nearly two miles from the beach, probably due to the intensity of artillery shelling from the enemy guns. Twenty seven of the twenty nine tanks sank. Without tank cover, the American soldiers suffered terrible losses from attack by the German machine gunners.

Sources… Armoured Crusader, Taurus Pursuant, Trevor Constable, The Black Bull and Wikipedia

9… Mulberry Harbours

Mulberry was the code name given to the two artificial harbours built off the coast of France following the D-day invasions. Their purpose was to help supply and support the Allied Forces as they fought to regain Europe from the Germans. The Harbours were built by the Royal Engineers. The floating breakwaters (Bombardons) were the responsibility of the Royal Navy.

Mulberry Harbour 'A' was assembled at Omaha beach at Saint Laurent sur Mer for use by the American Invasion forces. Mulberry 'B' was build at Gold Beach at Arromanches for use by the British and Canadian forces.

Mulberry 'A' had a very short life as it was destroyed by channel storms in late June 1944 because it was not securely anchored to the seabed. Parts of it were salvaged and used to reinforce Mulberry 'B'.

This was used for six months until the allies had secured Antwerp which was then used for supplies. Visitors to Arromanches can still view the fragmented remains of the Mulberry Harbour 'B' in the bay.

The harbour's construction included large concrete caissons (Phoenixes) which had been built in secret in the UK and then deliberately sunk at Dungeness, the Cant and Pagham to hide them. When they were needed, they were refloated and towed across to France, to form the main part of the breakwaters. They were re-sunk along with blockade ships called Gooseberries.

The Royal Engineers erected pier heads (Spuds) which lifted up and down with the tide. These enabled ships to unload. They were used by medium size cargo ships and hospital ships. Dock piers (Whales) were the floating roadways which connected the pier heads to the land. Each Whale had a span of eighty feet and floated on pontoons called Beetles. After the war some of these Whale bridge spans were used to repair bridges in France, Belgium and Holland.

Source…Wikipedia

10… 11th Armoured Division (known as The Black Bull).

It was formed under the guidance of Percy (Hobo) Hobart to react to the success of the German Panzer divisions and their Blitzkrieg tactics. The 11th Armoured Division used rapid advance strategies to drive the enemy into confusion.

The Cromwell tank used extensively by the Armoured Division had a 75mm main gun which fired high explosive shells and two 7.92mm

Besa Machine Guns. Many were built by the Birmingham Railway Carriage and Wagon Company.

Hobart suggested the design for the 11th Armoured divisional flash. He utilised the family crest of the Blickling Hobarts and developed a Bull Sable – a Black Bull on a yellow field.

The 11th Armoured division (The Black Bull) suffered 10,000 casualties during the 1944/5 charge across Europe. Of these 2000 were killed.

Source...Armoured Crusader, The Black Bull, Taurus Pursuant and Wikipedia.

11... Argentan

The city of Argentan was freed from German occupation during the morning of 20 August. The city was burnt and in ruins. This action opened up the route for the allies to liberate Paris.

Source...Wikipedia

12... Birmingham Accident Hospital and Rehabilitation Centre

Birmingham Accident Hospital formerly known as Birmingham Accident Hospital and Rehabilitation Centre was established in April 1941.

The hospital, thought to be the world's first trauma centre, used the existing buildings of Queen's Hospital, a former teaching hospital in Bath Row, Birmingham.

Director Sir Ashley Miles was joined by Leonard Colebrook who moved with his burns unit from Glasgow Royal Infirmary. Colebrook was an expert on the earliest antibiotic Prontosil, which was active against streptococcus. A joint project led to the development of Moisturising Renewal Cream no 9, which became the main burns treatment at that time. Work with burns victims during the Second World War led to the recognition that infection was the main cause of death. This resulted in the development of new treatments.

Source...Wikipedia.

13... Operation Sonnenblume (Sunflower)

In the latter part of 1940 the British forces launched a counter offensive (Operation Compass) against the Italian 10th Army in North Africa. This offensive took the Italians completely by surprise and within two months the British had captured 130,000 of their enemy's troops at the cost of 2,000 casualties. Throughout this campaign the Italians believed they were massively outnumbered. In fact the reverse was true.

Anthony Eden, British Foreign Secretary at that time, paraphrased Winston Churchill's proud statement about the Battle of Britain. He joked, 'Never has so much been surrendered by so many, to so few'.

Hitler was very alarmed by this turn of events, and following consultation with Mussolini created Operation Sonnenblume (Sunflower). In early 1941 he dispatched the newly formed German Africa Korps, under the command of General Erwin Rommel, from Naples to Tripoli, Libya, to support the remnants of the Italian Army.

Rommel's first offensive was a success and he destroyed the British 2nd Armoured Division.

Source.. Wikipedia

14... Photograph of Land Girl with Shire horses

This photograph (taken in 1941) hung on the wall of the author's home when he was a child. The land girl is Doreen Alderson when she was 18 years old. She was the author's mother.

15... Badges for 15th/19th Kings Royal Hussars

These belonged to the author's father William Durham. He served with the 15th/19th from 1940 until 1945 when he was discharged due to his war injuries. His service record is shown as exemplary. He was a modest man who rarely spoke about the war.

Bibliography

16 'Armoured Crusader' by Kenneth Macksey. The Biography of Major
    General Sir Percy 'Hobo' Hobart one of the most influential military
    commanders of the Second World War. Published by Hutchinson
    1967. ISBN: 1 904010 64 4

17 'The Black Bull' by Patrick Delaforce. Published by Sutton Publishing
    1993. ISBN: 0 7509 3183 3

18 'Club Route in Europe' Printed by Werner Degener, Hannover. 1946
    Army publication.

19 'Taurus Pursuant. A History of the 11th Armoured Division' Army
    publication.

20 'Short History of your Regiment XV – XIX The Kings Royal Hussars.'
    Army Publication.

21 'The Little Known Story of Percy Hobart' by Trevor J. Constable.
    Published by the Institute for Historical Review.

22 'Regimental Magazine (January 1946)' 15th/19th The Kings Royal
    Hussars.

23 'The Illustrated History of British Steam Locomotives.' by David
    Ross. Published by Parragon. ISBN: 978-1-4054-8290-5

24 'The Observer's Book of Railway Locomotives of Britain' by H. C.
    Casserley. 1958 edition.

25 'Not Lost for Words' by Gunter Helft. ISBN: 1 479142712

26 'Land Girl…A Manual for Volunteers in the Women's Land Army.'
    by W.E. Shewell-Cooper. English Universities Press.

27 'Land Girl' magazine December 1941 issue.

28 'From a Railway Carriage' poem by Robert Louis Stevenson 1850-1894. After research presumed out of copyright due to age.

29 'Fascination Waltz' Music (1904) by Fermo Dante Marchetti and lyrics (1905) by Maurice de Féraudy (English lyrics by Dick Manning).

30 'Chattanooga Choo Choo' written by Harry Warren, recorded by Glenn Miller. Featured in the 1941 movie 'Sun Valley Serenade.'

31 'Heart and Soul' written by Hoagy Carmichael and Frank Loessor. 1938.

As a boy the author was always singing and whistling. His versions were incomplete, with free interpretation of the lyrics (and tune). He hopes that the fragments reproduced in this book, with the exception of 'Les Toreadors' and 'We'll Meet Again', are reasonably accurate. The following were great favourites.

32 'Les Toreadors' From the comic opera *Carmen*, by Georges Bizet

33 'Run Rabbit Run' Sung by Flanagan and Allen. 1938. Popular throughout the war years.

34 'Lay a Little Egg for Me' Anonymous 1928? Sometimes attributed to Ted Weems.

35 'The Stormy Winds do Blow' Traditional Shanty. Lyric by Laura Alexandrine Smith 1888, from 'The Music of the Waters.'

36 'The Runaway Train' by Robert E. Massey and Harry Warren. 1928.

37 'See You Later Alligator' Bill Hayley and his Comets, 1955, Decca records. This song was originally entitled 'Later Alligator' written by Robert Charles Guidry and recorded by him earlier in 1955.

38 'The Ballad of Davy Crocket' by George Bruns and Thomas W Blackburn. In 1955 Walt Disney productions launched an intensive marketing campaign in the UK, to publicise their film 'Davy Crockett, King of the Wild Frontier'. This was released in Britain in 1956.

39 'Puffing Billy' the theme tune for 'Children's Favourites', which was broadcast on the BBC Light Programme from 1954–1967. The music was written by Edward White, who was captivated by an old steam locomotive, while on holiday on the Isle of White. He decided to

capture the rhythm in music. 'Children's Favourites' was introduced by 'Uncle Mac' (Derek McCulloch) with the words 'Hello children, everywhere.'

40   'We'll Meet Again' 1939. Composed by Ross Parker and Hugh Charles. Sung by 'Forces Sweetheart' Vera Lynn.

41   'O Sole Mio' 1898. A Neopolitan song with lyrics by Giovanni Capurro and music composed by Eduardo di Capua. Popularised in the early twentieth century by opera singers Enrico Caruso and Beniamino Gigli. It was also performed by the Marx Brothers with a harp accompaniment in their film 'Monkey Business' (1931).

42   'The Keeper of the Eddystone Light' Folk song, lyric from Charles Wingate.

43   'Little White Bull' 1959. By Tommy Steel and Lionel Bart. Featured in the film 'Tommy the Toreador.'

Alan Durham is an old bloke who writes a bit. He enjoys writing short stories and the occasional rhyming thing. He is happily married to Tana.

The Hen Race book has been floating around in his mind for over forty years; some would say writing it was overdue. It is set in the 1950s, a decade roughly coincidental with the early years of Alan's life. He was brought up in the East Riding of Yorkshire but now lives in the West Midlands.

He enjoys eating things he knows he shouldn't, watching the world walk by and drinking red wine at pavement cafes.